An Ignominious Burial for a Long-dead Jester King

It was not hard for Abderian to find the castle trash midden, from its location near the kitchen, and the smell. Here and there in the mess, Abderian thought he saw pieces of stained ivory that might be old bones. From within a mass of fruit rinds, a dark skull grinned back at him.

Abderian felt tears welling up in his eyes. "I don't care what you did. You were my great-grandfather. They shouldn't have done this to you." He drew the Sword of Sagamore from his belt and saluted the trash midden. "I, Abderian, Prince of Euthymia, do honor you, O once mighty king. May your spirit rise beyond this sorry place into a worthy heaven."

No sooner had he said "rise," than there was a strange stirring in the midden. The heap of garbage shuddered once, twice, and then a whole skeleton emerged from the mess to stand before the prince.

"As a jester, I often had garbage thrown at me," came a hollow voice from within the skull, "but this is the first time I have been thrown at garbage." With bony fingers, the skeleton picked orange peels off his frame and flicked them away.

"King Sagamore!"

Books by Kara Dalkey
from Ace

KARA DALKEY

THE SWORD OF SAGAMORE

ACE BOOKS, NEW YORK

This book is an Ace original edition,
and has never been previously published.

THE SWORD OF SAGAMORE

An Ace Book / published by arrangement with
the author

PRINTING HISTORY
Ace edition / November 1989

ISBN: 0-441-79429-7

Ace Books are published by The Berkley Publishing Group,
200 Madison Avenue, New York, New York 10016.
The name "ACE" and the "A" logo are trademarks
belonging to Charter Communications, Inc.

PRINTED IN THE UNITED STATES OF AMERICA

10   9   8   7   6   5   4   3   2   1

PROLOGUE

Portion of Private Correspondence from Queen Mother Pleonexia of Euthymia to the Lady Willenemma, Countess of Bullmarket:

> 10th of Slush
> Year One of the Reign of King Cyprian the First

My Dear Willi:

Greetings and good health to you! How very kind of you to write. It has been entirely too long, and so much has happened this past year, I've scarcely had time to put ink to parchment. You may have heard that I have become a hermit in the service of Our Lady of the Twinkling Firmament. In that capacity, I suppose it is not really proper for me to receive and send letters. But I'm finding hermitage to be somehow lonelier than I expected, so I could not resist responding to you. I will doubtless have to do some sort of penance for it, though. I shall have to ask my High Priestess, Entheali, what she would recommend as suitable self-abasement. Perhaps skipping dessert at this evening's meal would do.

Thank you for your sympathies on the death of my Lord Valgus. Yes, it was quite tragic, and how my daughter's toy pull-dragon got on his chamber stairs I simply cannot imagine. No, I am not of the opinion that Amusia should have become Queen because it was her toy. I don't care what tradition says, assassination by pratfall is not a proper method for accession to the throne. Besides, Amusia is only six years old—hardly fit to rule. Our family may be descended from a court jester, but that does not mean we should be foolish about who wears the crown.

Speaking of the children, they are quite well, thank you, those that remain to me. Alexia, my twelve-year-old, complains that there is no one of her age at court to be her play-companion. Sometimes she can whine most dreadfully. But she will soon blossom into a young woman and we can marry her off to some fat, aging, wealthy duke whom she can torment to her heart's content.

Amusia is mischievous as ever, and is being quite a trial to her older sister. Her last prank was to slip tadpoles down the armor of the castle guards. She said she liked to watch the guards dance. I suppose she's trying to top Alexia's triumph last year of putting dragonlets in Cook's meat pies. I hope it's just a phase. Amusia has said she wants to write a history of our family and Euthymia. As long as it keeps her busy, I'll not complain.

As for the boys, I'm afraid we still don't know how Paralian passed away. Your suggestion that the priests of the Lizard Goddess might have sacrificed him is, I think, a bit over the edge. The Lizard Priests were unpleasant and wrongheaded men, and I'm quite glad they disappeared to who-knows-where, but I don't recall that their rituals required the blood of a royal first-born son. They told us it was plague and even offered to show us his ashes, so I suppose we must believe them.

Despite your misgivings about Cyprian, I believe he is turning out to be a fine king. He has stopped his skirt-chasing entirely and has settled down with his new Queen, Horaphthia. I confess, I don't quite know what he sees in her. She is twice his age, if I am any judge, and I think she is too much of a sorceress to be a proper wife. But what does it matter, so long as he's happy? Cyprian bears the Mark of Sagamore, you know, so a happy Cyprian makes for a happy kingdom. Now, if only those troublesome, rebellious noblemen would see that and stop bothering him.

Well, I mustn't dwell on politics. I am supposed to have left such worldly cares behind me. Ah, but my greatest joy this past year has been my youngest son, Abderian. Who would have guessed that such a shy little wimp would have amounted to anything. And yet, Willi, the Goddess Tritavia, blessings on her name, promised me he would serve our cause well and he has. Ever since he returned from being kidnapped months ago, he has done the most amazing things. Abderian found Cyprian his sorceress queen, drove the Lizard Priests out of the castle temple, slew a dragon with a magic sword (utterly ruining the sword in the process, I understand, but then one can't do everything right).

I do worry about the boy, however. He has brought a young lady to court and gotten her in a . . . condition that should properly be preceded by marriage. And he has a little bird for a pet that he calls Paralian. I know Abderian took his brother's death hard, but I do hope he gets over it. And I hear he's taken up magic studies with that strange fellow Valgus used to keep shut up in the cellars—Dolus, I think his name is. I worry that such interests may lead to . . . necromancy. Oh, you may think this is merely a mother's exaggerated concern, but not long ago I overheard his young lady mentioning that he once conjured up skeletons to save her from a dragon. And I've heard how a little spell or two can lead apprentices to experiment with "the harder stuff" in search of greater thrills. I'll have to see that he is watched for the symptoms.

Yes, the demons did make a bit of a mess after the Lizard Priests left. We who worship She of the Stars aren't well equipped to deal with such things. Fortunately, the larger demons have returned to their realm. They left quite suddenly, in fact, as if there were some important business to attend to. Some of the smaller ones have stayed and made themselves more or less useful. Abderian keeps one, for example.

The weather these past months has been quite normal for autumn, which is remarkable in itself, if you'll recall the past few years. Except there seems to be a storm brewing outside. I hope it isn't one of our resident sorcerers being troublesome again.

Dear me, the room seems to be shaking. I shall have to leave off . . . .

ONE

Catastrophes would make superb weapons of war, except that they tend to get out of hand and never seem to happen to the other guy.

—GENERAL MUNGO THE SLOPPY

"WHAT'S WRONG WITH me?" young Prince Abderian grumbled as the magical texts blurred and swam before his eyes. He squeezed his lids shut and rubbed them.

"You've been at the books too long," said the little brown bird perched on his shoulder. "So much study is unnatural for a lad your age. When Cyprian was sixteen—"

"Is that what you thought when *you* studied sorcery? And Cyprian at sixteen liked close work too, only he preferred wenches to books." Abderian massaged his middle and groaned. His stomach was beginning to feel queasy.

He gazed around his tower room, and watched the bed, the shelves, the wardrobe, and the tapestries wavering as if seen under water. A window shutter slammed open and a great gust of wind that smelled incongruously of the sea riffled the pages of the sorcery book in front of the prince.

"Oh, bother," said Abderian. "Where was I?"

4

"Page six," said the bird. "Haven't you had that window fixed yet?"

"So someone else can throw a rock through it?" Abderian snapped. "I've been busy, Paralian, for your sake, you know." Abderian paused, wondering why he felt so irritable and anxious.

"I'm not ungrateful," said the bird, ruffling his feathers, "but you needn't drive yourself like this. I've gotten rather used to being a bird, after all."

Abderian flipped to Page six of his text and stared at it. The top of the page read "Furrier Transformations: The changing of an animal spirit to higher or lower states of being."

"If I could just concentrate on this," muttered the prince, "I'm sure it could give us some—"

Thunder cracked and rumbled outside and the sunlight streaming into the room changed from gold to an ominous green.

"What in the twinkling eyes of Tritavia is going on?" peeped the bird.

Abderian's stomach lurched and he felt an intense itching on his right arm. *Oh, no,* he thought, *Not that. Not again.* He scratched at his puce velvet sleeve, but did not look beneath. He did not need to see the intricate, cinnamon-colored mark that lay just below his elbow. *Haven't you caused enough trouble for one lifetime?* Abderian said silently to the mark. *I wish I really had given you to Cyprian.*

The prince braced his hands on the silverwood desk and stood. With effort, he walked to the window and looked out past the colorful broken shards. His mouth dropped open in amazement.

Beyond, viridian clouds roiled and billowed across the sky. Sticky, purple raindrops sprinkled on the prince's face. A howling wind whipped away the last of the late autumn leaves.

"It's not my fault!" Abderian said, fearing that it was.

"I didn't say that," piped the bird, clinging grimly to Abderian's shoulder.

"But others will, Paralian. You can bet your pinfeathers on it. It will be like last spring all over again." Struggling against the wind, the prince pushed the thick oak shutters closed. He leaned back against them and closed his eyes, sighing. *Lord Sagamore, now what? Is it illness or anger or all of this magic I'm studying?*

"Why should anyone blame you? They all think *Cyprian* bears the Mark of Sagamore."

"Face it, Paralian, that tattoo you did on his arm won't fool everyone."

"It fooled Cyprian."

"That isn't difficult. But with all this happening, certain people are going to look closer at the mark. When they see it's a fake, guess who they come to visit next?"

With a bang, the window shutter slammed open again, pushing Abderian forward. He stumbled, flinging his arms out, but found his fall neatly checked by the weight of a leather-winged demon clinging desperately to his back leg. Tears coursed out of the creature's narrow eyes and down his bulbous nose, and his triangular ears were folded back in distress.

"Oh, my Master! Oh, my Queen! Woe, oh woe!" the demon cried.

"What is it, Mux? Get off!" Abderian shook his leg but the demon held fast.

"Calamity! Mishap! Ruin! The Powers of Earth are mixed with the Powers of Fire! The flames shall be smothered and the land shall be scorched! All is lost, oh woe!"

"Will you calm down? Let go of my leg!"

"Disaster! Tragedy! Perilous misadventure! A gaping wound in the sweet visage of Fate!"

"You've been listening too much to Dolus."

"Alas for the world! Oh, sweet Khanda, my Demon Queen!"

"I doubt that prayers to her will be helpful," said Abderian. He had been briefly betrothed to the beautiful Khanda before she ran off with the Demon King, and his feelings toward her were decidedly ambivalent. "Look, if you know what's wrong, Mux, just tell us, all right?"

"I dare not speak of it," said Mux, covering his face.

Abderian sighed. "Can you give us a hint?"

Suddenly the floor rolled and undulated like the back of a flying dragon, and there came a deep rumble from under the floor. Abderian was knocked to his knees despite his counterweight demon.

"Earthquake!" Paralian chirped, fluttering among the rafters overhead. Bits of stone and mortar came raining down as the walls shuddered. Abderian dragged himself and the still-clinging Mux under his silverwood desk for safety.

"Paralian! Fly out or get under here!"

The little bird swooped beneath the desk to join them just as one end of a roof beam lost its moorings and came crashing down. All around them the furniture rocked and rattled and danced to the tune of continuous thunder.

Abderian closed his eyes tight and hugged the demon close, not caring about the ugliness of its wrinkled leather face or the foulness of its smell.

"If this is a hint, I don't want to know," Paralian peeped. "Can't you do something to make it stop?"

"It's too big for me!" said Abderian. "In my sorcery studies I've only gotten as far as Easing Minor Mishaps, not Reversing Major Disasters."

"Couldn't you use the cursemark?"

"You know I can't control that."

"But your emotions—"

"You expect me to be calm at a time like this?"

"Oh. Never mind."

"It is inevitable," Mux whimpered into Abderian's shoulder. "It is Fate. It is Destiny. We are doomed."

"Shut up, mushroom breath," said the bird.

Abderian ignored them and worried about Maja, his young, pretty, and very pregnant fiancée. *There are people with her*, he thought, to console himself. *She'll be all right*. Still, he wished teleportations weren't such complex and tricky spells, or he'd send himself to her chambers, demon leg-ornament and all.

In time, the rocking of the room slowed and stopped, and the thunder faded. The only sounds were the occasional rattle of falling bits of mortar and the ragged breathing of those under the table.

The prince opened his eyes. Nothing moved in the room except drifting clouds of dust. "It's done," he whispered.

"Huzzah," sighed Paralian, fluffing his feathers.

"Aye, done," grumbled Mux. "And we are done for."

"Anyone ever tell you that you have an attitude problem?" said the bird.

Abderian crawled out from under the silverwood desk, disentangling himself from the demon's embrace. He stood and dusted himself off, noting that the floor still seemed steady. He turned toward the chamber door and found it completely blocked by fallen stone. *Drat. How will I get to Maja?*

Abderian went to the other window, which faced out over Castle Mamelon, and opened the shutters. He blinked in the unexpected bright sunshine pouring through the colored glass. Abderian undid the latch and let the pane swing open, then whistled in amazement at what he saw.

Castle Mamelon, even at its best, had never been a gem of

architecture. It had been designed long ago by the Jester King, Sagamore, who was better versed in jokes and japes and tricks of the eye than in structural engineering. As a result, the castle had been embellished with stairs that led nowhere, windows that faced walls, and archways that supported nothing. Now, after the earthquake, the stairs had crumbled, the windows had unexpected views, and the archways could not even support themselves. And the towers . . . Castle Mamelon had been a pincushion of towers, of all shapes and sizes. Now the straight ones were askew, the twisted ones were tilted, and the Wizard's Tower—whose former point of interest was that it had no stairs—now also had no visible means of support. The upper third of the tower sat steady-as-you-please in midair, looking like an unfinished painting.

"It's a good thing," Abderian mused, "that most of this place is held up by magic."

Paralian fluttered to his shoulder. "Shall I take a flit round?"

"Yes. Will you go see if Maja's all right?"

"Of course. What are big brothers for?" Paralian chirped and he flapped away out the window.

There came a curious pounding from the center of the room behind the prince, and a muffled voice called out, "Abderian!"

He whipped around but saw no one in the room. Then the pounding came again and a section of the floor rose an inch or so and fell.

The chute. Someone's in the chute! Abderian went to the center of the room and knelt, brushing away dust and bits of wall. Finally he found the fingerholds and he lifted a square stone slab out of the floor.

"Ah, there you are," said a mild-eyed, brown-and-grey-bearded, middle-aged man peering up at him from the black pit in the floor. "Give me your hand. I feared you had been injured or worse."

"It's all right, Dolus, I'm not hurt." Abderian grasped his wizardry tutor's arm and helped pull him up out of the chute. Then he gasped and jumped back, as he saw that Dolus's brown robe was covered with the dried carcasses of spiders, scorpions and centipedes.

Dolus shook out his robe, releasing clouds of dust along with the insect husks. "All's well because you're not hurt? As if you were the only denizen of this castle. Your housecleaning, my boy, leaves something to be desired. And you do not treat your pets well, it would seem."

"Pets? Oh, the spiders and things. They weren't mine. Cyprian put them in the chute last year, as a jest. I think they were alive then."

"Let us hope Cyprian treats his subjects better than these." Dolus shook the remaining bits of mummified creatures out of his greying shoulder-length hair.

"Have you seen Maja? Is she well?"

"Oh, I suppose she fares about as well as those whose souls drift in the yawning Abyss between the Peaks of Englightenment and the Cliffs of Despair."

"*Do*lus—"

"How should I know? I scarcely had time to look, did I? I had to come racing up here to stop whatever shenanigans you were performing. And just what in the Seven Dark Heavens of Tritavia have you been doing?"

"Nothing! I haven't, I mean this isn't—"

" 'Tis not the Master's fault," said Mux, finally crawling out from under the silverwood desk.

"Aha!" said Dolus, wrinkling his nose. "Do the denizens of the Fiery Realm know the cause of these events?"

"We are doomed," Mux intoned, his knobby hands clasped pitifully over his little potbelly. "The elements of fire have mixed—"

Abderian's hand slapped over the demon's lips. "Don't get him started, Dolus. He'll go on like that all day."

"Perhaps, then, Abderian, *you* would like to explain the situation to me, before you have to explain to the King, the Queen, the nobility, and the rest of Euthymia why you have brought wrack and ruin down on our heads!"

"I wasn't doing anything! I was just reading in the transformation texts how to change Paralian back from a bird to man. That's all."

"Hmmm."

"Look, I'm not the only wizard in Euthymia," Abderian said, "or Mamelon, for that matter. Maybe Onym's up to something."

"Possible. The chaotic quality of these events would suit his madness. But I think the High Priestess Entheali keeps too close an eye on him to allow him such excess."

"Maybe Queen Horaphthia, then. She's powerful enough."

"What possible reason would Her Majesty have to cause such a mess?"

Abderian shrugged. "Maybe Cyprian hogged all the bedsheets last night and she's upset."

"No, lad, the scope of this disorderly calamity points to only one source, I fear."

Abderian defensively covered his arm. "You mean the cursemark."

"Of course I mean the cursemark. How have you been feeling?"

"I'm fine! I haven't been upset until now. Except . . . I was feeling a little sick just before the storm began."

"Mmmm. Did you feel anything from the cursemark itself?"

"Just some itching."

Dolus scratched his beard, then laid a hand across Abderian's brow. "Well, you do not seem to be feverish. If a mere disagreement with your lunch caused this disaster, we're in bigger trouble than I thought. We'd better have a look at your arm."

Reluctantly, Abderian began to roll up his sleeve. The fluttering of wings at the window made them both turn.

"I'm back!" sang Paralian, perched on the sill. "The Lady Maja is in good health, and she and Her Royal Majesty, Queen Horaphthia, demand to see you both in the Lady's chambers at once."

"We're on our way," said Abderian, pushing the sleeve back down. He looked up at the blocked door. "That is, if we can find a way."

"Might I suggest the route by which I arrived?" said Dolus, indicating the chute.

Abderian frowned at the square black pit in the center of the floor. "If my having an upset stomach causes earthquakes, that might not be a good idea."

" 'Tis a thought, true. But what might your mood be should you incur the wrath of the most powerful sorceress in Euthymia?"

Abderian paused and considered a moment. "After you," he said, with a generous gesture toward the pit.

TWO

Excerpt from *A History of the House of Sagamore*, as dictated to her Royal Secretary by Her Highness, Princess Amusia:

My great-granddaddy was King Sagamore. He used to be a jester, but his master, King Thalion, made Sagamore the next king because Thalion didn't like any of his own children. Some people called him King Thalion the Foolish because of that. But I think it was pretty smart, because if Sagamore hadn't been made a king, I wouldn't have been a princess. . . .

THEY SLITHERED AND skittered down the dark chute, Abderian holding his arms across his face. He might have found it fun had he not been aware of what he was slithering on. The spiders and snakes had been the result of Cyprian making good on a big-brotherly threat, some months before. Due to the former occupation of their illustrious forebear, jesting was the family tradition. Abderian was glad, however, that Cyprian had ceased his pranks after becoming king. Sibling relations in a royal family were uncertain enough without having to always be on guard against sudden meat pies in the face or fruit peel on the stairs.

Abderian's feet slammed into Dolus's shoulders and the tutor let out a loud "Ooof!"

"Sorry."

"Couldn't you use the walls to slow your descent, lad?"

"I didn't want to touch the walls!"

Dolus sighed and guided Abderian down beside him. "Here's the bottom. Mind your feet."

"There's nothing still alive here, is there?"

"We haven't really time to look, have we? If you're worried, you'd best step lively." Dolus's voice moved away in the darkness.

"Wait for me." Abderian leapt forward and grabbed a handful of the back of Dolus's robe, following right behind him as he shuffled ahead in the dark.

"You know, I'm almost grateful—easy on the velvet, there—that your father kept me secluded belowstairs. As a result, I probably know these passages better than anyone else in Mamelon."

"Is that why you're not bothering to use a light?"

"Do you really want to see our surroundings, lad?"

Aware of the crunching sounds beneath his feet, Abderian said, "No."

"Thought not. Besides, a little traipse through the unknown is good for the character. Stimulates imagination. Induces awe."

Abderian stumbled over Dolus's ankle. "Ouch."

"And encourages clumsiness in some cases. Pick up your feet, lad. They're still there, even though you cannot see them."

"Thank you, Dolus. What would I do without you?"

"Let go and you may find out."

"Uh, no, thank you. I'll use my darkness-stimulated imagination." Abderian sniffed the mould-scented air. "Dolus, do any of these passages lead to Castle Doom?"

"Sagamore's haunted underground swamp? Undoubtedly."

"And you are sure you know where we're going?"

"Do *you* want to lead?"

"Uh, no."

"All right, then." The floor slanted upwards and Dolus stopped suddenly. Abderian stumbled into his back. "Have a care. You'll do more damage to me than your earthquake."

"It wasn't my earthquake." Abderian blinked as a door was opened and light flooded into his eyes. As Dolus pulled him through, Abderian recognized the East Wing by the fresco on the wall. It showed a scene of a beautiful river gorge—a straight-down view, as if one were falling toward it. Vertigo, apparently, had been one of Sagamore's favorite sensations.

Two doors down the hallway, passing frantic servants and frightened courtiers, they came to the Lady Maja's lancet-arched door.

Abderian's knock was answered by a handsome middle-aged woman. She wore a *houppelande* of black silk lined with crimson satin, with gold threads on the borders and hem. Her raven hair hung in a thick plait over her shoulder and on her brow was a gold circlet from which dangled rubies on delicate gold chains. As usual, Abderian was uncertain whether to address her as his sovereign Queen, his sister-in-law, his great-aunt, his fiancée's sometime guardian, or the mightiest sorceress in Euthymia. "Um," he said.

"The Lady Maja and I are fine, thank you," said Queen Horaphthia, a glimmer of amusement in her dark eyes. "Which, I see, is more than might be said for you. Do come in."

She stepped aside and Abderian bowed past her. Dolus followed, murmuring, "Your Majesty."

On a huge round bed in the center of the vaulted chamber sat a girl of sixteen, with chestnut-brown hair that was half falling out of an elaborate coif. She frowned at the bedsheets as three ladies-in-waiting fussed over her voluminous green velvet gown, which did not quite match her hazel-green eyes. Abderian thought she looked splendid and stood in relieved admiration as the serving women plumped and arranged pillows around the Lady Maja.

"Will you stop that?" said Maja to the ladies. "I'm fine. Just leave it alone." She lightly slapped the hand of one lady who was artfully draping the hem of the green gown over the pillows.

"Please, Mistress," said another one of the ladies, "you must stay calm, for the baby's sake at least."

"The baby isn't going to notice if my dress is perfect or not, and I certainly don't care."

Queen Horaphthia cleared her throat and said, "The Lady Maja has a visitor."

Maja looked up at Abderian and her eyes widened in delighted surprise. All the ladies' efforts went for naught as Maja jumped up, scattering pillows and rumpling her gown. She ran to Abderian, arms outstretched, and stopped two paces short. Her eyes opened even wider and her mouth gaped. "Bugs," she said.

"What?" Abderian looked down at himself and saw that his tunic and hose were covered with the dangling carcasses of spiders, scorpions and centipedes. "Oh. It's all right, Maja. They're dead."

"Dead bugs," she said, wrinkling her nose. "Abderian, if this is some kind of jest, it's *not funny*."

"Actually, it's Cyprian's jest from about a year ago." Abderian smiled sheepishly.

"Wasn't funny then, I'll bet, either." Maja folded her arms on top of her burgeoning belly. "And I suppose you think the weird weather and the earthquake were a hundred yuks a minute, don't you?"

"No, I don't—"

Behind Maja, a lady-in-waiting whispered to another, the word "necromancy" plainly audible.

"What was that?" Maja snapped, whipping around to face the ladies.

"There have been rumors," one lady with a long, narrow nose said diffidently. "Something about attempts to bring His Highness's departed brother back to life."

Maja covered her mouth, and glanced back at Abderian, clearly suppressing laughter.

"Where did this rumor come from?" said Abderian, bewildered.

"Your demon, Highness," said one of the ladies, "while delivering a message to our Mistress, did indicate that it might be so."

Abderian wondered how well his hands might fit around Mux's scrawny little neck. "Mux doesn't know anything. He's just a demon."

"And you know," Dolus added, "that the speech of demons is like the fire that is their element—quick, capricious, fascinating, and likely to cause damage if you aren't careful."

Before Abderian or Maja could stop her, one of the ladies said, "Is it really, Master?"

"No," said Dolus, with a serene smile. "But it seems like it ought to be, doesn't it?"

Abderian said to Maja, "You really should have warned them about him, you know."

Maja shrugged. "Why? If they're going to walk right into it—"

"Methinks," said the lady, "that the Master takes advantage of those of lesser station."

"Alas," said Dolus, with a regretful but lecherous expression, "I am no longer so young—"

"I think," Horaphthia said, "that the danger to our Lady Maja is past and you ladies may be needed elsewhere. Try the Office of the Steward, where you may find more respectable company." With gracious gestures, Horaphthia shooed the servants out the door and closed it. She turned to Abderian. "Now, if we may return to more pressing matters, I would be very interested in your theory of the cause of this little calamity, Abderian."

"It's not my fault," Abderian said. "I didn't cause the earth-quake."

"We were not so certain about that, as I recall," said Dolus.

"Maybe Onym—"

"My father has cast some odd spells," Horaphthia allowed, "but usually it's something he finds amusing. Somehow, I don't think earthquakes are his idea of fun."

"It's the cursemark," Maja said. "It has to be."

"No, it isn't," said Abderian as pleasantly as he could between clenched teeth. "I've been feeling fine. Really."

"Maybe your studies have kept you from noticing some ache or illness," Horaphthia suggested.

Dolus said, "You did mention feeling sick this morning, lad."

"Yes, but that only started when—"

There was a knock at the door and a servant in the gravy-and-wine-blotched livery of the Office of the Steward bowed his way in. "Please pardon me, Your Majesty, my lords and lady. Your Majesty, your sorcerous skills are needed throughout the castle. People need healing, and repairs must be made."

"I trust there have been no deaths?" said Dolus.

"It appears not, my lord, whatever gods be praised."

Abderian sighed with relief. It would have been too unjust for anyone to have died as a result of his stomach's disagreement with an underdone beef stew.

"I thank you for your report," said Horaphthia. "But as for your request, I fear I must remain here to give my energy to *that*." She gestured toward the wall on which a complex diagram had been sketched in black and white chalk. Abderian had learned enough magic to recognize it as a powerful spell, involving forces of support, binding, and preservation.

"I see," said Dolus. "Perhaps no gods need be thanked, but a sorceress. Well, Abderian, looks as though it is time for you to apply your learning to practical tasks. That is, assuming you've sufficiently ascertained your lady's well-being."

"Very well." Abderian turned to Maja and considered how he might hug her without the baby getting in the way. Maja, it seemed, was trying to figure out how to avoid the arachnid ornaments on his tunic. Finally, Abderian leaned forward and kissed her on the forehead.

"You idiot," she sighed fondly. "Try to visit more often than just when there's a disaster, or else I'll have to ask Horaphthia to conjure more disasters. I'm due any day now, you know."

"I'll visit. I promise. I'll come back tonight and stay with you until the baby comes."

"That's more like it," said Maja, grinning.

Dolus cleared his throat loudly.

Abderian squeezed Maja's shoulders and gave her a brave wink-and-a-smile. Maja wrinkled her nose back at him. Unable to think of anything more to reassure her, Abderian turned and followed Dolus and the steward out the door.

The corridor was a chaotic, flowing river of people and objects. Servants carrying brooms, baskets filled with broken stone, and pots of tar or quick-mixed mortar bustled by. Abderian wondered if it wasn't a waste of sorcery, not to mention a traffic hazard, for the baskets and pots to be allowed to trundle about on their own stout little legs. *Probably Onym's idea.* As an opening presented itself, Abderian and Dolus joined the moving throng.

"You really ought to marry the girl, you know," Dolus said.

"What? Oh, I've intended to," Abderian said, trying not to trod on debris, trip over the walking receptacles, or jostle the workers going past. "But there wasn't enough money left over from Cyprian's wedding. And I wanted to wait until I could change Paralian back so he could stand with me. But by the time I learned that would be harder than I thought, Maja was getting big and I figured we ought to wait until she had the baby."

"I see. So it does not bother you that the next ruler of Euthymia might be called King So-and-So the Bastard."

"Um. I didn't look at it that way. Maybe Maja will have a girl."

"Queen Such-and-Such the Bastard would be rather worse, don't you think?"

"Oh. Hmm. But why should a child of mine end up on the throne?"

"Queen Horaphthia is too old to have children. Even the best sorcery cannot help that."

"She could adopt."

"Yes, but heirs of the blood are generally preferred over adoptees. The nobility tends to think there's something mystic about it."

"But if Paral—if a certain someone . . ."

"The factionalism that would cause would shake this kingdom worse than your earthquake."

"It wasn't *my*—"

"No, Abderian, I have a hunch Maja's babe may be very important indeed. You must take care to treat them both well."

"Of course," Abderian said, frowning. "Dolus, what makes you—"

"Hush, now. We have much to do, and the busy ant cannot worry about the rotting fruit that may drop on his home from above."

"Uh, right."

"This way, my lords," said the steward.

They were led to a gaping hole in the floor of one of the lesser audience chambers. Blue-green vapor issued from it and the room was full of the smell of mud and rotting things. "Another portal to Castle Doom is opened," Dolus said. "We'd best close this quickly, lad. Who knows what might crawl out."

Abderian nodded. He remembered the one visit he had made to the vast underground chamber, decorated to appear like a ruined castle sunk into a haunted bog, and infested with all manner of strange creatures. It was said that toward the end of his reign Sagamore used to enjoy long sojourns in that place, melodramatically named "Castle Doom." It was also said that, in those final years, Sagamore went mad. Whether the swamp or the madness was cause or effect, no one could say.

"Ordinarily," Dolus went on, "I'd have set a Lizard Priest to guard it and move on, but Tingalut's minions seem to be in short supply right now."

"Do you think the Lizard Priests might have caused the earthquake in revenge? I did give their goddess something of a setback when I killed her dragon."

Dolus shook his head. "I think not. The Lizard worshippers set a certain style and ritual to their viciousness. Well, the stones that made up this part of the floor are no doubt sunk beyond retrieval in the swamp below. We'll have to make a new floor. Stand here and do as I tell you."

Abderian and Dolus worked together, Dolus advising and directing as Abderian chanted the mystical words and made the near-impossible gestures. Dolus had little sorcerous power of his own anymore. It had been drained by Lizard Priests—punishment for helping Abderian to escape the wrath of his now-dead father, King Valgus. Abderian had managed to accidentally absorb Dolus's magic while meditating in the temple, much to his surprise and Dolus's supreme annoyance. This made their magical teamwork very successful, but it sometimes put a strain on their friendship.

"No, no, no!" cried Dolus. "The word is *Plotzfizzle*, and the hand must be pointing up, not down!"

"Oh. Sorry."

"Why Fortune ever entrusted you with my talent, I'll—"

"I said I was sorry, Dolus." Abderian tried again, and a sheet of crystal grew across the hole, sealing it. "Well, it looks solid." He tapped his foot on it experimentally. The crystal made a hollow ringing sound, and suddenly myriad pairs of tiny, feral eyes stared back at them from the other side. "Maybe we should make it opaque, too."

"Nonsense. The lords and ladies will no doubt find it an amusing diversion at the next masked ball. Let us move on."

In the Great Hall, the Grand Staircase and Sliding Banister had crumbled and was suspended in pieces in midair, thanks to Horaphthia's spell.

"I almost think Sagamore would have liked it this way," Abderian mused. "Imagine the court clambering over it like mountain goats."

"You've got the Jester King's blood in you, aright," said Dolus sardonically. "But the nobles would complain about the lack of the banister, though their tailors would no doubt appreciate not having to mend so many breech-bottoms. Let's get on with it."

After the staircase, they moved on to restoring the lower portion of the Wizard's Tower, so that it was not quite so disconcerting to look at. Then they went to the kitchens and restored the bread kilns to their proper three-pointed jester-cap shape, then to the castle cobbler's to raise some fallen arches, then on to healing innumerable broken legs on benches and chairs, restoring walls, and . . .

Hours later, Abderian sat alone and exhausted on a bench in the dining hall. *I feel as though I did all that with my bare hands instead of my mind,* he thought. He sighed and leaned his elbow on the great U-shaped table that filled most of the room. He let his head roll back, and his gaze drifted upward—and his eyes snapped wide open as they beheld the ceiling.

It did not surprise Abderian that there was an exact duplicate of the U-shaped table and its attendant chairs nailed overhead. That had been another of old King Sagamore's decorating innovations:

allowing the poor noble who had drunk too much of the dinner mead to believe that perhaps he was actually seated on the ceiling and was looking *down* at the floor. What startled the prince was that the chairs on the ceiling were empty—or nearly so. Usually there were mannequins tied to the chairs. It had been a game among the servants to dress and pose the mannequins in ways that reflected the mood of the court. When the demons got loose from the lower depths of the castle, they took over the game, with strange and amusing results.

But this night there were no mannequins on the ceiling. Instead, strips of orange and yellow cloth had been tied to the chairs, hanging down like banners and pennants. Whenever a draft disturbed them, the rippling of the bits of cloth made them resemble flames dancing on the seats of the chairs. The illusion made Abderian uneasy. The words Mux had spoken came back to him: "The Powers of Earth are mixed with the Powers of Fire." *What is it the demons know, I wonder?*

"Abderian! Are you all right?" There came a loud fluttering and the prince felt a slapping of feathers against his cheek. He sat up, having been lying on the table for a better view.

"Yes, Paralian, I'm fine. I was just staring at the ceiling."

"Rather pretty, isn't it? I suppose it was the best the demons could do after all the mannequins had fallen down and broken."

"I hope that's not an omen. Something about this bothers me."

"Perhaps it's the color combination. All that fiery orange excites the blood. Maybe it needs some pink for proper balance. But what do I know? I'm a bird, not an interior decorator."

Abderian sighed as Paralian hopped off his shoulder and onto the table. "That's not what I meant, but never mind. I have bigger things to worry about."

"Oh?"

Looking around to be sure they were still alone, Abderian said, "What if I did cause the earthquake, Paralian? What if the cursemark has become so uncontrollable that even my feelings have little to do with what it does? Maybe I shouldn't have kept it after all."

The little bird cocked his head sympathetically. "If it no longer responds to feelings, it makes little difference who owns it."

"Horaphthia could control it."

"She is not of Sagamore's blood. I doubt the mark would stay with her."

"You wore the cursemark most of your life, didn't you, Paralian? Did weird things like this happen while you had it?"

"Well, strange things happened all the time in our father's reign. But you must remember no one knew what the cursemark meant back then. I was treated no differently than any other royal first-born male child. Which might explain some of the problems our father, Time rest his ghost, had with running the kingdom. You recall the drought, don't you?"

"Yes. When I first had the cursemark, I thought it had been my fault."

"You may have prolonged the drought, but you didn't start it. If Father had been kinder, Euthymia might have suffered less."

King Valgus the Brutal had earned his name in many ways. Diplomacy had eluded him and sorcery had baffled him. The only instruments of rule he had felt comfortable with were the rack and the sword. And he had treated his family little better than the peasants, priests, and nobles who had constantly threatened revolt. Abderian wondered how many of the upheavals in Euthymia had been incited by the moods of a headstrong child-prince subjected to his father's "discipline."

"You really ought to marry the girl, you know."

"What? Paralian—"

"Your Highness?" called a page standing in the doorway.

Abderian quickly looked around, trying not to blush. "Uh, yes?"

"His Majesty asks that you come at once to the Throne Room. It is most urgent."

The prince slowly stood, feeling sore all over. "Very well. I'll be there."

The page bowed and left.

"I wonder what Cyprian wants now," Abderian groaned, running his hands through his hair.

Paralian fluttered onto his shoulder. "Answers, I would guess. Now that the crisis is past, people are seeking the cause. Cyprian, I'm sure, would rather not take all the blame himself."

"What joy. I always was his favorite whipping-goat."

"I'll be with you."

Abderian smiled weakly at the little brown bird. "My thanks. But you're not quite the big brother you used to be."

Paralian shrugged his wings. "Nothing is quite as it used to be."

"True enough, brother. True enough." Abderian straightened his shoulders and went to meet the King.

THREE

I hate surprise. The man who surprises me has too much advantage. To be surprised is to be a rat cornered in the cheese box with his little furry pants down, and he wants to bite when cornered. Now, are you sure it's my birthday?

—KING VALGUS THE BRUTAL,
   on the occasion of his first and only surprise party.

THE THRONE ROOM was full of frightened and angry people. Noble men and women from the southern duchies, wearing tall leather headdresses and stiff linen trousers, huddled together and whispered. Fur-clad merchants from the northern counties shouted and shook their fists. Short-skirted patricians from the mountainous border known as The Edge of the World muttered to themselves, fingering parchments of writ. The velvet-clad denizens of Mamelon itself shouted wisecracks and epithets across the room. All were in various states of dishevelment, and casting furtive, angry glances toward the Royal Dais.

Abderian tried to blend in with the tapestries on the wall, not wishing to look like an obvious target. Fortunately, for the moment all their ire was directed at the blond young man sitting on the golden throne.

The eighteen-year-old King Cyprian, wearing the harlequin parti-colored Cloak of State and the three-pointed Jester Crown, sat with his chin in his hand, staring back at the turbulent mob with an expression of helpless concern. Abderian felt a little sorry for him, even though they had never been truly close as brothers. But in the eight brief months of his reign, Cyprian had proved himself to be no worse than any previous king of Euthymia, and some had hopes he might even turn out to be better. He had already earned the name "King Cyprian the Fair," though the rowdier women guards of the castle tended to use "King Cyprian the Hunk" instead. The support and affection of his people, however, was now clearly under a strain.

"It is The Cursemark!" a lord in dirty ermines shouted.

"My wizards send me word there are thirty dead cattle in my duchy! What will you do about this?"

"And my keep is in ruins!"

"Our graneries have collapsed! Who will pay for their repair?"

This is more serious than I imagined, Abderian thought.

King Cyprian leaned forward, as if to speak.

"It is that witch, Horaphthia, who has caused this!" called out one of the linen-clad ladies.

Cyprian suddenly half stood up from his throne. "Who dares accuse my beloved Queen?" he thundered. "Let him speak again and use his tongue for the last time!" The room instantly fell silent.

I guess the love spell is still in effect. Abderian felt amusement and pride at having engineered that particular jest. Their mother, Pleonexia, had insisted Cyprian marry before accession to the throne. Maja's mother, the priestess Entheali, had maneuvered to betroth Maja to Cyprian. Neither Maja nor Abderian wanted any of this, and they conspired to set up Cyprian with the sorceress Horaphtia instead, using an elegant two-stage love spell. Cyprian was enthralled, Pleonexia had no choice but to condone the wedding, and Maja was spared an unhappy marriage. Many had had misgivings about the young prince's taking an ancient sorceress to wife, but Euthymia had since had the most peace and prosperity in living memory.

"One moment, Your Majesty," a woman called out, and the crowd parted to let her through. She wore a hooded gown of black velvet studded with chips of crystal and polished silver that shone and sparkled, as if the gown were a piece of a winter night's sky made into a garment. The woman sketched a brief but graceful curtsey to the King and pushed back her hood, revealing fair-but-greying hair and a fair-but-aging face.

Entheali! What does she want? thought Abderian. *I see she's changed her holy robes again. Maybe the white one was too hard to keep clean.*

The priestess turned to face the assembly and raised her arms. "Good people of Euthymia, hear me. We do falsely accuse our good king. It is true as you say, Lord Carfax, that the Mark of Sagamore is the cause. But His Majesty does not deserve the blame."

Uh-oh, thought Abderian. *They've figured it out.*

Entheali gestured at the crowd, and it parted again to let through a round, balding little man with a bulbous nose, dressed in a yellow silk robe carrying a long wooden box.

Onym, Abderian thought, getting queasy with worry. *Naturally the wizard who created the Mark of Sagamore would figure out the King's mark is a fake. And what will he do about it, given that he is so ancient, so powerful, and so completely crackers?*

"Your Majesty," Entheali continued, turning back to the King, "Onym and I have discovered, through the means of his most potent sorcery, that you have been the victim of a cruel and dangerous jest."

Here it comes . . .

"Indeed?" said King Cyprian, raising his fair brows. "And what might this jest be?"

At least he doesn't trust her any more than I do, thought Abderian.

The priestess pointed at the King's right arm. "Someone has removed the true mark from your arm, Your Majesty, and replaced it with a false one."

The assembled crowd gasped and whispered to one another. Onym rubbed his nose and looked smug.

Half right, Abderian thought, with no pleasure at all.

King Cyprian frowned and rolled back his puffed goldcloth sleeve. "It appears genuine," he said, staring at the liver-shaped mark revealed beneath.

"But we have learned that it is not." Entheali gestured at Onym, and the wizard opened the box he carried. The priestess reached into the box and reverently removed from it a gleaming, golden sword. The hilt was shaped like a jester's stick, its terminus a jester's face complete with a three-pointed belled cap. The incredibly long nose of the jester face wound around the base of the blade to become the bell-guard. "Do you recognize this, Your Majesty?"

Abderian did. It had been a gift to him from the ghost of

Sagamore himself. Entheali had "borrowed" it during her mach-
inations with Maja. So far as the prince knew, the only magic the
sword could do was to animate dead bones. *I'd forgotten she still
had that. Has she found some other power in it?*

"This is the Sword of Sagamore," Entheali intoned. "Given to
the Temple of Tritavia upon our triumphal return to Castle
Mamelon, for our support of Sagamore's royal line."

And how many lies can I count in that sentence? thought the
prince.

"How nice," King Cyprian said with a smirk. "What does a
trinket of the Jester King have to do with us?"

"Most of the powers of this blade escape us, because it is
attuned to those who are of Sagamore's blood. But it was this very
quality that allowed Onym to seek the whereabouts of the true
cursemark."

Abderian looked around for the nearest door. *Can I escape in
time?* he wondered. The crowd was thick in all directions, but he
began to edge along the wall.

"We have learned," Entheali went on, "that the true cursemark
lies not with the King, but with his brother, His Highness, Prince
Abderian!"

Ulp! Too late. Abderian wanted to sink into the floor as all the
nobility around him turned and stared.

"Ah, there you are, little brother," Cyprian said. "I was hoping
you would show up."

Abderian bowed nervously to the King. "Always at your
service, Your Majesty."

"Uh-huh. Do you know what she's talking about?"

"I've no idea, Your Majesty."

"Liar!" Entheali cried, pointing at the prince.

Cyprian turned a dangerous expression on the priestess.
"Madam, you had better have a good reason for calling my
brother a liar."

"Let him bare his arms before the court," said Onym, "and I
will be proven right."

What now? Can I stall the inevitable? Abderian attempted a
nonchalant smile. " 'Tis against all courtesy, sir, to carry weapons
before the King. Therefore it would be most remiss of me to bear
arms here."

After a moment, titters and chuckles rippled through the crowd.
Onym scowled and said "Don't play the fool with me, boy."

"Why not?" Abderian riposted. "Sagamore did, and you were happy to serve him."

Shaking a finger, Onym said, "Take not in vain the name of—"

Entheali caught the wizard's sleeve, and regarded Abderian with a cold smile. "It is appropriate, for a grand-whelp of Sagamore. But your jests will not save you now. Roll back your sleeve!"

In his most haughty tone, Abderian said, "Madam, you do not have the right to command me. I will accept such an order only from my liege, the King." Abderian turned toward the Royal Dais with outward confidence. *Call her off, Cyprian!* he thought frantically. *If you ever had any love for your little brother, save me!*

"Well," said Cyprian, with an expression of suspicious curiosity, "there's no harm in proving her wrong, if you have nothing to hide. Go ahead, Abderian. Push up your sleeve."

That's it. I'm doomed. Abderian closed his eyes as his stomach went hollow and his blood tried to hide within his bones. Reluctantly, he pushed back his right sleeve. He heard gasps nearby and he sighed.

"Well, will you look at that," someone said. "The prince was right."

What? Abderian looked down at his arm.

The cursemark was gone.

FOUR

Excerpt from *A History of the House of Sagamore*, as dictated to her secretary by the Princess Amusia:

There have been lots of kings and queens with funny names. My favorites are King Zhlub the Sad, Queen Baffona the Hairy, and Queen Stalko the Poorly Dressed. Sometimes my great-granddaddy was called Sagamore the Shrewd. My grandfather was King Vespin the Sneaky. My daddy was called King Valgus the Brutal, because he was big and strong and liked to yell a lot. I don't know much about Grandpa Vespin. He was sneaky, I guess.

ABDERIAN BLINKED AND fought to conceal his astonishment.

"What jest, what sorcery is this?" hissed Entheali, running her hands roughly over the smooth skin of his forearm.

"No jest, madam," Abderian said softly. "I do not bear the Mark of Sagamore." He looked back at Cyprian and wondered. *Has he got it, after all? I must get a closer look. Why would it leave me for him, though? And why now?*

The King glared at Entheali through narrowed eyes. "Are you quite satisfied, madam?"

Onym rubbed his bulbous nose and frowned at Abderian's arm. "Perhaps he's hidden it somewhere else on his body. Abderian, would you mind terribly removing the rest of your clothing?"

"You idiot!" Entheali whipped around to face Onym, the gems on her robe swirling like a cloud of falling stars. "You told me you were certain!"

Onym jumped back, abashed. "I swear, Entheali, that is what the sword told me only last night. I don't know what happened. If

26

the cursemark isn't on him now, it must have moved to someone else—jumping, like a flea, perhaps, from one host to another. It would be odd, though. I don't remember giving the spell such fickle tendencies."

Entheali clapped a hand over her face. "Tritavia spare me from this madness!"

King Cyprian slowly stood, saying, "Though we thank you, madam, for your supportive intentions, we are not pleased by your disruption of our court in its current state of distress. We suggest that you retire to your temple cell and meditate on the possible consequences of possessing such a wayward tongue. In fact," he added with a cold smile, "we will send guards to accompany you, and to assure that your meditation is not disturbed." He gestured toward the door and two burly women in leather cuirasses approached.

Onym turned, brandishing the golden Sword of Sagamore at the guards. "Do not dare to touch the holy person of Entheali!"

"Onym, behave yourself," said Entheali. "And get rid of that thing." She grabbed the sword out of Onym's hands. "Useless trinket," she grumbled and she threw the sword on the floor. "Come along now, Onym. Let us allow these nice people to escort us home, where we can have a nice, long talk, shall we?" Her tone indicated the "nice talk" would be anything but. She took Onym's arm, leading him as if he were a recalcitrant child, and allowed the guards to escort her and the confused sorcerer out of the hall.

There was a collective sigh among the gathered nobles, and they did not seem as angry as before. Instead they chuckled and made embarrassed, clumsy remarks about the priestess and the mad mage:

"There goes a star-crossed pair."

"Do you suppose she has to tuck him into bed at night?"

"From the wrong side of the sheets?"

"How many wizards does it take to change a wall sconce?"

Abderian stared down at his naked arm. *It's gone. It's really gone.*

"Depends upon what you want him to change it into."

"None. It makes them soggy and hard to light."

Something metal rolled across the marble floor and bumped against Abderian's left foot. He glanced down and saw the Sword of Sagamore resting against his ankle. The prince picked it up and carried it over to the Royal Dais. "Your Majesty, I believe this is rightfully yours."

Cyprian made a face as though Abderian were offering him a rat on a stick. "Uh, no thank you, brother. You may keep it. As a sign of our royal esteem."

"You are too kind, Your Majesty. Thank you," Abderian said, bowing low. As he did, he looked closely at the part of the mark on his brother's arm not hidden by the gold sleeve. *Nope. That's still the tattoo. So where did the real one go?*

Cyprian faced the rest of the court. "We thank you, good subjects, for bringing your troubles to our attention. This calamity touches us deeply, and we promise you we will do everything in our power to see that all damage is repaired and all wrongs redressed. We go now to confer with our advisors, to seek the cause of this tragedy and to determine what should be done. You will all be informed of matters as they progress. Go now and be of good cheer, for all may yet be very well."

Murmuring among themselves, the lords and ladies bowed and slowly rustled out the doors. A page called out, "Your Majesty, Queen Horaphthia awaits a conference with you in your private audience chamber."

"I'll be there anon," the King replied. To Abderian he added, "You come too. I think it's time we had a 'nice, long talk,' so to speak." Cyprian gestured to a page to follow and, with a flourish of his multicolored cloak, strode from the room.

I know how Onym must feel about now.

Paralian fluttered down from the rafters and lit on Abderian's shoulder. "Could have been worse," he chirped encouragingly.

"It *is* worse," whispered the prince through clenched teeth. "Cyprian still has the tattoo. Where did the real cursemark go?"

"Don't look at me," said the bird. "It wouldn't fit on my itty-bitty wing."

"This isn't funny, Paralian. We've got to find out who has it. I'll bet whoever that is was the one who caused the earthquake." Abderian fumbled with the golden Sword of Sagamore. "And what do I do with this thing?" he grumbled. Finally, he stuck it through his belt.

"It looks quite dashing on you."

"Thanks. Well, got any ideas?"

"Hmmm, a jeweled scabbard might—"

"I mean about the cursemark!"

"Oh. Well, if I don't have it, and you don't have it and Cyprian's is still the fake—maybe we'd better check Amusia and Alexia."

"Uh-oh. You're right. If one of our sisters has it, we're really in trouble. You go try to find out—I'll go try to soothe Cyprian. Maybe Horaphthia will have learned more about what's going on."

"Let us hope. Later." In a flutter of feathers, Paralian was gone.

Though the King's private audience chamber had a perfectly straightforward door down the hall and up a flight of stairs, by habit Abderian sought out the nearest secret passage. Its entrance lay behind a tapestry in the rear of the Throne Room. Normally, Abderian paid little attention to the all too familiar furnishings, but this time he stopped a moment, something about the tapestry catching his eye.

The weaving depicted a charming family scene, entitled, according to a banner woven into the bottom border, "Baby's First Jest." It showed King Sagamore, who apparently had been a small, dark, wiry man, standing with his head thrown back in laughter and pointing at an infant in an opulent cradle. *Probably little Prince Vespin,* Abderian decided. The baby was reaching up to snatch at a string of beads hanging from Sagamore's tunic. And on the infant's arm was a discoloration, which Abderian recognized instantly as the cursemark.

Abderian wondered why the scene was so arresting at the moment. *I can't even tell what "jest" it is that the baby is supposed to have made. Sagamore seems to be pointing at the baby's arm. I wish you could point to where the cursemark is now, Great-Grandfather.* Shaking his head, Abderian gently pushed the tapestry aside and squeezed into the small passage revealed behind it.

The passage was an exceedingly narrow stairway built into an airspace between two stone walls. Abderian had to turn sideways to negotiate it. Though he was not trying to be silent, the prince made little noise as he came up to the arras that covered the exit to the passage, in the private audience chamber.

"It's not my fault!" Cyprian moaned beyond the arras. Abderian cautiously peeked around the edge of the wall-hanging and saw the young king kneeling before Horaphthia, his fair head pressed against her bosom. "I've been feeling fine!" Cyprian went on. "I couldn't have caused the earthquake."

"There, there," said Horaphthia, stroking his golden curls. "I know." Her long black hair hung loose over her shoulders, framing the angles of her handsome face, and she had changed into an ungirdled gown of scarlet silk. "Others will know, too, when we learn the truth." Suddenly, Horaphthia looked up and her eyes met Abderian's. She scowled at him.

Abderian ducked back behind the arras and loudly cleared his throat. He heard Cyprian start. Horaphthia said, "I believe one of your 'advisors' has arrived."

Abderian marched in place on the stair, as if he were still approaching, then flung back the arms and stepped in. "Here I am, Your Majesties, as requested."

Cyprian had stood and was smoothing his tunic and hair. "About time you got here," he said.

"Don't you believe in using doors in this castle?" Horaphthia asked with a sweet-and-sour smile.

Abderian shrugged. "We like to keep up the family traditions."

Horaphthia's mouth quirked. "Some traditions might best be left to die an unmourned death. But now that you are here, make yourself comfortable."

The darkwood-paneled chamber was small and intimate. Benches strewn with red velvet cushions lined the walls, and a huge oak chair, covered with carved laughing faces, dominated the room. Abderian sprawled out on a bench while Cyprian settled into the chair. Horaphthia went to open the one tiny window in the room, revealing a patch of indigo evening sky. A gust of unseasonably hot, dry wind blew in, fanning her hair until it resembled a raven's wing.

"Summer again so soon," murmured Cyprian. "It's from no mood of mine."

"As I have said, my lord," said Horaphthia, "you are not the cause of these events."

"So it is some sorcery other than the mark of Sagamore?"

She didn't say that, thought Abderian. *It's the cursemark, all right. But whose mood is it that brings summer when winter is due, and earthquakes and green clouds?*

There was a rapping at the door and Abderian jumped.

"Enter," said Cyprian, and a page walked in. He carried a silver tray, on which were a flagon and cups, a wheel of cheese, three small loaves of bread, and some steaming chunks of meat in what smelled like a garlic-and-ginger sauce.

"The cooks extend their apologies, Your Majesty," the page said, "for the humble fare. With the quake and all, this was the best they could do."

"No apology needed," said Cyprian, greedily digging into the meat dish with one of the loaves. "Right now, this is easily a meal fit for me."

Abderian answered the grumbling of his stomach and sliced himself some cheese. Horaphthia stood by, seemingly uninterested in the food.

"Am I invited to this party?" said Dolus, standing in the doorway, a much ruffled Paralian perched on his shoulders. Most of the centipedes and scorpions had fallen off his brown velvet robe, and out of his beard and hair.

"You are," said Cyprian, as garlic sauce dripped down his fingers. "Come in."

"Will there be anything else, Your Majesty?" asked the page.

"I think," said Horaphthia, "some towels and finger bowls would be a good idea."

The page bowed out and Dolus closed the door behind him. Paralian fluttered unsteadily over to Abderian's shoulder.

"What happened to you?" the prince whispered to the bird.

"I checked the girls. Neither of them has it. But Alexia tried to pluck some of my feathers out for a necklace she's making and Amusia chased after me with a featherball racquet."

"Poor fellow. Well, I suppose that's some good news."

Cyprian smirked. "When did you start talking to birds, Abderian? Or has wizardry driven you batty, like Onym?"

"Some birds," Abderian said, "are better conversationalists than some people. This fellow here was just explaining why his feathers are such a mess. Our sisters played a little roughly with him, that's all."

"Hmm," Cyprian said through a mouthful of cheese. "Not surprised. Serves you right for having a wimpy bird for a pet. The girls like cats better. Maybe you ought to get a dog—"

"My lord," said Horaphthia, "forgive me, but we should be dealing with our immediate problem. Dolus, you have had time to listen to others in the castle. How do you see His Majesty's position?"

"Well," said Dolus, "his position is no worse than that of the frog whose lily pad rides the spring torrent."

Good old Dolus, thought Abderian.

"Thank you, Dolus," Cyprian sneered.

"So," said Horaphthia, "he will not be unseated immediately, but danger threatens on all sides."

"Exactly."

"But this frog," grumbled Cyprian, "is being blamed for the

torrent. They'll think I deserve to be swept away." The young king sighed and settled back in his chair. "We've got to find the explanation for all this. It's been only hours and my subjects have come up with several of their own, most of which are not favorable to me."

"What did you expect?" Horaphthia asked gently. "Gossip is the lifeblood of any royal court. Malicious or demeaning gossip, in particular."

"Yes," said Dolus. "I remember reading that during King Vespin's reign gossip had it that he would lock himself in a tower at night and play chess with ferrets."

"That hardly seems malicious to me," said Cyprian.

"It is if you love animals," said Dolus. "Ferrets play dreadful chess and hate to lose. It would be torment for them."

Cyprian frowned and Horaphthia caught his arm as he was preparing to throw a chunk of cheese at the tutor.

"Be that as it may," said Abderian, hoping to bring some sanity back into the discussion, "let's think about which schemers might do the most damage." Abderian wished desperately he could discuss the missing cursemark with Dolus and Horaphthia, but he dared not while Cyprian was there. And one can't really shoo a king away from his own council.

"What about that priestess and the wizard? They seem up to something strange," said Cyprian.

"Well," Horaphthia said, "I doubt that Entheali would go so far as to conjure a disaster, for whatever motive. Entheali is mostly concerned with firmly entrenching her cult as the royally sanctioned faith of the kingdom, and in gathering sorcerous power to keep their sorceress/goddess, Tritavia, well supplied in her starry retirement heaven. Onym's motives, of course, are a mystery even unto himself."

"Perhaps some firm questioning might bring his motives to light."

"Perhaps, but that is not possible at the moment. While returning to the temple, Onym, in his shame and embarrassment, 'threw his soul' into one of the chickens in the courtyard."

"Poor dumb cluck," said Paralian.

"A foul fate, indeed," murmured Dolus.

"A poultry excuse," said Abderian.

"Think you I should arrange for a chicken banquet?" Cyprian raised his brows at Horaphthia.

"Please forbear," said Horaphthia. "He is my father, much as I would like to forget it."

"Sorry, my dove." Cyprian patted Horaphthia's hand. "What about that goddess of theirs?"

"Tritavia has little interest in this mortal realm and prefers to keep herself apart."

Abderian knew that was not always the case, but decided now was not the time to mention it.

Cyprian looked back at Abderian. "Any others?"

"There's Tingalut," Abderian said. "Remember him?"

"That Lord High Priest of the ugly Lizard Goddess? Skinny little prune of a guy with beady black eyes?"

"That's the one. Who knows what he's up to? I . . . severely inconvenienced his goddess when I killed her avatar, that dragon, in the temple."

"But by so doing," said Dolus, "you diminished the power of the Lizard Priests, and they are far from their temple in which much of their power is stored. I don't think Tingalut could be much more than a nuisance."

"But a nasty nuisance," Cyprian said. "Well, the reason I called you all here is that these events are clearly magical, and you are the best advisors on magic at hand. Or the only ones I trust," he added softly.

Abderian felt touched. Signs of regard from his brother were rare and always surprised him. "I'll help however I can."

"How long will it take the three of you to learn the source of this sorcery?"

Abderian looked at Dolus and the Queen. They both wore pensive expressions that revealed nothing. "I guess we don't know."

"You don't know," Cyprian said flatly. "Then my situation seems straightforward enough." A wild edge grew in his voice. "I must simply hold the kingdom for an indefinite period of time against traitorous noblemen, a vengeful priest, a scheming goddess, a senile sorcerer, and the curse of a dead jester king. What could be easier?"

"My lord," Horaphthia said soothingly, "it has been a day of trials for you and you are doubtless tired—"

As the Queen tried to calm Cyprian, Abderian's mind wandered back to the tapestry: ". . . the curse of a dead jester king." *What did Sagamore find so funny about*—And then he felt as though struck in the stomach as the answer hit him.

FIVE

Love and magic have much in common; their source is mysterious, their benefits are dubious, and their potential to disrupt all logic and order is incalculable. In short, with few exceptions, both are far more trouble than they're worth.

—LORD JAVEL, DUKE OF NIKHEDONIA,
father of Lady Maja

ABDERIAN STOOD ABRUPTLY, his foot bumping the food tray and setting the goblets to wobbling. Garlic sauce dripped unheeded off his fingers onto his tunic, and Paralian fluttered, off balance, from his shoulder as the prince suddenly turned and started toward the door.

"What is it?" asked Cyprian, frowning.

"Are you all right, lad?" said Dolus.

"Uh, no. Got to go. I don't feel . . . the food just . . . bye." Abderian flung open the door and began to run down the hall, trying to keep his panic from blooming into hysteria. *I've got to get to her first. Nobody else ought to know. Gods, what are we going to do?*

The hallway dipped and swayed before him, which was normal in Castle Mamelon, but for once Abderian cursed Sagamore's dislike of the straightforward. He pushed servants and nobles aside in his headlong run, and didn't notice the frantic fluttering of wings behind him until Paralian had his talons dug into his shoulder.

"What is wrong with you?" chirped the bird. "If you're sick, the *garde-robe* and the healers are the other way!"

"No," Abderian gasped in a loud whisper. "Don't you understand? It's the baby. The baby!"

"Nonsense. If Maja was in labor, we'd have heard of it by now. There's no need to panic."

"No, it's—never mind." Abderian reached the end of the corridor, which stopped before reaching the wall. In the gap stood a brass pole that reached one story up and one down. Abderian flung himself onto the pole and slid down to the ground floor. The footing was more solid here, and he made better speed to Maja's door. Breathlessly, he shoved the latch and stumbled in, unable to stop until halfway into the room.

Maja looked up from her round featherbed and the tray of food on her rounded lap. "Another disaster already, or are you just happy to see me?"

Abderian flung himself down at her bedside and took her left hand in both of his. Paralian fluttered over and perched on Maja's pillow. "Maja . . ." Abderian began, gasping to regain his breath.

Two ladies-in-waiting entered through a side door. "My lady?" they asked with worried frowns.

"It's all right," Maja said. "As long as you're here, take this away." She handed her tray, on which sat a bowl of some greenish broth, to the ladies.

"Oh, your dinner . . ." Abderian said.

"Never mind. It was just some spinach-and-turnip soup. Tasted awful. Now what's *wrong?*"

Abderian looked worriedly at the serving women, and Maja shooed them away with her free hand. Reluctantly, the ladies turned and left. Abderian reached over and ran his hand gently over Maja's belly. "It's the baby, Maja."

Maja made a face and sighed in mock exasperation. "We'll be fine, Abderian. That is, if the midwives give me something real to eat instead of that green pond-scum. Horaphthia says the birth should be no trouble at all. So don't worry, silly." She affectionately mussed Abderian's hair.

"No," Abderian moaned. "It's . . . Maja, look." His hand shaking, Abderian rolled up his sleeve and held out his bare right arm.

"It's gone. Oh, no. Abderian, how did you lose it? Or has Mother done something dreadful again?"

"No, Maja," Abderian said in a loud whisper. He wanted to laugh and scream at the same time. "It's the most obvious thing in the world. The *baby* has the cursemark!"

Maja's lips formed a silent "Oh" and she stared down at herself. Softly she said, "Is that why things have been so strange?"

There was noise at the bedchamber door and Abderian turned to see Dolus rushing in. The tutor turned and closed the door behind him. "I see that you have reached the same conclusion that I did," he said.

"What are we going to do, Dolus?"

"It would seem," the tutor said, walking up to the foot of Maja's bed, "that there is not much to do but wait."

Maja said, "But Uncle Dolus, if the earthquake happened just because the baby got the cursemark, what's going to happen when it's being born?"

Dolus shrugged. "That is impossible to say."

"Wait. Paralian," Abderian said, "when you were born with the cursemark, did terrible things happen?"

The little bird hopped onto Maja's hand. "I'd scarcely remember," he peeped. "I was very young at the time."

Abderian rolled his eyes. "Did anyone tell you of such things later?"

"Abderian, court historians always invent portentous events coinciding with royal births. It's expected, but that doesn't mean they really occurred."

"As I recall," said Dolus, "there was a heavy rainstorm. It had the midwives worried as to whether your mother would catch cold. But that was all."

"Still, something isn't making sense," Abderian said. "There were no strange happenings when you transferred the mark to me, were there, Paralian?"

"No. No outward effects at all, that I noticed."

"Well," said Dolus, "that may mean that a magical transfer of the curse is more smooth than the natural." He threw up his hands and sighed. "Considering the complexity of the idiotic spell, we may not be able to predict *anything* it may do."

Maja slapped the bedclothes. "This is stupid. The person we should talk to is Onym. He created the curse."

"We can't right now, Maja. Onym's a chicken."

"I don't care how scared he is—"

"No, Maja, really, he threw his soul. You remember how he does that."

"Then we'll just have to find that chicken."

Dolus was vigorously shaking his head. "No, no! Onym above all must not know where the cursemark has gone. He would never keep it secret. And then you and your child, my dear, would be subjected to the same fate Abderian has suffered; to be chased by all manner of ambitious folk seeking the power of the cursemark. That is a fate you must avoid, for the safety of the babe and the peace of the kingdom. In fact, no one outside of those now in this room should know."

Damn, thought Abderian. *And to think I once believed magic would make life simpler.*

"What about Horaphthia?" asked Maja. "She's been like a mother to me, and she knows most everything about the mark already."

"Well," Dolus conceded, "yes, I suppose she should be told. But no others."

"This will be awkward, you know," Paralian piped up. "Abderian and Maja have to pretend there is nothing special about the baby, while doing all they can to see that the child is protected."

"And what will we do during the birth itself?" said Abderian, feeling despair start to rise like an incoming tide. "The midwives will see the mark on the baby's arm. So will anyone else who is present. And it will look awfully suspicious if they aren't allowed to help with the birth. Oh, Dolus, this is impossible."

"Nay, do not fear so just yet. Remember, my lad, the way out of a maze is never the most straightforward path. Or as the Gorgorrians say, 'Tis the jewel that lies behind walls of utmost darkness that will shed the clearest light into the hearts of those who persevere.' Or they would say it, if they had the wit."

Maja smirked. "I knew living in this castle was going to be interesting."

"It shall become more interesting as time goes on, I suspect," said Dolus. "Horaphthia has put His Majesty to bed, and I suggest the rest of us get some sleep as well. The days ahead will be challenging enough, without our facing them like the walking dead."

"Well, the sooner you stop pestering us with your strange quotations," Maja said in a playful, didactic tone, "the sooner we might get the rest we need."

Dolus tilted his chin as if insulted. "Well, if it requires my

departure to get you to heed my advice, I can do no greater service
than to leave forthwith. Good night to you all." He bowed and
swept grandly to the door. There he paused and looked back a
moment, winked at Maja, then opened the door and went out.

Abderian sighed. "I wonder if he can ever be serious for long."

"I'm glad he isn't," said Maja, nestling back into her pillows.
"He looks too much like my late but little lamented father as it is.
I wouldn't want him to be so deadly serious as well."

Abderian leaned his head against Maja's arm and realized he did
not want to leave her side. "Would it be all right if I stayed with
you?" he asked softly. "The baby has to be protected, after all."

"So long as you don't invade the baby's privacy," Maja said
with an arch grin, "I think we'd appreciate your company."

"Wait," chirped Paralian. "Won't people start wondering if you
begin to treat the child as special?"

"Dumb bird," said Maja, "*all* mothers think their babies are
special, and deserve all the attention in the world. No one could
be suspicious of that. Even if it didn't have the cursemark, I'd
think it was special." She looked fondly at Abderian.

Abderian felt a joyous fluttering in his middle and a silly grin
spreading across his face. Partly to hide his blushing, he kissed
Maja's hand.

"Well!" said Paralian. "Shall I stay and sing for you a romantic
lullaby?"

"Beat it, worm breath," said Abderian, still grinning. "Find
yourself a drafty rafter and do a courtship dance with a pigeon."

"Hmpf. No appreciation of musicianship. Open the window for
me, then, and I'll be gone. G'night, Maja."

"Good night, Parry."

Abderian opened the shutters of the bedchamber's one window,
and Paralian soared out on the soft, balmy air, "Good night!" the
prince called after him, and closed the shutters again. He turned
back to Maja, thinking, *If it's a happy baby bringing us summer
weather, I'll see that we have many long summers indeed.*

SIX

You can never forget your past deeds.
In the Garden of Life, they're like seeds;
They will sprout, grow and flower
At the most awkward hour,
And many turn out to be weeds.

—LADY CHEVALINE

ABDERIAN FLOATED, SUSPENDED between heaven and earth. Above him, the vault of the night sky was a coal seam littered with diamonds. Beneath, the earth was a barren plain, spreading out to the horizon, where jagged mountains indicated the edge of his world. Abderian felt off balance, as if on the brink of falling. But though he struggled and flopped and spun, his location did not change.

"Tritavia! Burdalane!" he shouted toward the sky. But no inquiring face appeared among the cold stars, and he knew no one heard him.

He reached toward the ground and clawed at the air as if he could dig his way down. But he could bring himself no closer to the earth. His arms felt ugly and naked. *It's the cursemark,* he thought in despair, *I don't have it anymore, so the land won't have me. And I don't have the Nightsword, so Tritavia won't take me in either.*

Then Abderian heard the beat of approaching wings. *Paralian?*

39

he thought with hope. But no, the wings were too large, and the sound they made was muted thunder. He felt a wave of hot air rush by his face, the scent of death borne upon it. Looking up, Abderian saw with horror a great pale dragon circling overhead. *Not again!* thought Abderian. *You're dead!*

"The next time we play this game," said the dragon, in a voice curiously like Cyprian at ten years old, "*I* get to win." The dragon made another close pass and caught Abderian's upper right arm in its talon. "Come," it said, "the Queen awaits."

But even the mighty dragon could not move Abderian from his airy trap, and the powerful thrust of its wings only jerked Abderian's arm a bit. "The Queen, Master," said the dragon, "you must awaken for the Queen!"

"Huh?" said the prince, and suddenly he came free and found himself sitting up in bed. There was still a tugging on his right arm, and he turned his head. The demon Mux was standing beside the bed.

"You have awakened, Master?"

Abderian rubbed his face with his left hand. "What does it look like? What do you want, Mux? Leggo my arm."

"The Queen would speak with you."

"Wha?" Abderian uneasily felt his dream bleeding into real life. He shook his head. "What does Horaphthia want at this hour?"

"Nay, not *thy* Queen, Master. *My* Queen."

"Your—" Abderian began. Then he noticed the flickering orange light coming from beneath the door to the handmaids' chamber. "Oh." *The Demon Queen. Khanda.* He flung back the covers, then looked beside him to see if Maja had been disturbed. She seemed asleep, her peaceful face vaguely demonic in the fiery light.

Abderian slipped out of bed, and Mux released his arm. The little demon led the way to the handmaids' door and pulled it open, bowing. The brilliant firelight in the room beyond made Abderian squint and he crooked his arm before his face. It seemed the chamber was filled with flames, but there was no smoke, and little warmth. He took two unsteady steps into the room.

Mux rustled in and shut the door behind them. "I have brought him, my Queen."

"Khanda?" Abderian said. Blinking, he lowered his arm as much as he dared.

In the middle of the room, within a pillar of fire, sat a young woman on a throne of glowing coals. Her gown was rippling white plasma and her hair was molten gold. A crown of flames encircled her head and firelight danced in her eyes. But despite her glory, the woman on the throne seemed fatigued. "You remember," she sighed with a little smile.

Abderian considered that it would be a trifle difficult to forget the first girl he had loved, particularly since it had been only some months ago. But as Khanda had used his ardor to prepare herself for the wedding bed of another, Abderian's affection for Khanda had soured somewhat. "Yes, I remember. What do you want?"

"I am sorry to have so intruded into your earthly realm this way. This visit is taking what remains of my strength. It was not until this hour that I had recovered enough to even attempt this."

Abderian frowned. "Is there something wrong?"

"My sweet prince, I bring you good tidings and bad tidings."

"Oh. What's the good?"

"I bring you tidings of great joy. You have a baby daughter."

"Thank you, but how do you know what Maja is carrying? And why—"

"Oh, no, no, my sweet prince. It is *our* daughter. Yours and mine."

"*Our* . . ." Abderian's stomach did flip-flops again, not pleasantly this time. "You have a baby too?"

"Yes. It was a likely consequence of our time together, you know." Her warm smile only irritated Abderian more.

"How do you know it's mine?" Abderian said. "Couldn't it be your husband, Belphagor's?"

"We are certain, Belphagor and I. Though the child absorbed demon-nature as she grew within me, still her features are wholly mortal. She is yours."

"I see. Um, doesn't Belphagor mind?"

"Of course he minds. That is why I am here."

"You want me to take the baby." *Oh, lords, what will I tell Maja?*

"You must," said Khanda, leaning forward on her fiery throne. "For hear my other tidings. Our child bears upon her arm the very mark I had once seen on yours. The Cursemark of Sagamore, I believe my father had called it."

Abderian felt his stomach plummet to the floor. "Oh. Oh, gods. And I had thought . . ." he whispered.

"The child was born this morning," Khanda went on, "and

since then there have been strange events in your world and ours
below."

"The earthquake."

"The Powers of Earth have mixed with the Powers of Fire,"
Mux said softly.

Abderian turned toward the demon. "You knew!"

"Hear me, sweet prince," said Khanda, "while I still have the
strength. Belphagor was willing to allow me to give birth, but he
intends to destroy the child. My midwife was to take the baby to
the Soul Eater, but I offered her payment to hide the babe in this
realm instead. Belphagor is searching for the child and if he finds
her, he'll kill her."

"If he kills the baby while she still has the cursemark . . ."
Abderian remembered, with growing fear, dire warnings of doom
to the kingdom if the bearer of the Mark of Sagamore should die.

"You must find our little girl! Save her!"

"But where is she?"

"I will show you." Khanda extended her hand and a picture
formed in Abderian's mind: a rustic village of small, thatched
houses above which towered jagged, snow-capped mountains. A
little sign at the edge of the scene bore the word "Pokelocken."

"There," said Khanda, "is where you will find her. And here is
her appearance. Remember it well."

Another vision formed in Abderian's mind. He saw, asleep in
an orange blanket, a tiny infant with a head of fine, red hair
surrounding a sweet face. For reasons he could not fathom,
Abderian wished he could reach out and run his fingers along her
soft little cheek. *She is mine*, thought Abderian, with wonder. *My
little girl*. "Khanda, why didn't you just bring her here to
Mamelon?"

"That is where Belphagor would search first. Please Abderian,
find our daughter. Save your kingdom and our child."

"Yes, of course." Abderian nodded, knowing he had just
stepped into water higher than his head.

Khanda sighed and smiled, and she slumped back upon her
throne. "I knew you would. You are good and gallant, Abderian.
My father's choice of bridegrooms might have been wisest, after
all. But who can see these things before they are past? I must go.
May the best of fortune follow you, as do my hopes. Good night,
my sweet prince."

In a great puff of black, sooty smoke, Khanda, her throne, and
her fires all disappeared.

Abderian coughed and rubbed his face. *Good and gallant? Heh. I'm a sucker and an idiot.* He blinked in the darkness and heard the chambermaids snoring in their beds, oblivious to anything that had happened. *But how can I get to the baby in time—?* The little demon rustled in the dark beside him.

"Mux," Abderian whispered, "you have wings. You can fly out to this place and grab the child before Belphagor gets there."

"No, no, no, Master. Do not send me. Do not even tell me where it is. Belphagor is my king and I would have to obey any command he gives me."

"Oh." Abderian realized he didn't know much about the politics of the demon realm. Who were Mux's ultimate loyalties to? Abderian sighed. "Well, then. Guess I'll have to go myself." He turned around and fumbled at the latch, finally opening the door.

A stray beam of moonlight angled in through the shuttered window. Maja still rested on her side, fast asleep. *I can't tell her,* he thought. *Not when she's so close to having her own.* "Mux," he whispered, "bring me some paper and something to write with."

"Aye, Master." Mux's leather wings rustled and presently he returned with a scrap of parchment and a small lump of charcoal.

"You expect me to write with this?"

"Demons use it all the time."

"Oh. I suppose demons don't care if their hands get all smudged."

"We rather like it, Master."

"I was afraid you'd say that." Abderian went to the bed table and scrawled on the parchment:

> Dear Maja,
> Something came up and I had to leave.
> Won't be gone long.
> Don't have the baby 'til I get back.
> I love you.
>
> Abderian

The last line was painful to write. He felt as though he were deceiving her, though that wasn't true at all. In the dim light he examined the black, smudgy handwriting. *Heh. Looks more like Amusia wrote this. I hope Maja won't think it's one of her pranks. It will have to do.*

Abderian set the note on the bed table. He found his pile of clothes in the dark and struggled into them, hoping nothing was inside-out. As he went to the door, he turned to gaze fondly one last time at Maja and tripped over something that clanged on the floor. His hands slapped hard on a sharp metal object and he heard Maja stir on the bed.

"Mmmm, Abby-dabby?" she murmured softly.

"Just going to the *garde-robe*," Abderian said, not moving.

"Mmmmm." Maja rolled over, and sighed, seeming to return to sleep.

Abderian slowly stood, picking up whatever it was his hands had fallen on. Moonbeams glistened on the jester head that was the hilt of the Sword of Sagamore. By a trick of the light, the jester face winked at him.

"It likes you, Master," Mux whispered hoarsely.

"Great." *Well, I might find it useful.* Abderian stuck the sword through his belt and went out the door as quietly as he could, Mux following closely after.

The twisted corridor was dim, lit only by two wall torches that were burning low. No one was in sight.

As Abderian tiptoed down the hall, Mux began to make choking, coughing sounds. The prince turned to look at him. "What's wrong, Mux?"

The little demon's eyes were wide, and his knobby talons were clapped over his mouth.

"Mux? Are you all right?"

Suddenly the demon took his hands from his mouth, revealing an enormous grin, and wrapped his arms around his belly. "Abby-dabby!" he gasped. He rolled, laughing helplessly, onto the floor. "Abby-dabby abby-dabby abby-dabby abby-dabby!"

Abderian rolled his eyes heavenward. "That's enough, Mux."

"Abby-dabby!"

"Shut up, before you wake everyone in the castle."

"Abby-dabby!"

"Stop! *Sigas tumur ilixit!*"

At the magical words, Mux instantly jumped to his feet, silenced and pouting.

"That's better. Now be off with you. Go find Paralian and tell him . . . tell him to look after Maja while I'm gone."

"Yes, Abby—Master."

"That's right. Go."

Mux flashed him a wicked grin and lifted his wings, whose span was just wide enough to fill the width of the corridor. The demon turned and flapped away. But in the distance, Abderian could hear him squeak "Abby-dabby! Abby-dabby!" all the way down the hall.

Abderian shook his head. *Almost makes me wish the Lizard Priests would come back.*

He continued down the hallway, which more and more had begun to resemble a corkscrew. Just before it took a discomfiting twist to the left, Abderian found a narrow door and pulled it open, revealing what appeared to be a deep broom closet. He stepped inside and lit a small, sorcerous blue flame in his right hand. He pulled on a broom hanging on the wall and a panel slid aside in the back of the closet, revealing a stairway going down. Abderian descended and was relieved to find that the stairs were only two flights long. Dolus had been known to make it far worse for unexpected visitors.

The prince came up to a beautiful, deeply carved bloodwood door embellished with designs of herbs and flowers useful in sorcery. Abderian raised his hand to knock, but it slowed in the air, meeting some strange resistance. Suddenly the air just in front of the door shimmered, and golden letters appeared glowing in the wood:

"You have reached the abode of the sorcerer Dolus. I'm sorry, but I am occupied and cannot come to the door right now. If you will state your name and a brief message after the tone, I will endeavor to get back to you. Please wait for the tone. Thank you."

There came the sound of a gong in the distance.

"Dolus!" Abderian shouted. "This is urgent! Turn this spell off and . . . Oh, shuck it." Abderian waved his arms in a simple Spell Disruption pattern. The gold lines twisted into chaos and the door emitted a high-pitched "*Skreeeee!*"

Moments later, a very disheveled Dolus threw wide the door, exclaiming, "Who in the demon-blasted—Oh, it's you. Abderian, I hope you are not going to tell me something else has gone wrong. I'm not sure my constitution could take it at this hour."

"Who is it, Dolus?" called a feminine voice from the depths of his chambers.

Dolus reddened and called back, "Nothing to worry about, my dear."

"It's not my husband, is it?"

"No, Lady Maduro, fear not."

Abderian opened his eyes wide. "Sounds to me like your 'constitution' is doing just fine."

Dolus stepped out beside him and shut the door, wrapping his dressing robe tighter around himself. "She came to me needing some healing ointments."

"And of course you had to give her a thorough physical examination."

"Well, she stayed for . . . conversation."

"Yes, General Maduro isn't much for witty repartee."

"I presume, lad, you did not disturb me for the sake of gossip. What do you want? It had better be important."

"Is knowing the true location of the Cursemark of Sagamore important enough?"

It was Dolus's turn to widen his eyes. "Eh, hum, yes. Where? Not on your babe, then?"

"On my babe indeed, but not Maja's."

Dolus sighed. "It's too early in the morning for riddles, my lad. Has she given birth already?"

Abderian shook his head. "Do you remember your other niece, Khanda, Maja's sister?"

Dolus scratched his beard. "I remember her as a pretty little blond child. Devoted to her father. Didn't you once say she'd become queen of something?"

"Queen of the Demons, Dolus. Did I tell you how she earned the title?"

"No. Is it relevant?"

"Very. Apparently the Demon King, Belphagor, could only wed a maiden deflowered by a male who was also pure. Guess who the lucky boy was."

Dolus raised an eyebrow. "I . . . see. And there has been a child from this?"

Abderian nodded. "A little girl. Khanda just told me tonight."

With a frown, Dolus said, "And was this babe born before or after Khanda became the Demon Queen?"

"Well after. The baby was born just this morning."

Dolus slapped his brow. "So a demon child has been born bearing the cursemark."

"You got it."

"Almighty Earthmother! So that was the cause of the earthquake. Oh, Abderian, this is not good at all. Demon sorcery mixed with the cursemark! We must persuade Khanda to give us the babe so that we may remove the mark at once!"

"That's the problem. She's already had to give the baby up because Belphagor wants to destroy it. Khanda hid the infant somewhere. That's why I came to you. You have to show me how to do a teleport spell so that I can find it and bring it back."

"Teleport?" Dolus groaned. "Oh, lad, I can't. It's far too complex to explain in an hour or two, and I was never good at it anyway. If I tried to teach you, the result would probably be purée of Abderian spread all over the eastern plain."

"But we've got to find the baby, and soon! If Belphagor kills her—"

"I know, lad, I know. That earthquake will seem like a minor annoyance in comparison. Well, there is only one person who can help."

"You mean Horaphthia. But she's almost a mother to Maja. What would she say?"

Dolus clapped a hand on Abderian's shoulder. "My boy, you are kin of the great Jester King himself. Your blood is that of the greatest tricksters Euthymia has ever known. It is your very heritage to lie, prevaricate, and cheat when called upon for the good of the kingdom. I'll go dress. Meet me by the Queen's chambers in a quarter-hour." Dolus slipped back into his rooms.

Sagamore, inspire me now, thought Abderian as he turned and trudged back up the stairs, his heritage weighing heavily upon him.

SEVEN

Excerpt from *A History of the House of Sagamore*, as dictated etc., by Princess Amusia:

There are lots of places in Euthymia with funny names, too. There's the Forest of Forgetfulness, and the Stylus Wood. There's a big mountain range called The Edge of The World—it really isn't, people just call it that. And there's a big waterfall called the Veil of Giant's Tears. And Abderian says there's a swamp underneath Mamelon called "Castle Doom," but I think he was just teasing me—

"A TREASURE HUNT," said Queen Horaphthia, tapping the arm of her high, straight-backed chair. "While Mamelon is still in ruins and Maja is due. What considerate timing." Though she wore only a plain black satin night robe and her hair was disheveled from sleep, she looked every inch the puissant sorceress queen. Abderian preferred to stare at her patterned rug rather than meet her gaze.

Dolus, standing at Abderian's right, cleared his throat. "Your Majesty oversimplifies what I have said."

"I have found, my dear Dolus, that when dealing with you that is often the best course. Abderian, would you say my interpretation is correct?"

"Not exactly . . . Your Majesty." Abderian felt as though he were again before his history tutor, having forgotten to memorize his lessons. *Ohhh, this was a mistake. I should have just ridden off and hoped the babe survived until I got there.*

"Indeed? In what way, pray tell?"

Abderian stared at a russet curtain and his hands flopped in helpless gestures as he tried to explain. "You see, it's not really just a game—it's more important. What we seek really is a treasure, and we have to find it first, but—"

"Stop that!" Horaphthia's voice froze him in mid-gesture. "I'm not so great a fool, even at this hour of the morning."

"What?"

The Queen let her breath out slowly. With exaggerated patience, she said, "Kindly clasp your hands behind your back and keep them there."

Abderian did so, bewildered.

"Did you really think to teach your grandmother how to gut goats?"

Abderian opened his mouth to protest, then shut it. *I was trying to bewitch her, and I wasn't even aware of it.*

"He meant no harm, Horaphthia," Dolus said. "This happens upon occasion because he absorbed my sorcerous power. There's a bit too much of it for his corporeal vessel, so to speak, and sometimes it leaks out. You know how magic can have a will of its own."

"Yes, I know," said Horaphthia, rubbing her brow. "Now, before I lose my patience entirely, I will ask you to tell me truly just what in the darkness of Tritavia's Heaven is going on."

Abderian took a deep breath. "We . . . I can't. Not yet. But believe me, it's very important that we find what we're looking for."

Horaphthia stared at him intently. "It concerns the earthquake. And the cursemark. Doesn't it?"

"Please, I shouldn't say anything more. It's not safe."

The Queen slowly shook her head. "Do you feel I am that untrustworthy?"

"That's not it!" said Abderian. "It's just that we don't know—" Abderian looked around him and said more softly, "who might be listening."

"If you had asked," Horaphthia said, her lips twisting in a wry smile, "I could have set a spell to foil eavesdropping before we began this discussion."

"And that might seem suspicious itself to any who watched," said Dolus. "You are in a very public position, Your Majesty. Were you to give more aid than what we ask, or join us on our quest, your activities or absence would be noted."

"While people are used to my disappearing now and then," Abderian added.

Horaphthia stood and paced slowly past Abderian. Softly she said, "Maja will be very hurt if you are not here when your child is born."

"Don't worry," Abderian said. "This should take scarcely an hour or two. We'll be back this evening at the latest." In fact, he had no idea how long their expedition would take. *How easy is it to find a little baby in the middle of nowhere?*

"I should hope so," said Horaphthia, standing. "It would break Maja's heart not to have you near."

Abderian stared at the rug again. *It might break her heart more if she knew the truth.*

Horaphthia went to a simple but elegant darkwood chest and took from a drawer two sticks of chalk, one white, one black. She motioned Abderian and Dolus off the rug and onto a part of the floor that was plain stone. "Now, where do you need to go?"

"I . . . shouldn't say it out loud."

Horaphthia put her fists on her hips and rolled her eyes. "Don't like to make it easy for me, do you? Shall I choose a location at random and have you go from there?"

"No, I . . . I have a vision I was given of the place. Can't we use that?"

"Hmmm. Touchy." Horaphthia began to draw a wavy circle around Abderian and Dolus. "I hope you trust who or whatever gave you this vision. If the recollection is too vague, or if the place doesn't actually exist, there's no telling where you'll end up."

Abderian felt his mouth go dry. *What if Khanda wasn't clear about the village? What if becoming a demon drove her crazy? What if she's trying to trick me again?* The prince was suddenly aware of Dolus's considering stare. "Yes. I'm certain of the place." He tried to smile and wink at Dolus, managing only some nervous twitching in his cheeks. His tutor did not seem reassured.

"Good," said Horaphthia. She finished the circles with a flourish. Then, somehow, one of the chalk lines became a length of string in her hand and she pulled it up from the circle until there was enough loose twine to reach over to where Abderian stood. She bound the end around Abderian's brow. "Now, hold still, close your eyes and think of wherever it is you want to go. Allow no distractions to enter your mind. Think only of your vision."

Not knowing why, Abderian clung tightly with both hands to the hilt of the Sword of Sagamore, and stood as close to Dolus as he could without standing on top of him. He shut his eyes tightly and tried to bring the image to his mind. It was there, but seemed a bit fuzzy, as if seen in the rain.

"You know the routine," said Horaphthia. "Tug three times on your hair when you are ready to return. Try not to make me come chasing after you. It would not improve my temper, believe me."

"Yes, ma'am," Abderian mumbled.

"Courage, lad," said Dolus.

And then the room went topsy-turvy, and the colors of the walls and curtains blurred into muddy shades of twilight darkness. Abderian concentrated on the scene Khanda showed him, and on the sign saying "Pokelocken," on the mountains in the distance. Tried to imagine himself there—

Abderian blinked several times as the colors before him again resumed recognizable shapes. Something felt odd about his hands, and then he realized he was clutching Dolus's sleeve as though it were his mother's apron.

"Easy there, lad," said Dolus.

"Sorry," Abderian mumbled, letting go. He took a breath of cool air and shivered. To their left rose a dark wall of mountains, whose jagged peaks were haloed by the pale pre-dawn glow. "The Edge," he murmured.

"Heh," coughed Dolus. "It is only called The Edge of the World because early Euthymian mapmakers were notoriously provincial. The Gorgorrians, you know, call it The Caterpillar."

"Do they really?"

"Well, maybe not exactly that, but that is the *sort* of name they'd give it."

"Dolus," Abderian sighed. He peered around in the gloom, making out what appeared to be thatched houses not far ahead. His feet felt cold and uncomfortable. Abderian looked down and saw that he was ankle-deep in mud. "Dolus!"

"An unfortunate point of arrival," Dolus commented. "Good thing we remained standing. Let us seek drier ground, shall we?"

With effort, they sloshed their way onto what seemed to be a raised road. As the dawn gave them more light, Abderian could see that much of the land around them was covered with mud and rivulets of water. "This isn't exactly what Khanda showed me."

"It would seem," said Dolus, "that there has been a flood here recently." He looked up at the mountain peaks. "Yes, there should be more snow up there at this time of year."

"It was warm at Mamelon last night," said Abderian with

growing worry. *If the demon baby can do this with the curse-mark—* "Dolus, what if the baby's drowned herself in all this?"

"I think we would have noticed the cataclysm that would have resulted, don't you?"

Abderian saw something sticking up out of the muck by the side of the road. He walked over and examined it. It was part of a sign, the visible portion reading "-locken." "Well, this seems to be the right place. But how do I find her in all of this?"

Dolus turned and frowned. "You mean you brought us all this way without—"

"I thought she'd be right here! Or nearby. I didn't think I'd have to search." *I didn't think . . . I didn't have time to think. Oh, hell.* Abderian flopped cross-legged onto the road and rested his chin in his hand. "Maybe if we listened for a baby crying."

They were both silent a moment.

"Unless your babe is so precocious she can imitate chickens or cows," said Dolus, "I don't seem to hear her."

Abderian had to admit that distant clucking and mooing was all he could hear, too. He ran a fingertip through the dirt of the road. "So what do we do now?"

Dolus squatted down beside him. "Has the frenetic pace of things garbled your wit, or have you forgotten that you are a sorcerer?"

Abderian blinked up at his tutor. "No, I hadn't forgotten. But I haven't studied any spells for finding people. Just transformations and repairing things. How can that help me?"

Dolus gave him a measuring gaze. "Study cannot tell you everything. There are times when you must improvise your own spells."

"Isn't that dangerous?"

"Always. But very educational, too, and sometimes it yields surprising results."

"I'll bet. But I don't have any equipment or books with me, anyway."

"The greatest of wizards, Salvia the Sage, carried no other equipment than the knowledge in her mind and the clothing on her back. It was said she could work wonders with a single blade of grass."

Abderian looked at Dolus skeptically. "Is that true or are you just making that up?"

"Does it matter? I'm making a point. The creative wizard uses what he has at hand."

"So, how can I find a demon baby with mud?"

Dolus shook his head and eased himself into a more comfortable sitting position. "You've much more available than that. Let us examine the situation. One: The baby must be nearby or has been nearby; otherwise Khanda would not have sent you here—assuming she's honest."

Abderian nodded, wondering how large an assumption that was.

"Two: You yourself are a close relation to that which we seek. You at least remember the laws of similarity and contagion, don't you?"

"Like attracts like. Things closely associated take on each other's qualities, and retain an association even when separated."

"Close enough. And there are few associations closer than relation by blood."

"But that's just a figure of speech," said Abderian. "We don't really share each other's blood, and we've never been near each other."

Dolus chuckled. "Well, much about the generation of life remains a mystery. But a scholar friend I had at the University of Rodomontade, in the Phenomenology Department, once told me that there were little bits of stuff we carry around in us that determine what we look like, act like, and so on. He called these bits 'trousers' because he believed they come in pairs, and one gets a different pant leg from each parent—"

"So we're all born with a patch-quilt wardrobe," Abderian put in, disgusted. "Dolus, that is the stupidest idea I ever heard. What do trousers have to do with finding Khanda's baby?"

"Scoff at science if you wish. I only meant that there is more connection than you think. Use it."

"I guess I don't have much choice." Abderian glanced down at the drawing he had been idly making in the dirt and noticed it was a sort of spiral with lines radiating out from it. He felt a chill in his spine. "I wish I would stop doing that," he murmured.

"Doing what, lad?"

"I think I've just drawn a magical symbol, without knowing it."

"Let me see." Dolus leaned over. "Hmmm, looks unfamiliar to me. What do you think you have drawn?"

"I don't know. It's sort of like those direction arrows they put in the corners of maps." Ideas began flitting through Abderian's mind almost faster than he could catch them. "Maybe if I put a little of my blood into these grooves . . ." He rose onto his knees and moved around the diagram.

A smile lit Dolus's face and the tutor moved back to give Abderian room.

"I need a purified blade to cut myself with," Abderian thought aloud. Then he noticed his right hand was on the hilt of the Sword of Sagamore. "Of course! This sword has association to any of Sagamore's kin. It should help, too." He grinned triumphantly at Dolus.

"Ah. Now you are thinking like a creative wizard!"

"But I have no pure water or fire."

"One moment." Dolus pulled a slender flask from beneath his robe and handed it to Abderian. "It's a good thing I travel prepared."

Abderian pulled off the stopper of the flask and caught a whiff of sweet wine. He raised a brow at Dolus. "For medicinal purposes?"

Dolus frowned. "In case I need a drink. But it should serve the spirit of your purpose well enough."

"Right." Abderian paused a moment to consider the proper words. Then he drew the gleaming sword from his belt. The rosy morning light seemed to give the blade a warm, golden glow. Abderian held the blade over the diagram and slowly poured the wine over the blade. Remembering Mux's words, he said,

> "Fire and Earth, water and mud,
>   Help me find that which is blood of my blood.
>   Show me the hiding place here in the wild,
>   That Khanda had chosen for our newborn child."

Abderian then rested his left hand under the blade in order to cut the fleshy part of his thumb. But before he could draw blood, the sword leapt out of his grasp and fell onto the diagram in the road. Abderian jumped back as the sword spun around madly. Then it stopped, the blade pointing straight at a clump of bushes on the north side of the road.

Abderian and Dolus rushed over to look, and found within the bushes an empty basket. A few strands of fine, red hair clung to one of the woven reeds.

"Well," said Dolus, scratching his beard, "unless Khanda steered you very wrong, it would seem someone else has found the babe already."

"Oh, gods. Now how do we find her?"

"Hang on, your blade is acting up again."

Abderian glanced back to the road, where the Sword of Sagamore was spinning on its point like a top. Suddenly it leapt into the air and the blade aimed straight down the road into the village. A shimmer of golden light pulsed down the blade, as if the sword were saying, "Thataway."

"It appears," said Dolus, "yon clever sword is willing to be of some service in the matter."

EIGHT

Countless souls, seeking their own selfish ends, daily work their will upon the world. So why is it we are so surprised when we don't get our own way?

—SALVIA THE SAGE

IF ANYONE IN the village of Pokelocken thought there was anything strange about the sight of a richly dressed adolescent running down the road behind an outstretched, glowing golden sword, followed by a bearded middle-aged man in wizard's robes, there was no sign of it. What few inhabitant's Abderian and Dolus passed gave them scarcely a glance. The villagers seemed more concerned with clearing the mud from their homes and extricating stranded cows from the flooded pastures.

Abderian could spare little time to look at them as he struggled to keep up with the sword's urgings and tuggings. *Where am I going? Which house has the baby?* They passed a little shrine, a blacksmith's, an inn and various shops, until, to Abderian's utter bewilderment, they came out on the far side of the village, with the sword still pulling him onward.

The prince dug his heels into the road and managed to slide to a stop, leaning against the sword's pull. As he gasped to catch his

56

breath, he heard Dolus come puffing up behind him. "This is ridiculous, Dolus. The baby isn't in the village at all!"

Dolus paused, winded, before answering with a worried frown. "Perhaps she has been taken by an outlying farmer."

"Or a traveler that was just passing through?"

"Let us hope not, lad. These old legs ache enough as it is."

The bare trees rattled off to their right and a farmer in a long cotton smock and floppy hat emerged onto the road, leading a sad-looking, mud-stockinged cow.

Dolus called out to him, "A gracious good morning, sir. Could you give us some assistance?"

The farmer squinted back at them and Abderian felt very self-conscious about the sword and arm stuck out at his side. He wished there was some position he could stand in that would make it look natural.

The farmer said nothing, but stopped, regarding them as though they were someone's idea of a bad joke.

"Muuuuh," said the cow.

"Ah, such eloquence in one utterance," said Dolus. "Pray tell me, good squire, what farmers might live northwards beyond this village?"

The man frowned bushy eyebrows and pursed his lips. "Nobody," he said.

"Ah, well then, has some traveler perhaps passed through here, with a child?"

The man tilted his head back and thought. "Nope."

"Muuuuh," said the cow.

"I see. Clever animal you have there. I don't suppose there has been word of a foundling discovered hereabouts and carried off that way?"

"How'd I know such a thing?" said the farmer. "D'I look like a gossip?"

"Yuuuuh," said the cow, nodding.

"Aw, who asked ye?" said the farmer to the beast. Turning back to Dolus and Abderian, he went on, "There's a caravan passed through here last night. Ye might ask them."

"Aha! And is that caravan now to the north?"

"Should be. Went through despite the flood. Might still be hereabouts if the road's washed out."

"Excellent! Thank you, most observant and gracious fellow."

"A word o' caution to ye, though, sir."

"Yes?"

The farmer nodded at Abderian. "Tell yer young'un there that it's impolite to point."

Abderian pulled his lips into an embarrassed smile and tried to force his arm down against his side—to no avail.

"Uh, most certainly, wise sir. Thank you. Goodbye."

"Buuuuh," said the cow, following the farmer down the road.

Dolus grabbed Abderian's shoulder. "Let us go. A bit more leisurely, this time, if you please."

Abderian managed to keep their pace to a rapid walk. "Did you have to flatter him so much?" he asked when out of earshot of the farmer. "He might have been insulted."

"Compliments, my dear boy, are never wasteful. Most people need all the compliments they can get. Kind words wash away the tarnish on one's spirit, allowing the inner beauty of the soul to shine again."

Abderian sighed. "Yes, Dolus."

Beyond the north end of the village, the road wound up and down through the foothills of The Edge. Over the second rise, Abderian and Dolus stopped and looked down in the vale before them. There, a cluster of wagons, oxen, horses, and shouting people cluttered up the road. They were clearly mired in a wash of mud from the mountain. The Sword of Sagamore hummed and sparkled as it pointed into the midst of the wagons.

"She's there," Abderian said. "We're lucky the flooding kept them from getting farther. Let's go."

"Not so fast, lad. This is no ordinary band of mendicant merchants or roving entertainers. They're of the Grey Guild. See the wolf's head insignia burned into the side of each wagon?"

"Yes. So what?"

"Shhh! Not now. And put that sword out. The light will give us away."

"But—Oh, well. Mission accomplished. Thank you, sword. Dismissed." The golden light immediately went out and Abderian's arm flopped to his side. With aching muscles, he stuck the blade back through his belt. "So what do you suggest?"

"Ho, there!" someone called, and a man dressed in loose, dark blouse and trousers stepped out of the trees and onto the road before them. "What business have you observing us?"

"Most specific business, sir," said Dolus. "We would speak to your Caravan Master."

"She is busy"—the man looked over his shoulder at the morass behind him—"as you can see."

"One of the Grey Guild is never too busy for business," said Dolus. "We are interested in a certain item discovered in a basket by the side of the road last night. It is most important to us. Have her meet us at the inn in the village to discuss terms."

The dark-clad man rubbed his chin and nodded. "I will tell her."

Abderian opened his mouth to protest, but Dolus caught his arm and spun him around, marching him back down the road.

"Say nothing," Dolus hissed in his ear.

Abderian fought to keep his questions from escaping until a hill separated them from the caravan. Then he stopped and rounded angrily on his tutor. "What in Tritavia's Holy Heaven is going on here!"

Dolus looked sadly patient. "The Grey Guild is unique among merchant and transport associations. They are powerful, stubborn, and arrogantly independent. They are also trusted with handling the most dangerous, valuable, or unusual cargoes. There are rumors that a Master of a Grey Guild caravan must also have certain unusual abilities in order to fulfill his or her duties. It is no ordinary trader we will be dealing with, I can assure you."

Abderian felt so confused and angry that he sputtered a moment before the next words came out clearly. "But, but, this is my child we're talking about. A royal baby! What do you mean business, dealing, trading? She's mine and they just have to give her back!"

Dolus sighed. "I understand how you must feel. But believe me, if you hope to retrieve the infant, you must trust me and do as I direct. It will be hard, I know."

"But what if Belphagor shows up?"

"Abderian, these people are far better equipped to protect the child from murderous demons than we are. Now calm yourself. It will look better if we get to the inn before the Caravan Master does." Dolus put a consoling arm across Abderian's shoulders and they continued back to the village, Abderian kicking stones angrily the entire way.

Some time later they were standing before a two-story ramshackle cottage. Above the door hung a weatherbeaten sign on which were rough paintings of a horse and a pig. Beneath these were the words "Neigh-boar-ly Inne."

The inn door opened and a stout woman emerged, carrying a

barrel nearly as big as she was. She set this beside the door and gave Dolus and Abderian a nod of greeting.

"Well," Dolus murmured, "we can hope that the ale here is not so bad as the name, and as full-bodied as its matron. Good morning, good alewife!" he called out.

The woman rubbed her broad hands on her apron and stuck a corncob pipe in her mouth. She nodded once at them again.

"The volubility of the inhabitants of this village is astounding. We wish to rent a private meeting room, if you please."

The woman narrowed her eyes at them and seemed to be studying their clothes. "If yer here for the Harvest Festival," she said, "yer two months late."

"No, madam. We are here to confer with the Guild Caravan Master over an important item of business."

The alewife's eyes grew wide. "Well, why dint ye say so in the first place. I got the best rooms in the duchy. I'll set ye right up. Come on in."

The magic effect of mentioning the Guild was not lost on Abderian, and he wondered what manner of people they were. *Maybe they just leave big tips.*

The back room of the Neigh-Boar-ly Inne was sparsely furnished, but hospitable, and the ale was indeed quite good. These did nothing, however, to soothe Abderian's dark mood, and the unnatural, humid warmth of the day made it all the worse as they waited in silence for the Caravan Master.

The arched door to the room creaked open and two dark-clad men, similar to the one they had met in the road, walked in. The first one had dark blond hair and deep-set eyes that looked a little wild. The man behind him was shorter, with shoulder-length black hair and a droopy black moustache. His step bounced and his dark eyes sparkled at the prince as though delighted at the prospect that Abderian might try something untoward.

"Let me search the room, Little Uncle," said the blond one.

"No," said the dark one as he swaggered around the room, looking under tables and chairs. "You will guard the door."

"Aww, why do you always get the fun jobs?" said the blond.

"Because, you livid lump of lamb's liver, you would botch them up."

"Aww, I would not."

"Are you quite finished?" called a husky voice from the main taproom beyond.

"Clear," the dark one said through the doorway. The blond

made an almost graceful sweep of his arm to welcome in whoever
it was.

The shorter man stepped aside and took up a position beside the
door.

And an extraordinary woman walked in. She was of moderate
height, and her face was handsome, tanned and weathered. She
had large grey eyes, and her pale, ash-brown hair hung in a thick
braid down her back. She wore tunic and leggings of soft grey
leather, and carried a grey leather whip at her side. She nodded at
Abderian and Dolus. "I am Vulka," she said in a rough but not
unpleasant voice, "seventh-year Master for the Guild." She sat
with muscular grace across the table from them.

"I am called Dolus," the tutor said with a nod that was almost
a bow. "Counselor of Sorcery for the Court of Mamelon."

Vulka gave a brief nod in return, then turned her gaze on
Abderian. "And the young man?"

"An apprentice. He is not important in this."

Vulka blinked, her face showing the barest hint of disbelief.
Abderian bristled at being called an apprentice, even if it was, in
a way, true, but he said nothing. He nodded and smiled at her. He
wasn't sure if he liked or despised her, but she was very
interesting. She looked back at Dolus, expectant.

"Has your man told you of the item that interests us?"

"He has, but perhaps you should remind me so that we are
certain there is no confusion."

"The item I seek is a found object, discovered by the side of the
road south of this village very early this morning."

"Ah, yes." The barest hint of a smile crept onto Vulka's face.
"That item. Continue."

Abderian ground his teeth at the word "item."

"Have you decided to put this item on the market?"

"For the right price," Vulka said cautiously.

"And what might that be?" Dolus asked blandly.

"I could not let it go for less than a million scepters."

Price? thought Abderian. *A . . . million . . .*

Dolus smiled politely. "That is impossible. No one would pay
such an amount."

"The item in question has certain unusual and unique qualities.
There are those who would pay well for it," Vulka said.

They're going to sell the baby. Abderian gripped the edge of the
bench until his hands hurt.

"Would you accept something in trade, service perhaps?" offered Dolus.

Vulka's grey eyes looked dubious. "It would have to be an object or service of most rare value."

"Ah, but if you deal with us now, we can spare you the cost of upkeep that the item will require over a long journey."

"For such a small item, the upkeep is minimal and will easily be covered by the purchase price—"

"Enough!" Abderian stood and pounded the table with his fist, unable to contain his growing rage. "This is a *baby* we're talking about, not an *item*! My baby! I'm the father and that child rightfully belongs to me!"

The short, mustachioed man danced up to the prince and laid a hand lightly on his shoulder, smiling. Abderian wanted to punch him, but doubted he'd survive the attempt.

"Let be, Stad," Vulka said, gazing at Abderian. "This interests me. I like to know the background of my commodities."

"She's not a commodity!" Out of the corner of his eye, Abderian saw Dolus bury his face in his hands. "Slavery is unlawful in Euthymia. You've no right to sell her as if she were a . . . a . . . statue or something."

Vulka gave him a patient smile. "The child is a foundling, and even in Euthymia, adoption fees are permitted. However, the clients who I think will have an interest in her are in Gorgor, where there are no laws against slavery."

"As the father, I have the right to claim the foundling before she is given to another!"

"As the current guardian of the child and responsible for its welfare, I must tell you that the burden of proof lies with you. If you attempt to bring local authority against us, I assure you it would be in vain."

"I will have you know," Abderian growled at her, leaning over the table, "that I *am* the highest authority here. I am His Royal Highness, Prince Abderian, brother to King Cyprian, son of the late King Valgus. I order you to hand the child over to me!"

Dolus stood suddenly, knocking over the bench behind him. He glared down at Abderian and said in a voice more low and deadly than the prince had ever heard from him, "Your Highness, as you have seen fit to ignore and reject my counsel, I will absent myself from these proceedings. The problem is now your own to handle as you see fit." Dolus strode to the door, and the dark-clad men made no effort to stop him as he left.

Abderian stared helplessly after Dolus for a moment. *But . . . but . . . don't leave! What will I do? No, I mustn't appear weak now.* Summoning all the resolution he could muster, he again faced Vulka. He took a deep breath and cleared his throat.

The Caravan Master looked pleasantly patient. "It is hard to find good help these days, isn't it? Pray continue your story . . . Your Highness."

"You don't believe me? Well here is proof, and I will give this for the child's return." Abderian drew the blade from his belt and flung it on the table. "This is the Sword of Sagamore."

Vulka examined the sword a moment, turning it gingerly but not picking it up. She observed the jester-head hilt and chuckled. "An amusing trinket, to be sure. Beyond The Edge, they'd consider it a quaint decorative item, but the price it would command would not be close to equaling that of the child. And this in no way proves your royalty. For all I know, this could be fake or stolen."

Abderian paused. *Maybe Dolus's way was the easiest.* He leaned on his elbows and said in a loud whisper, "I could make you very rich."

Amusement in her eyes, Vulka said, "I understand the Euthymian court treasury has not been the same since King Cyprian's wedding."

She's well informed. Should have expected that. "Perhaps. But we could make special trade arrangements for your Guild."

"The Guild is pleased enough with the arrangements it has, thank you. And if I were willing to consider your offer, I would of course want to make inquiries through proper channels to ensure that you were authorized to make such an offer. I would have to inform various offices in Mamelon and the Guild as to who you are and the nature of the request and so forth. The process would take time, which I cannot afford, and would require exposure of the situation, which I believe you cannot afford."

Damn. She's sharp. And she's right.

Folding her arms across her chest, Vulka said, "You might help your cause considerably if you could tell me the true reason for your interest in the child."

Abderian fought hard to keep from shouting. "I have told you. I am the baby's father."

Vulka closed her eyes and sighed. "I am losing patience for ill-considered lies. I will break my oath of discretion to tell you that the child is demon get. To my knowledge, human and demon cannot interbreed. So unless there has been some miracle, magic, or other interference with nature, you cannot be the child's father."

Abderian sat again, feeling miserable. "I know she's a demon. It . . . it's a long story."

"I am sure," said Vulka. "But only a story, nonetheless."

"No!" Abderian again smote the table with his fist, but he did not meet the Caravan Master's eyes. *Dare I tell her about the cursemark? Would that be proof enough?* "The child . . . has a birthspot on her right arm."

"This tells me only that you have seen the child before, or have had her described to you," Vulka said blandly, though she sat up, more alert.

Abderian felt at a complete loss. Softly, he said, "Please. The child is in danger."

"What sort of danger?" Vulka said quickly, laying one hand on Abderian's arm.

"The Demon King, Belphagor, will kill her if he finds her."

"Why?"

"I can't tell you. But if he succeeds . . . the consequences will be disastrous."

Vulka released his arm and sat back. She seemed to come to a decision and stood abruptly. "I thank you for your timely warning, young master. And I assure you that we will do all in our power to protect the child while she remains with us. We will discreetly look into your allegations—"

"No! He mustn't find out!"

"I did say 'discreetly.' We have our methods. But I sense you do have an emotional investment in the situation. Therefore I will break my oaths once more to tell you this much: We will take good care of her. Those who would pay for her would treat her well, also. But if she is not spoken for among my clients, I have a mind to keep her and apprentice her to the Guild when she is of age. A demon in our ranks could be most advantageous to us. I will see her talent is not wasted. Fare you well, young master."

Abderian said nothing, watching Vulka and the two men leave.

NINE

Magical spells are like the warm tears of a maiden's first heartbreak. Just why, I can't recall at the moment, but let me think. . . .

—ONYM THE SORCERER

ABDERIAN STEPPED FORLORNLY out of the back room and went up to the counter of the taproom, pulling splinters out of his right hand. He said to the alewife behind the counter, "I broke one of your chairs. I guess I was a little angry. I'm sorry and I'll be sure to see that you're reimbursed—"

"Not to worry," said the alewife with a broad grin and a wink, as though such things happened all the time. "The Grey Mistress, she's paid for it all. They be fine folk, the Guild."

Heh. Fine folk, thought Abderian, *who sell babies.* He left the inn, stepping into the warm, humid air. He walked back to the road. wondering where Dolus might have gone. *Maybe he went back to Mamelon already.* Abderian ambled back through the village, watching the dust kicked up by his feet. A shadow fell across his boots and he ran into something hard that reeked of horse sweat.

"Watch where you're going, lad," someone growled at him.

Abderian looked up. He had bumped into a skinny pack-pony

65

laden with pots, pans, brooms, and other household items. Beside it rode a grizzled old man atop an only slightly better fed nag. Abderian blinked in the bright sunlight. "Sorry. Who . . . Dolus?"

"Shhh! I know it's not a great disguise, but it was the best I could do on short notice. I spent my travel money buying all this from a passing tinker."

"I'm sorry I angered you. I thought you'd gone—"

"Yes, yes, I was furious, but righteous anger on either of our parts will not solve this problem. Hurry now, hop on behind me."

Abderian struggled onto the horse, and sat on the back rim of the saddle. Dolus nudged the nag into motion and the prince fell forward and clung to his tutor's back. "I've been thinking, Dolus. Maybe I shouldn't worry about the scandal. Maybe I should go back to Mamelon and borrow from Cyprian a regiment or two of guardsmen and make Vulka give up the baby by force. She won't seem to listen to anything else."

"Have you lost every last semblance of sense?" Dolus growled. "The Grey Guild is quite well set up to defend itself from attack—that is why they are trusted to deliver valuable or dangerous cargo. And they are protected by so many laws and treaties and agreements that they are nearly a sovereign power themselves. Any attack of the sort you mention would not only bring on bureaucratic nightmares, but would likely plunge Euthymia into war with allies of the Guild. Force is not the answer."

"Then what is?"

"You'll see."

They rode uncomfortably to the north end of the village, then Dolus turned off the road onto a deer track through the brush.

"Where are we going? And why did you buy all this tinker's junk?"

"All part of the plan, lad."

"Plan?"

"Abderian, Vulka is not your ordinary wagon-train boss. She has skills other than just whip-snapping. For example, she's a shape-changer."

"You mean, she could look like anything she wants to?"

"No, only the most skilled of sorcerers can do that. Most shape-changers have just one particular form they change to. Vulka's is a wolf. That's the mascot of the Guild, you see."

"Oh."

"The Guild's familiarity with magic makes it difficult to use enchantment to get our way. At least, directly."

"Directly?"

"That's what the tinker's gear is for. At least we can be reassured that the child will not be harmed. The Guild never damages important merchandise. But we can do something to help keep our options open even if we cannot get the babe now."

"I . . . I told her the child was in danger. I said Belphagor wanted to kill the baby, though I didn't tell her why."

Dolus sighed heavily. "I suppose you felt that it was necessary. Of course this means their defenses will be even stronger, which is good for the child, but not for us. Well, we'll just go ahead and see what happens."

"Go ahead and do what?"

"Hush, we're drawing close."

They came out of the underbrush onto a wide mud flow between two hills. Abderian heard faint shouting and other noises upslope to his right.

"Here is where you get off, my boy," said Dolus. "I've no disguise for you. Wait here in the bushes till I come back."

"What if you don't come back?"

"Don't be melodramatic, lad. The worst they'll do is toss me out on my aging rear end, I'd expect. Fear not."

But fear Abderian did as he watched Dolus ride up the dried mud river and over the rise. The prince sat among the bushes and waited, sweat dripping down his forehead. The minutes dragged by. He found the heat of this summer-in-winter disconcerting and wondered what was happening to the baby. *At least there aren't any biting insects as there are in summer.* Abderian wished he carried a wine flask as Dolus did. *What's keeping him?*

Presently, he heard shouts from over the rise and he stood. Dolus came cantering down the mud flow, pony in tow, with various flying objects hurtling after him. The dark-clad men flinging the objects at Dolus shouted epithets and certain suggestions as to which bodily functions and orifices the objects might be put to. "And don't come back!" they finished before disappearing once more beyond the rise.

Dolus stood in his stirrups and looked around as Abderian stepped out of the undergrowth. "There you are, lad. Come along. Step lively, they might think twice and get curious."

Abderian ran over to the now burdenless pony and clambered atop it. The pony had a bridle and reins but no saddle, and its back felt both lumpy and slippery to the prince's posterior. He squeezed with his legs and they trotted down the hill. "Now, will you tell me what's going on? I can see you didn't get the baby."

"That was not my objective, Your Highness. As I believe I explained, we have to work circumspectly. I posed as a tinker and tradesman so that I could sell them a hairbrush or two."

Abderian waited a moment, refusing to lose his patience immediately. "A . . . hairbrush. Or two."

"Yes. Of course, I had to prove my hairbrushes were better than their hairbrushes, in order to encourage them to bring out and show their hairbrushes to me."

"I see. Dolus, you don't suppose the heat has addled your poor brains more than usual, do you?"

The once mighty ex-wizard sat up in his saddle and fixed Abderian with the same steely glare he had used at the inn. "No, but it would seem to have affected yours. You discourage me, lad. I had such hopes for you, but you still seem unable to think like a sorcerer."

Abderian swallowed, humbled. "Well, what do you mean? What do hairbrushes have to do with sorcery?"

"Not the brushes! What's on them. It is a given of witchcraft that any part of an organism has much juju, as they say."

"Juju?"

"Potential for power, because of its intense association with the person or animal it comes from."

"Oh . . . Oh! The hair!"

"That's better. Yes, the hair. I managed to make Vulka's personal attendant so incensed at my boasts that she practically thrust Vulka's hairbrush under my nose. Naturally, as a courtesy, I had to clean the brush for her." Dolus pulled a wad of silky light-brown strands from his pocket.

"Vulka's hair. So we can do a spell on her! But I thought you said she was familiar with magic."

"Certainly any aggressive form of magic she could notice and counteract immediately, yes. So we must be extremely circumspect."

"You mean sneaky."

"Leave your grandfather out of this. I'll explain when we come to a suitable spot."

They continued riding westward, down across the widening mud flat as the muggy afternoon dragged on. "Why is it so hot,

Dolus? What can they be doing to her? Smothering her in blankets?"

Dolus snorted. "She is of demon nature, lad, remember? They like it hot. I'm sure your daughter finds this quite comfortable. Ah, here's a good place." The tutor guided his nag over to the shade of some pines, where a puddle of water remained from the flood.

"Good place for what?" asked Abderian, gratefully sliding off the pony's bony back.

"Our spell. Come over here, lad."

Abderian squatted beside his tutor at the muddy puddle. Dolus reached in and scooped out handfuls of the wet muck and tossed it onto the drier ground. "More of your 'creative sorcery'?" the prince asked.

"Of course. Creative, but simple—as the best spells are, if I do say so myself." Dolus leaned over and patted the mud into an odd shape, flattening some parts of it and pushing up others.

There was something familiar about what Dolus was forming, but Abderian couldn't quite recall what. "Is there some meaning to that shape?"

Dolus turned a disbelieving stare on the prince. "Let me guess. You were the despair of your geography tutor as well, were you?"

"Geography?" Abderian looked again at the mud and realized it was a crude but recognizable map of Euthymia. "Oh."

"Not a hopeless case, at least. Now I will need your help for the next step."

With Dolus's coaching, Abderian performed some mystical phrases and gestures over the map. Then Dolus took the strands of Vulka's hair and rolled them into a ball. He teased out a few of the long hairs and put the ball in the center of the map. The remaining strands he pressed into the mud along the edges of the map. Then Abderian waved his hands and mumbled some more.

"That should do it," said Dolus, pleased.

"Do what?"

Dolus sighed. "As an exercise for the student, I will allow you to tell me."

"Thanks." Abderian grimaced at him and thought for a moment. "Well, you have a map of Euthymia made out of the earth of Euthymia, which combines both the qualities of similarity and contagion."

"Very good. Go on."

"You put Vulka's hair in the map, which, for the sake of the enchantment, locates and affixes her in the kingdom."

"Keep going."

"You put a border of her hair around the edge, or border, of the kingdom. I don't understand that. As if something about her will rule or determine Euthymia's borders."

"No, no, you've got it backwards, lad. Weren't you listening to the words I had you say? The borders determine the limits for Vulka. With this spell, she will be unable to leave the kingdom. By the nature of their contract, the caravan will not be able to leave without her, so this ensures your babe will not be taken out of the kingdom. This will not solve your problem, but it gives us time. And we need not worry about what will happen if the cursemark is taken out of Euthymia."

"That's brilliant, Dolus."

The tutor smiled. "Yes, well—"

"But won't she be angry?"

"Undoubtedly. But we now have something to bargain with and it will force her to deal with us. The Grey Guild will not be pleased either, but the wheels of commercial lawsuits can grind amazingly slow."

Abderian felt hope buoy him up once more. "Wonderful. So what do we do next?"

"Wait. Hers is the next move. While we wait for her to make it, we must carefully consider what our reaction should be. Heading back to Mamelon would be my suggestion."

The idea of returning home empty-handed and having to make explanations to Horaphthia did not appeal to the prince. "There's something I'd like to do first."

"Hmm?"

"We're not far from Castle Nikhedonia, are we?"

Dolus frowned. "It is, perhaps, a day's ride from here. But why do you wish to go there? I thought it had been deserted since my brother the duke died."

"Almost. But there remains someone I want to talk with."

"Who?"

Abderian looked at his hands. "The ghost of my great-grandfather. King Sagamore."

Dolus looked bewildered. "Why, in the name of all reason? Are you so in need of distracting entertainment that you would conjure the shade of the Jester King to caper about and tell you bad jokes about his reign?"

"He's not like that!" Abderian snapped. "He's given me helpful advice before. He gave me this sword. And the curse was first his, after all. I just think it would be useful to ask his opinion of our situation."

"From what I've heard, it seems his opinion on anything was rarely useful. Besides, Her Majesty will be worried."

Abderian set his jaw. "Horaphthia would like our failure less. I don't want to go back without some idea of what to do."

"What if Maja has her child while you're gone?"

"I don't know what I'll tell her. But I won't be very helpful unless I feel more confident about what's going on. The midwives have said it might be up to a week before it happens. One day might not make that much difference. If you want, you can go back and I'll go on alone."

Dolus sighed. "Surely you jest. Leave you out here by yourself? No, Highness, I will bow to royal whim."

"You didn't, back at the inn."

"There was nothing more I could do for you there, and much to be gained by leaving. Fear not, Abderian, I will never willfully abandon you. I am bound by compelling ties to your service."

Abderian felt touched and humbled by this statement of fealty. "Did you . . . swear an oath to my father or something? Is that what binds you?"

"No. The fact that you hold my magical power binds me. I've got to see that you don't misuse it. I won't let you out of my sight too long, believe me."

"Oh."

"Now if we're to head to Nikhedonia, we'd best be on our way."

TEN

Whoever said "good things come in small packages" was a braggart with a tiny wife.

—King Sagamore

AFTER A NIGHT spent trying to sleep on hard ground, and a day spent trying to stay atop a hard, bareback pony, Abderian was ready to call it quits. Several times he caught himself reaching up to tug a lock of hair so that Horaphthia would bring them home. "Is a chat with a mad ghost worth this?" he muttered to himself.

"Eh?" Dolus said over his shoulder, ahead of him.

"Nothing, Dolus." *At least the weather was warm last night. I wouldn't have survived it otherwise.* Abderian stretched the muscles in his back and felt each one twinge with a new ache. *I feel like I've been pinched by a hundred demons.*

They rode over yet another pine-topped rise, the sun setting behind the hills to their left. To their right, The Edge rose up, a rocky, jagged bulwark against the oncoming indigo night. As they reached the summit of the rise, Abderian sighed with recognition and relief. Ahead of them lay the Vale of Nikhedonia.

"There it is," said Dolus with a sweep of his arm. "I hope it is worth the trip for you, lad."

72

"So do I."

The Edge curled around this corner of Euthymia to take a westward march to the sea. Across the vale, Abderian saw the road that led down from the dragon's gate. There had actually been a dragon there once, set by Lord Javel to defend against an invasion of dwarfs. The first time Abderian had come to Nikhedonia, the dragon, Kookluk by name, had tried to claim Maja as its "maiden." With the help of the Sword of Sagamore, Abderian had managed to rescue Maja, but the sight of the gate still sent shivers up his spine.

In the center of the vale lay the ruins of Castle Nikhedonia. It had been crumbling even when Maja's father, Lord Javel, had lived there, as he had had more compelling things on his mind than housekeeping. But something looked different to Abderian's eye.

"Place has really fallen to pieces since I lived here," said Dolus.

"Your brother liked that lived-in look," said Abderian. "But do you see those green patches down there?"

"Hmmm. Yes, that is odd. There hasn't been any cultivation in this valley since Javel kicked the dwarfs out twenty years ago. You don't suppose—?"

"Let's go see."

Sunset had faded into cool twilight by the time they reached the castle. The stone walls showed signs of recent repair. "Even the moat is clean!" said Abderian, who remembered it as dry and choked with weeds. Now it ran with clear water, and fish leapt about in it. Abderian and Dolus rode around the castle to the southwest wall and rode through the open portcullis. The drawbridge was down, and on the far side a scaffold leaned against the castle's inner wall. On the scaffold, two little men worked scrubbing away at the stones.

"Ho, there!" called Dolus. "May we enter?"

The two dwarfs jumped at the sound, nearly losing their fo on the scaffold. "Who? What?" said one.

"Hey, we got visitors," said the other. He clambered down the drawbridge and approached. Suddenly he stopped and turned pale. "Eeeeh, Ambert," his voice wavered, "It's Javel come back for revenge! We didn't mean it! Don't kill us, lord!" The dwarf fell on his knees and bowed till his head struck the wood of the drawbridge.

"Get up, my friend," said Dolus. "I may resemble my late brother, but I assure you my temperament is quite different."

The other dwarf waddled over to the kneeling one and tugged at his sleeve. "It's not Javel, you ninny. It's his brother Dolus. And the young man beside him must be"—this time it was Ambert who turned pale as he looked at Abderian—"the prince," he finished with a squeak.

"The prince?" said the kneeling one. "Yipe!" And they both turned and ran down the drawbridge into the castle.

"Excitable lot, aren't they?" said Dolus.

"I guess they weren't expecting royalty for dinner. Shall we invite ourselves?"

"I've rarely known a royal guest to be turned away." They rode their mounts across the drawbridge into the castle courtyard. Here they dismounted and left the animals to graze on the greensward. It was easy to find the Great Dining Hall from there—one needed only to follow the sound of high voices singing.

Abderian remembered the dining hall of Nikhedonia as a dark, foreboding place, dusty and cobwebby. It was there that he had been forced into a not-so-unwilling betrothal with Khanda, Lord Javel having wanted control of the cursemark and an heir on the throne all at the same time.

But now, as Abderian stepped into the dining hall, he was charmed by what he saw. Now the hall glowed with the light of a hundred candles. The old statues had been cleaned, and some made into f untains. Colorful frescoes lined the walls, and the ceiling was in the process of being finished in floral designs of gold and silver leaf.

Filling the hall was a great horseshoe of a table, lined with little people in elegant clothes. All fell silent as the prince and Dolus entered, and they stared. Abderian smiled and nodded at them. y all nodded in return, apprehensively.

derian walked to the center of the horseshoe and faced a g, pot-bellied figure he recognized—Lord Undertall, who nayor of the dwarf cave to the east. This worthy stood and ed his throat, then jumped over the table to face the prince, ms folded tightly across his chest. "Now look here," said Lord Undertall, "you may be a prince and all, but we have rights. This place is rightfully ours, by previous ownership and right of conquest, and right of restitution. We're not leaving."

Abderian smiled at him, bemused. "I'm not asking you to."

"And furthermore," Undertall continued, "we deserve to stay because—What did you say?"

"I said I'm not asking you to leave. I think this is great! You folk can stay here as long as you like. I'll even ask my brother the King to cede it to your families, or something."

"You—you would?"

"Of course. Although, strictly speaking, it belongs to Maja, I've never heard her say she wanted it."

"The Lady Maja! Naturally we are happy to consider her our duchess, after all she has done for us. If you could just see that I am titled Viceroy, or Lord High Steward, or some such, we will happily take care of her duchy until the Lady Maja decides to return."

"Done!" said Abderian with a grin. He looked around at the table laden with food and rubbed his stomach. "Um, if you don't mind—"

"Oh, how rude of me," said Lord Undertall. "Please be welcomed into Castle Nikhedonia. Nani! Set two more places at table for our honored guests."

Lord Undertall escorted Abderian and Dolus to the head of the table, where he had been sitting, and indicated they should take a place at either side of him. This did not appear to inconvenience the dwarf lords and ladies who had to move aside for them. In fact, they seemed relieved and pleased to do so. Unlike the last time Abderian was a guest of the dwarfs, the chairs were not too small. *Must be Javel's leftover furniture.*

Plates heaped with joints of braised game, stewed potatoes, vinegared green beans, and creamed turnips were passed to the prince and he took plenty of each. His cup was filled with a tart but pleasant wine that managed not to clash on the palate with any of the meat or vegetables. It was fare that easily rivaled that of Castle Mamelon, and Abderian dug in greedily. Out of the corner of his eye, he noticed Dolus wasn't stinting himself either.

"Not such a bad idea, was it?" Abderian said to Dolus across Lord Undertall's bow.

"Riding a day and a half for a decent meal? Could be argued, lad, but right now I'm not inclined to. We'll see if the rest of your plan bears similar fruit." Dolus stuffed his mouth with potatoes and said no more.

"Now," said Lord Undertall, "where were we before, uh, our honored guests arrived?"

"We were singing," said a little lady to Abderian's left.

"Quite right! We must have another song for out guests. Kanti! Choose a song for us. Something appropriate for our special visitors."

A dwarf in a russet and green tunic, wearing a peaked green cap and carrying a mandolin, stepped before Lord Undertall and bowed. "Well, m'lord, I was thinking they might like to hear 'The Taking of Nikhedonia,' seeing as they're letting us have it and all."

"Perfect, Kanti. Let our lordships hear the story of our victory."

The minstrel dwarf bowed again and picked an arpeggio on his mandolin. He began to sing in a powerful tenor voice:

> I'll sing to thee of our victory,
> When dwarfs, with great huzzah,
> Brought about the fall of the rummy-tum Hall
> Of Nikhedonia.

(and the rest of those gathered at the table echoed, "Of Nik-hedonia!")

> To the dragon's lair did our company dare,
> So we might pass beyond,
> But we came too late to the rummy-tum gate,
> The dragon it was gone.

Abderian chuckled to himself. *Of course it was gone. Maja and I had taken it for a little ride.*

> So we marched down the road to our foe below,
> Our thirst for vengeance high,
> But when our boat crossed the rummy-tum moat,
> No Javel did we spy.

Yep. He'd gone to set a trap with Tingalut at the temple.

> So we rushed the walls and the crumbling halls,
> Two serfs we held at bay,
> And we beat with our treads on their rummy-tum heads,
> Until they ran away!

Such chivalry, thought Abderian.

> The castle was ours through our valorous powers,
> But yet for vengeance sweet,
> There remained one deed we did rummy-tum need,
> To make our day complete.

"To make our day complete," Abderian joined in with the others.

> So we made our way to where Sagamore lay,
> Beneath his marble throne,
> And we wreaked foul doom on his rummy-tum tomb,
> And scattered all his bones.

"And scattered all his WHAT?" shouted the prince, as he realized what he had just heard.

The hall instantly fell silent, and the dwarfs looked at each other with embarrassment and fear. Abderian stared, shocked, at the singer, then turned to Lord Undertall. "My lord, is this true?"

The mayor rubbed a napkin across his perspiring brow. "Well . . . in a matter of speaking, Your Highness—"

Abderian stood and glowered at him. *"Did your people desecrate my great-grandfather's tomb?"*

Lord Undertall was shaking. "W-well, we didn't do much damage, really. Just nicked the marble a bit, that's all." Then he seemed to gather some resolve and went on: "He did give us cause, you know. Made all of our ancestors short like this just so his royal house and descendants would always have dwarfs for their entertainment. Cause enough for a little righteous vandalism, if you ask me."

Murmurs of agreement spread around the table. Abderian squeezed his fists tight and shut his eyes, trying to forgive them. He understood they had had cause for anger against Sagamore. *But now I've come all this way for nothing.* As calmly as possible, he asked, "What did you do with the bones?"

"Eh? Old Saggy's bones? Kanti, were they really scattered like you said?"

The minstrel looked down at his feet a moment. "Well, they weren't scattered, really, your lordship. We just kind of dumped them on the trash midden out back, in case the dogs wanted something to gnaw on." He suddenly looked up at Abderian and fell silent.

"I've heard enough," Abderian said softly. He turned on his heel and walked around the table, back toward the entry doors. He did not look at any of the dwarfs he passed, though they craned their necks to regard him with apologetic faces. He did not notice if Dolus followed him. He did see Lord Untertall make futile gestures in his direction, which he ignored. The only sound in the room was the clack of his boots on the stone floor, and their echoes in the silent hall.

It was not hard for Abderian to find the castle trash midden, from its location near the kitchen, and the smell. Fat-bodied flies hovered around the detritus of the evening's dinner. Here and there in the mess, Abderian thought he saw pieces of stained ivory that might be old bones. From within a mass of fruit rind, a dark skull grinned back at him.

Abderian felt tears welling up in his eyes. "I don't care what you did." He balled his fists again, as the tears spilled onto his cheeks. "You were my great-grandfather. They shouldn't have done this to you." The prince took a deep breath, feeling this was an ignoble way to react to an ignoble deed. He drew the Sword of Sagamore from his belt and saluted the trash midden. "I, Abderian, Prince of Euthymia, do honor you, O once mighty king! May your spirit rise beyond this sorry place into a worthy heaven."

But no sooner had he said the word "rise," than there was a strange stirring in the midden. The flies beat a hasty departure, as the sound of clicking and clacking filled the air. The heap of garbage shuddered once, twice, and then a whole skeleton emerged from the mess to stand before the prince.

"As a jester, I often had garbage thrown at me," came a hollow voice from within the skull, "but this is the first time I have been thrown at garbage." With bony fingers, the skeleton picked orange peels and turnip skins off his frame and flicked them away.

"King Sagamore!" Abderian said, blinking with wonder.

ELEVEN

When asked which is worse, bankruptcy of one's treasury or bankruptcy of one's soul, the wise man would reply, 'the soul.' But the smart man would disagree. For the man with an empty soul but a full treasury is still a boon to society in the works he commissions and the taxes he pays. The man with an empty treasury, no matter how noble his soul, is still a debtor and a leech.

—LORD JAVEL

"OF COURSE I am Sagamore," said the regal skeleton, tiny lights blinking on and off in the eye sockets. "What did you expect, a skeletal pig? There are certainly two or three in there." He gestured at the midden. "You know what they say— 'when a man lies down among swine, it reflects poorly on the swine.'"

Abderian stammered, "I-I'd forgotten this sword could do that. Conjure skeletons, I mean."

"Oh, yes, yes, just about its only real use, besides looking flashy. But that's use enough in the right situation. I daresay I could have used it to summon skeletal troops against those dwarfs when they came tearing through."

"I'm sorry. Perhaps you shouldn't have given it to me—"

"No, no, my boy. From what little I could see from the Home for the Incurably Dead, you seemed to have made good use of it. And you will have need of it in the future, though for exactly what, I've no idea. The trouble with clairvoyance is there's

79

nothing 'clair' about it. Still, I can tell that it's more than just chance that you're here speaking to my ossified self."

Abderian nodded. "I came seeking advice, since you were so helpful the last time I saw you."

"Hmm. I'd thought you would have learned your lesson the first time. The dispensing of wisdom is not my strong suit. Now, if you'd like a jest or two to cheer you up—"

"Your Majesty," Abderian jumped in before losing his nerve, "it concerns the cursemark. Your cursemark,." As quickly as he could, Abderian explained his situation to the skeletal Jester King.

"On a demon babe, eh? There's a possibility I hadn't thought of. It would be just like a creation of Onym's to pick the most improbable place to be."

"Can you help me, Your Majesty?"

"What small wisdom and skill I may impart are, like this midden heap, at your disposal." The skeleton gave the prince a regal nod.

"Thank you!"

"However, I must ask one favor in return."

"Anything."

"Perhaps you know that there is a level below the ground floor of Castle Mamelon? Good, I see you do. It was my favorite haunt even before I was dead. Well, since the current occupants of Nikhedonia do not welcome me, I want these bones to be reburied in Castle Doom, that ruin in the basement swamp."

"That's where your spirit will find true peace, Your Majesty?"

"No, some diversion from the boredom of true peace, my boy. You've no idea how depressingly dull it is to be dead. No matter, you'll find out eventually."

"Yes. That is, I agree, Your Majesty. I will see that your bones are reburied in Castle Doom in return for whatever aid you can give me."

"Excellent! Ah, here comes another to pay homage."

Abderian looked to his left and saw Dolus walking quickly toward them, carrying a bundle of clothing in his arms.

"Perhaps there is hope for you as a diplomat after all, lad," said Dolus as he came puffing up to them. "The dwarfs, in their guilt, have given us these cloaks of Javel's, and . . ." He stopped, staring at the skeleton. "Is that who I think it is?"

"Lord Dolus," said Abderian, "may I present His Late but yet Royal Majesty, King Sagamore."

Dolus bowed as best he could with the bundle he carried.

Sagamore inclined his skull in return. "Ah, Lord Dolus, kin of King Thalion, I hope you are not as ill-disposed toward me as the rest of your family has been."

"No hard feelings on this end, Your Majesty."

"Good! From what I have seen of you from the Land of the Hopelessly Immaterial, I very much approve."

Dolus smiled with pride and bowed again. "I have done my best to guide your great-grandson."

"No, no, I don't mean that. I meant those . . . singular witticisms of yours."

Abderian rolled his eyes. *Naturally. I should have known these two would get along.*

Dolus's face lit up with a thoroughly smug expression.

The prince decided the safest thing to do was to change the subject. "His Majesty has agreed to help us in any way he can, Dolus. In return, I've agreed to rebury his bones in Castle Doom."

"Very thoughtful of you, lad. Though I am uncertain as to what assistance he can give in his current condition."

"You might be surprised," said the skeletal Sagamore. "I've got one or two tricks left up my noncorporeal sleeve, no bones about it."

This time Dolus rolled his eyes. "Well, we'd best be on our way, then. I think the dwarfs would be discomfited if we stayed here any longer. Tug on your hair, lad, and have Horaphthia take us home."

"But what about His Majesty?" said Abderian. "Horaphthia won't know he's along, so she won't bring him with us."

"Hmmm."

"Perhaps," said the skeleton, "if I become part of your baggage, I'll be brought along with you. Here, spread out one of those cloaks."

Dolus did so and Sagamore stepped into the center of it. "Now, my boy, flourish that sword again and wish me good night and good rest."

Abderian waved the Sword of Sagamore. "Good night and good rest, Your Majesty."

Immediately the skeleton collapsed into a pile of bones on the cloak.

"That was most effective," mused Dolus.

Abderian bent over the pile and gently gathered the corners of the cloak to make sure not even the tiniest bone was lost. As he looked at the skull, though, he saw glowing lights running around the circular rims of the eye sockets. "You're still here."

"Of course I'm still here," said the skull. "You don't think I want to return to that Great Retirement Home in the Sky, do you? No, thank you. I prefer to stick around to see what happens. This way, you may ask me for advice any time you wish."

"Ah, good point, Your Majesty," said Abderian. "Thank you." He continued gathering up the ends of the cloak until he could tie it into a bundle and sling it over his back. The bones rattled and a muffled voice said, "Gently there, my boy."

"Sorry." Abderian looked up at Dolus. "Are we ready?"

The tutor had bundled up the other cloak and held it under his arm. "Go ahead, lad."

Abderian reached up and tugged at his forelock three times. Nothing happened. He tried again, and waited. No result. "I don't understand. She's not responding."

"Is this some sorceress you're trying to reach?" said Sagamore's muffled voice from the sack. "Perhaps you've just caught her at a bad time. Even a wizard, if called while in the *garde-robe*, is not likely to drop everything, so to speak, and do your bidding."

"Even so, I do not like this," said Dolus. "Horaphthia would have responded somehow by now if she could. Well, if we must wait, at least we can find a decent campsite." Dolus whistled to the horse and pony still grazing in the courtyard. Under the watchful eyes of the guard dwarfs, Abderian and Dolus led their mounts across the drawbridge and out of the castle. The light from the flickering torches on the portcullis walls did not carry very far into the dark night.

"You must do a light spell, Abderian," said Dolus.

As the prince tried to remember from his studies how to conjure a guide flame, Sagamore spoke from the sack. "Try my sword, my boy. I seem to recall it did something along those lines."

Abderian drew the golden blade from his belt again. "What do I say?"

"Oh, dear me, I scarcely remember. It was something simple and obvious. Try 'Gimme a light.' "

Abderian said, "Gimme a light," and with a soft *whish*, the sword lit up so brightly that the prince had to squint to spare his eyes. The sword hissed, and little bits of pyrotechnic sparkle popped off the blade now and then, stinging when they landed on bare skin. Abderian had to hold the sword well ahead of him to avoid getting singed. But they had only traveled a few yards when the sword sputtered out, leaving them only starlight to see by.

"Well," said Sagamore, "it was intended more for display than usefulness."

"This area seems clear enough," said Dolus. "We might as well stop here."

They sat upon sandy soil, Abderian carefully setting the bag of bones down beside him. It was warm enough that a campfire wasn't necessary, so they sat in the starshine and waited.

"Shall I entertain you while we wait?" said Sagamore. "It's been so long since I played to royalty. Back in the Realm of Eternal Transparency, all the other kings and queens avoided me. They said my jests were out of place in the World of Gloom and Doom. Heh. Well, I'll sing you one of Thalion's favorite songs."

"Please, Your Majesty, don't—" Dolus began.

"You're very welcome. Here 'tis."

There was a young lady of Dragonsbroke Fen,
Of suitors to court her, this lady had ten,
T'were five that were short and t'were five that were tall,
She said, "Hell with custom, I'll marry them all!"

With a ring-diddle-diddle di do, all ladies are fey,
They'll do as they please, never mind what you say.

Abderian let his mind drift away, lulled by Sagamore's pleasant, if other-worldly, baritone. He watched the stars glimmering in the sky and felt himself becoming quite weary.

There was a young lady of Meadow-on-Tyne,
Of suitors to court her, this lady had nine,
T'were three that were ruddy, three dark and three fair,
So she made lovely weavings from locks of their hair.

Abderian slowly closed his eyes and curled up on the ground. Dolus placed the other cloak over him and he felt surprisingly peaceful.

There was a young lady of Ironburg Gate,
Of suitors to court her, this lady had eight,
T'were four that were rich and t'were four that were poor.
She took all their money and went off to war.

Abderian drifted into dreams, following the lady who went off to war, and watching her vanquish foe after foe. He saluted her with the Sword of Sagamore, but it seemed like tarnished brass compared to her gleaming armor, and she laughed at him. She gave him a nod of farewell and she rode away into a bank of mist.

Abderian walked down a road alone, feeling confident, if not powerful. A great wind came up and blew all around him, yet he was calm in the center of it, knowing the wind would not harm him. But as the wind blew away the mist, he saw before him a huge, four-headed hydra. As he raised his sword, the heads were transformed—each became a face of Horaphthia, in each of her different aspects. One head wore a golden crown, one was surrounded by a blue nimbus of sorcery, one was the ancient crone-face of Apu, and one was a motherly middle-aged woman. All the faces glared at Abderian, enraged. And when they spoke, it was with one voice. The hydra said, "Well, Abderian, I hope you have an excellent explanation for this!"

TWELVE

Excerpt from *A History of the House*, etc., as etc., by the Princess Amusia:

So my brother Cyprian is the King now. He's changed a lot since Mommy made him get married. But I don't know about his wife, Horaphthia. Some people say she 'witched him. And she can be real stern sometimes. Like, one time I asked if I could borrow some of her scarves so that I could tie them around the middle of the castle cats and watch the cats fall over. She looked at me like I was a monster or something. I don't think she understands our family very well.

ABDERIAN WANTED OUT of this nightmare. He blinked but it didn't help. Horaphthia's face was still before him, scowling ferociously.

"Go easily on him, I beg you, Your Majesty," Dolus said from somewhere behind him. "He has been sleeping. We have had a difficult journey."

Abderian felt hands under his arms, helping him to stand. He was on a hard floor and, as he looked around, he saw he was in Queen Horaphthia's chambers again. He rubbed his cheeks and brow as Horaphthia backed off a pace, her arms crossed and her scowl softening to a frown.

"He is not the only one who has suffered. It gives me little pleasure to inform you, Abderian, that you are a father."

"Yes, I know," Abderian mumbled. "Oh, you mean Maja—?"

"Of course I mean Maja. She had a bouncing baby boy."

"Is she all right?"

Horaphthia rubbed her chin. "Ten points in your favor. Yes,

85

physically she is fine, though it was a difficult labor at first. With my help, she only suffered for one hour."

"When did it happen? Why didn't you send for me?"

"It was the day before yesterday, at noon. I tried to summon you, but I could not. Whatever you had done to interfere with the magical bond, it was quite effective."

Abderian felt Dolus's hands on his shoulders. "'Tis not the lad's fault, Your Majesty. We were meeting with representatives of the Grey Guild. No doubt it was their protections against sorcery that interfered."

"The Grey Guild?" said the Queen, tossing her loose black hair. "This becomes even more interesting."

"Please, Horaphthia," said Abderian, "may I see Maja?"

"I doubt it," snapped the Queen, looking away.

"You . . . doubt it?"

"It isn't up to me, Abderian. Maja was very upset that you left so suddenly, and she was even more distressed to give birth without you there. When Entheali demanded to see Maja shortly after the birth—"

"Entheali?"

"She is the girl's mother, after all, though she picks damn few times to show it. So Entheali and some of her acolytes came sweeping in and surrounded Maja, then whisked her and the baby away in the fastest teleport spell I have ever seen in my life. Since then, she has kept the temple well-guarded, physically and magically, claiming that Maja needed rest and isolation."

"It would seem," Dolus said softly, "that the Star Cult has learned how to use the power contained in the temple floor."

Abderian shut his eyes. *So what I hoped to avoid has happened after all*—"Wait!" His eyes snapped back open. "That baby doesn't have the cursemark."

"I had noticed that," said Horaphthia. "Which should make Entheali very interested in talking to *you*." She turned and faced Abderian with an intense stare. "I assume by this that you know where the cursemark is."

Abderian reluctantly nodded.

"Who has it?"

The prince paused a long time, wondering whether to lie, evade the question, or blurt the truth. He was aware that Dolus was staring at him also. Abderian flushed with shame and opened his mouth, ready to give a full confession.

But Dolus spoke first. "Your Majesty, please believe me,

Abderian has his reasons for secrecy right now. Suffice to say that the cursemark is as safe as it can be, for the time being."

"Suffice to say," Horaphthia hissed, her eyes narrowed at the both of them. She walked up to Abderian, her arms outstretched. She placed her hands on either side of his head and slowly squeezed. "I could tear the thoughts from the roots of your mind," she said softly, her gaze more terrible than he had ever seen.

Abderian shuddered. "Please don't," was all he could say.

Horaphthia continued squeezing for a moment, then she sighed heavily and dropped her arms to her sides. "Ah, what does it matter?" she said, more to herself than to them. "Perhaps it is better that I not know. I must travel south to help repair the damage caused by the storms and the earthquake. Folk would take it ill if I abandoned them to run off on a mysterious errand." Horaphthia slumped into her straight-back chair, and for an instant Abderian saw her as a very tired, adolescent girl. She smoothed her hair back away from her face, stretching the skin of her brow. "I am sorry to have frightened you, Abderian. I don't know what it is with me. Maybe it's this heat."

Abderian nodded, not knowing what to say.

"We are sorry to have added to your troubles, Your Majesty," said Dolus. "Perhaps the King can be of some comfort—"

"The dotings of a teenage boy are no comfort at all," snapped Horaphthia.

It was Abderian's turn to stare at Horaphthia, astonished. He had never seen her in such a poor humor.

"You'd best be off about your business." Horaphthia stood and went to her window. Outside, the stars shimmered as if melting in the heat of the night.

"Yes, ma'am," Abderian said and stooped to pick up the cloak containing Sagamore's remains.

"Kindly remember," Horaphthia said quietly without turning, "that despite the dubious way I came to stand at the King's side, I do actually care about what happens to this strange little kingdom. As soon as it is possible, you will tell me what is going on."

"Yes, ma'am."

"Of course, Your Majesty."

Abderian raised the bundled cloak onto his back, and the contents rattled.

Horaphthia looked around. "What have you got there?"

Abderian shrugged and felt an embarrassed smile distort his face. "Just some bones."

"Bones," Horaphthia echoed with an expression of wonder and distaste. "What . . . Oh, never mind. Begone."

Abderian bowed, rattling the bones still more, and he and Dolus ducked out the lancet-arch doors. Abderian felt his muscles ache as well as his spirit. His only lofty goal of the moment became finding his bed to complete his night's sleep.

"So that is the current queen?" came a dour voice from out of the cloak.

"Yes, Your Late Majesty," said Dolus. "That was Queen Horaphthia, wife of King Cyprian."

"With a woman like *that* on the throne, no wonder you need my help."

"She's not usually like that," Abderian said, stung. "She's a good person, really." Abderian remembered how she, in the guise of the crone Apu, had nursed him back to sanity after he had escaped the Forest of Forgetfulness. And how Horaphthia had helped save him and Maja from the maw of the dragon Kookluk. He also recalled her rage as she avenged herself on Lord Javel.

"She feels powerless," Dolus said in a mild tone that startled the prince. "She is not in control of the situation, and it unnerves her. As someone who is always used to being able to *do something* about whatever disturbs her, she is at a loss now that she cannot."

"I see," Abderian said. "Should I have told her the truth?"

"And set her against the Grey Guild? The ensuing fireworks would be spectacular, but I doubt any useful purpose would be served and the repercussions would be endless. No, Vulka must make the next move. Then we will see what we can tell Horaphthia."

Abderian nodded. "I'm going to go to my tower, Dolus. If you think of anything new, let it wait till morning, all right?"

Dolus squeezed Abderian's shoulder and fabricated a smile. "Sleep well, then, lad. May the Dream Sprites weave you scenes of joy and beauty out of nightblooms and moonbeams."

A grunt of disgust came from the bundled cloak.

"You're a fine one to sneer!" said Dolus to the bag of bones.

"Dream Sprites, really!" said the skull of Sagamore. "If you wished this boy a pleasant night, you should have invoked the Dream Succubi to bestrew his bed with passionweed or some such."

Abderian felt too tired to be amused. "Good night to you both," he grumbled, and headed off to his chamber.

As Abderian trudged heavily up his tower stairs, Sagamore was saying, "You fell asleep at eight? Boy, you missed all the best verses! Here, let me repeat them for you."

> There was a young lady from Huddleston Tavern,
> Of suitors to court her this lady had seven,
> T'were three that were rogues, and three good men
>   by oath,
> But she picked the one that was something of both.
>
> With a ring-diddle-diddle di do—

"Sagamore," Abderian broke in, too tired to be polite, "do bones ever sleep?"

"Eh? Ah, I'm sorry. No, once dead, a spirit doesn't get tired, no muscles to wear down, don't you see? That is why boredom is our biggest problem in the Great Beyond. But I have forgotten what weariness is like. Forgive me. I am just a mad, sad soul too far removed from his brief span of years among the living."

Abderian decided he preferred the ex-king's humorous mood to his maudlin one. At the top of the stairs, he pushed the latch and shoved open the door. "Oh, no," he groaned.

The golden light from two oil lamps on the prince's desk revealed an unexpected but familiar shambles. In his rushing around after the quake, Abderian had forgotten entirely about seeing to the repair of his own room. A huge beam still angled down to the floor. There were holes in the walls, and dust and debris were everywhere. "What a mess."

There was a clap to his right and Abderian snapped his head around to see Mux looking at him, very surprised. The little demon was sitting on a stool by the prince's dusty desk. Between Mux's hands was a book he had evidently just slammed shut. An embarrassed grin spread across the demon's face. "Master Abby-dab—Your Highness!" Mux rasped. "I was just, er, dusting the place for you." The demon rubbed his gnarled hands over the red leather binding of the book and blew on it. He stuck the book back on the shelf and made cursory sweeps with his hands over the shelf and the desk. Clouds of dust billowed up and the demon sneezed.

"I'll go, now that you're back," Mux said when he recovered. With a self-deprecating shrug and bow, the demon waddled to the window and flapped out.

Abderian rubbed his brow and shook his head.

"Was that a demon I heard?" asked Sagamore.

"Yes. He's sort of a friend-familiar. We used to have more of them around." Abderian stepped into the room and carefully set the bundled cloak on his desk.

"*Urk,* careful there, m'boy. Hmmm, demons were rare in my day. Things have certainly changed."

"I imagine." Abderian reached up to the shelf for the red book that Mux had been reading. It was a slim volume entitled *Do-It-Yourself Demon Control.* "Now, why . . . hmmm."

"What's that, Abderian?"

"Never mind. Let's see, where can we put you for now?"

"The only part of me that really matters is the skull. I always knew I'd get a head in the world someday."

Abderian wearily clicked his tongue. "Yes, Your Majesty." Kneeling on the stool, Abderian gently unknotted the cloak and lifted out the skull. Faint red lights still danced a two-step in the eye sockets. For a moment, the prince had the irreverent thought of making the old king's pate a bookend, paperweight, or doorstop. Instead, he placed the skull on a clear space on the shelf that Mux had just "dusted."

"There. How is that?"

"Excellent! I have a lovely view of . . . Gracious! Does Mamelon have such poor maid service these days?"

"It seems that way, sometimes," said the prince crawling down from the stool. "But this is just left over from the earthquake caused by your cursemark's decision to change residence." He put the cloak with the rest of the bones under his desk.

"Ah."

Abderian went to his bed and snapped his coverlet to get the dust and rubble off. Then, pausing only to remove his belt, sword, and shoes and to blow out the lamplights, Abderian crawled into the bed. He had thought that sleep would hit him like a large boulder. But despite the weariness of his body, something kept his mind awake. He heard an odd sound.

Sagamore was humming.

Abderian's eyes flickered open and he saw the red glimmers of Sagamore's skull staring back at him. "Your Majesty?"

"Hmmm? Don't mind me, son, I'll just sit here in the dark."

"You're watching me."

"Well, I can't help that. I can't exactly turn my head easily, can I? And I can't close my eyes if I haven't got eyes to close."

"Oh. Should I turn you around?"

"And give me a lovely view of the wall? Is that any way to treat a guest?"

"Sorry. It's just . . . weird to have you watch me like that."

"Many people are comforted by the thought that someone is watching over them."

"Maybe I'm just not used to it. But, if you please, don't hum, Your Majesty."

"Oh. Sorry. Selfish of me. I'll sing it aloud."

> There was a young lady of Magetown on Styx,
> Of suitors to court her, this lady had six,
> They all looked much the same, even on close
>   approach,
> So she changed them to horses, they now draw her
>   coach.

> Singing ring-diddle-diddle di do—

Abderian groaned and rolled over and sighed into his pillow. And then sleep did hit him like a large boulder. And he dreamed no dreams at all.

THIRTEEN

Never become a scholar, boy. Reading will lead your mind astray faster than wild horses, loose women, or the Steward's rotgut ale.

—fatherly advice from King Valgus
to his son Prince Paralian.

"COCK-A-DOODLE-DOO! Rise and be glorious! The sun is up and so should you be. Cock-a-doodle-doo."

Abderian sat bolt upright in bed and looked around wildly, trying to find the source of the noise.

"Ah, there he is, face as red as the rising sun. Come greet the day, shining Highness!"

"Shut up!" Abderian yelled at the skull yapping on the shelf.

"Oh. Sorry, Your Majesty. I just—"

"That's quite all right. Part of the job. Why, I remember when I would wake my liege King Thalion. He would leap out of bed and chase me around his chambers, thrashing me with his pillow. It never hurt me, and it served to wake him very thoroughly. Ah, those were the days. And what kingdom-shattering adventures does His Highness have planned for today?"

"I wish you wouldn't put it that way," Abderian said. He saw that he had slept in his clothes, and they were sticky and reeking of sweat. "Why does it have to be so hot?" he muttered.

"Beg your pardon?" said the skull.

"Nothing." Abderian slogged through the rubble of his room to the window overlooking Mamelon. Leaning his elbows on the sill, he said, "I want to see Maja, and the baby."

"Hasn't Your Highness had his fill of baby-trouble yet?"

"Sagamore," Abderian sighed.

"I apologize. I had but one son, Vespin, and he was an annoying little brat."

Abderian remembered the tapestry in the Throne Room and snorted a laugh. "I can imagine."

There was a knock at the door.

"Enter," Abderian said, and Dolus stepped in, wearing a long, red silk tabard over a white linen robe. Embroidered on the tabard was a half-open silver eye, beneath which was a golden square.

"Good morning, Highness," Dolus said.

"You look splendid, Dolus," Abderian said. "I've never seen you wear that before."

The tutor looked a little embarrassed. "These were my student clothes at the university where I learned sorcery. I suppose, strictly speaking, I no longer qualify to wear them now. But, with the hot weather, the cisterns are drying up and the washermen say there's no water to be spared for laundry. This was the only clean outfit I had left."

"It looks simply dashing," said Sagamore.

Dolus looked down at the golden square. "I used to be able to make it light up and say 'Kiss me, I'm a wizard.' Those were the days."

"A lot of reminiscing going around," said Abderian.

"Well, when you get to be our age," Sagamore said, "memory is all you have left."

"Speak for yourself!" said Dolus.

Ignoring him, the skull went on. "Why, decades from now you will look back on these happy times with Maja and—"

"What happy times with Maja?" Abderian cried, striking the wall with his fist. "I've made her so mad she doesn't even want to see me. Dolus, have you heard anything new?"

Dolus shook his head. "I'm afraid Maja still will not see you. I'm sure Entheali has not yet done anything to change Maja's mood, and is probably adding fuel to the fire. On the other hand, Entheali hinted that if you came and had a chat with her, she would see what she could do."

"The last time I had a 'chat' with Entheali in the temple,"

Abderian grumbled, "I was drugged, robbed of the cursemark, and thrown at a dragon possessed by the Lizard Goddess."

"Tsk. Mothers-in-law," Sagamore said in a tone implying he would be shaking his head sympathetically if he had a neck to shake it on.

Abderian shrugged. "What *is* there to do? The person I want to see, I can't. You tell me we must wait for Vulka to do something, and everyone else I want to avoid."

"Perhaps," said Dolus, "you should simply get on with your life as it was, since these other factors you cannot control. What would you be doing had Khanda not visited you, and Maja not given birth yet?"

Abderian thought a moment. "I'd still be looking for a way to restore Paralian to his former shape."

"Then that," Dolus said, "is what we shall do."

"But I was getting nowhere with that," said Abderian. He stood and stretched, feeling disinclined to move at all.

"Yes, you were looking in *Furrier's Transformations*, weren't you? I think what we need is a different approach. And, of course, the best place to start for such research is the library."

"The library," Abderian said, he hoped, tonelessly.

"Yes, the library. Is there something wrong with that?" Dolus said.

"It's just that . . . I haven't been there in a while."

"All the more reason to go, then, lad. Find some fresh ideas for solving your problems, including perhaps, books on how to soothe a disgruntled wife."

"Maybe." Abderian stared at the floor.

"Aw, what is it, me bucko?" said Sagamore. "I had that library filled with the most complete joke books in the land. Onym collected obscure sorcerous texts from all over Euthymia and beyond. Hoo, boy, were some of them strange! You should be eager to go."

Slowly, Abderian said, "You put a Riddle-Beast at the library door."

"Well, of course. A scholar should prove he has a little wit before being allowed into a room filled with rare manuscripts."

"I'm not good at riddles. The one time I tried, I got them wrong. The beast threw me into the Pit of Itching Moss."

"Well, that wasn't so bad was it?"

"I couldn't stop scratching for two days and everyone laughed at me."

"What sort of descendant of jesters are you if you can't stand a little hilarity at your own expense? No matter. I will tell you a family secret: The riddles the Riddle-Beast asks are always the same. And because you are my favorite great-grandson, I will give you the answers."

Abderian relaxed somewhat and almost smiled at the skull. "Thank you, Sagamore. That will help a great deal."

"Mind you, I think it's cheating, but as my son, Vespin, was not above such a thing, it might almost be a family tradition. The answers are, in order of appearance: 'a lollipop,' 'swordfish,' and 'because it's there.'"

"Lollipop, swordfish, because it's there," Abderian repeated. "I think I've got it. Let's go."

"After we eat," Dolus said sagely. "Food for the stomach before food for the mind, I often say."

"Eat hearty," said Sagamore.

Their "hearty" breakfast, however, consisted of only some dry wheat bread, tepid porridge, and bacon, and a mug of ale since the water was running low. The air in the dining hall was still and stifling, and even the fiery pennants on the ceiling seemed limp and drooping. Few folk who came to dine in the room stayed long, and the cooks who attended on them seemed haggard and harried.

Paralian fluttered in through a window and settled on Abderian's shoulder. His feathers stuck out from his body and he was panting. "I used to always wish for summer, in winter," Paralian cheeped. "Now I can't imagine why."

"This is hotter than most summers we've seen," said Dolus, fluffing out his linen robe where it stuck to his skin.

"Any news?" Abderian asked.

"I've been to the temple," Paralian said. "I managed to fly into Maja's chambers."

"You've seen her? How is she? How is the baby? Did she say anything?"

"Yes, tired, fine, no. Maja seemed to want to tell me something, but the acolytes attending her shooed me out before she could."

"Damn. You say she's tired?"

"Yes, but fit enough to harangue the acolytes thoroughly, from what I could hear."

"And how does the baby look?"

"Very babylike."

"Thanks a lot."

"Well, I'm sorry. I've never been a father, and at this rate the closest I'll get is to sit on some eggs. Your son was under a blanket, beside Maja, so I really didn't see him too well."

"Thanks, anyway."

"What are big brothers for? I think if you just give Maja time, she'll see you again."

"I'll wait, then." Abderian noticed that there was a stocky, hirsute man with black curly hair and beard, seated across the dining hall, watching him.

"Who is that fellow across the room, Dolus?"

"He? Ah, that is the Duke of Rosymount, so named because behind his ducal manor, they say, he keeps a mountain of roses."

"His wife likes them?"

"His cat eats them."

"Oh."

General Maduro, a tall, swarthy man, entered and strode over to the duke. Abderian decided it must be hot indeed—the laces of Maduro's leather cuirass were all loose and dangling. The duke and the general each looked at Abderian and Dolus and pointed.

"If you will pardon me," said Dolus, a little nervously, "I think I will go have a talk with the cook about the quality of this porridge. I'll see you later, in the corridor."

"I understand," said Abderian, trying not to smirk as Dolus hurried out to the kitchens. And trying not to worry as the duke and Maduro got up and approached the prince's table.

"A gracious good morning, Your Highness," said the duke, in a jovial tenor. He bowed as much as his girth would allow. "I am Jorum, Duke of Rosymount."

Abderian regally inclined his head. " 'Morning, Your Grace. I have heard of you. You have a cat that eats roses."

"Yes. Splat likes them quite a bit. Long-stemmed ones, preferably. May we join you for a moment?"

Abderian could think of no way to politely decline, so he gestured for them to sit. "Good morning, General."

Maduro grunted and bowed and sat heavily beside the duke.

"What can I do for you good sirs?" said Abderian, hoping it was nothing consequential.

"Actually," said the duke, "it matters more what we can do for you."

"Oh?"

The duke leaned forward on his elbows and continued in a low, conspiratorial voice. "You are young yet, so you may not be entirely aware of the attitudes, the ebb and flow of the political tide, so to speak, that flows in court."

I've lived in court all my life. I know more about these "tides," from personal experience, than I ever wanted to know.

"So I hope," the duke went on, "it is not too terribly bad news to tell you that the tide is beginning to stink. Meaning no offense to your royal self, but while your brother the King may be a cutie in the looks department, he's not got much else upstairs underneath that crown, if you know what I mean."

Abderian held very still. "What are you saying?" *Don't tell me this is a conspirator trying to use me in his scheme. And why is Maduro sitting through this? Is this a test? Or does he want a palace coup?* Abderian leaned on his elbows, pushing up his sleeves to display his bare arms beneath.

The duke didn't even glance at the prince's arms. He waved his hands in the air as if to erase his words. "No, no, don't misunderstand me. I'm not talking overthrow here. I just think someone in your family ought to know what's going on. Maduro here agrees with me. I've been hearing nasty plots and insults from my fellow nobles, but I don't know who in your family to talk to. King Cyprian has locked himself away and won't talk to anybody—which is the worst thing a king could do under these circumstances. The Queen has gone south to give assistance for recovery from the quake there. The Queen Mother is a hermit for the Star Cult, and only talks to priests and goddesses. If Paralian were still alive, he'd be the best choice to get things done, but, alas, your dear brother is no longer with us."

Paralian, still perched on Abderian's shoulder, whistled a mournful tune.

"Cute," said the duke. "But kind of a wimpy pet for a prince, don't you think? How about a cat? I have a nice, big grey tabby I could let you have—"

Maduro nudged the duke hard with his elbow.

"Ooof. As I was saying, the only person available to talk to is you, and, hey, you slew a dragon in the temple, so I suppose you're qualified in the heroics department. And don't say I should talk to your sisters, either. That pull-toy on the stairs business was just a bit too underhanded for my tastes. More like your grandfather's style, if you ask me."

Abderian tried to make sense out of the barrage of words. "What do you want me to do?"

The duke's eyes widened and he struck the table with his fists lightly for emphasis. "Save your family! Bring respect back to the crown, even if it is on your brother's fair head. Believe it or not, I like you and your silly kindred and I *don't* want to see Euthymia in a mess the way it was during your father's reign. I wanted to let you know that if you should need military support, or a loan from my ducal treasury, you can ask me. Of if there's any other help you need, just ask. Now, I'm sure I've taken too much of your time and I'll leave you to finish your breakfast in peace."

The duke and Maduro both stood at once. Suddenly, the duke leaned forward once more and whispered loudly, "And if you require special help for a project that should not be common knowledge, seek out my secret agent, Eleanor of the Wood. I have found her advice to be very profitable. You'll find her in the Stylus Woods, to the east. Good luck." The duke nodded once more and walked away.

Abderian looked down at his porridge bowl, trying to sort out the hurricane of words he had just weathered, when a big, meaty hand grasped his wrist. He looked up into the scowling, sweaty face of General Maduro.

"I have a message for that craven wizard of yours," he rasped. "Y-yes?"

"Tell him that if he wants the old bag, he can have her."

"I'll tell him."

"Good." Maduro's mouth twisted into a smiling sneer. He roughly let go of Abderian's arm, and departed after the duke.

Dolus snorted when Abderian gave him the message, out in the corridor. "He's too late. She was most disappointed when I didn't have the prowess she was hoping for."

"Oh."

"*Magical* prowess," Dolus added hastily. "Come, if you're feeling ready, we'll be off to face the Riddle-Beast."

"Dolus! The answers Sagamore gave us. I've forgotten them!" The tutor sighed. "Lollipop. Swordfish. Because it's there."

"Oh, good. Yes, I'm ready. Let's get it over with."

The Riddle-Beast had the head of an owl, the body of a lion, and the tail of a fox, or a squirrel—Abderian wasn't sure. Its great saucer-sized eyes blinked at him, and although Abderian had never seen an owl smile, he could swear the Riddle-Beast was gloating at him.

Between the end of the hallway where Dolus and Abderian stood, and the book-shaped library doors was a large, square pit, spanned by a bridge made of narrow flagstones. The middle flagstone, Abderian knew, was hinged to drop away, allowing the unfortunate would-be-reader to fall into what lay beneath. The deep floor of the pit was lined with what appeared to be soft, dark green fluff.

"The Pit of Itching Moss," Abderian murmured. "You won't catch me this time."

In a voice high-pitched and irritating, the Riddle-Beast said:

"Friend or stranger welcome be,
To the castle library.
The door beyond shall ope to thee,
When you pass my riddles three."

"Did Sagamore write that for you?" asked Abderian, more boldly than he felt.

"Whooo are you?" said the Riddle-Beast.

"Is that your first riddle?"

"Don't get cute," said the Riddle-Beast. "This is a position weighty with tradition and worthy of respect. Now, come forward where I can see you."

"Right." Abderian was certain the Riddle-Beast could see him just fine with those saucer eyes. *But I guess I have to play the game.* Abderian stepped out onto the bridge that led to the library door, careful not to look down. "You've seen me before."

"Of course, Highness. I never forget a face. Another step closer."

Abderian sighed and crossed the line into the drop section. *No fooling it either, I guess.*

"Now. Here is your first riddle. Why does the medium wear ectoplasmic suspenders?"

"What!" cried Abderian. He was certain "Lollipop" was not the answer. He looked back at Dolus in panic. His tutor seemed bewildered, and shrugged. Abderian turned back to the Riddle-Beast. "That wasn't what you were supposed to ask! Your first riddle was supposed to have the answer "Lollipop"!

"Ah, yes, one of my first sets of riddles started off like that, long ago. But you know how it is—people get bored with the program if you keep it the same too long. So. Have you an answer?" The Riddle-Beast idly inspected one of its talons as it waited. Abderian could swear it was smug.

"Uhhh . . . because they're more her 'medium of expression'?"

"Is that your guess?"

Abderian swallowed hard and nodded. Only then did he see out of the corner of his eye that Dolus was shaking his head vigorously.

"Wrong!" sang the Riddle-Beast, and it chuckled to itself.

Abderian tensed, waiting for the drop and torment to come, but nothing happened.

"I tell you what," said the Riddle-Beast, "I'm a sporting sort. I'll let you have two out of three. How's that?"

Abderian nodded again, warily.

"Good enough. Here is the second riddle. "What are the white spots between a dragon's toes?"

Abderian blinked, completely befuddled. He rubbed his brow with both hands as if to massage out the answer. All that came to mind was the awareness of how fast his heart was pounding and how loud his breathing sounded.

"Think like Sagamore, lad," Dolus called out.

"No coaching!" said the Riddle-Beast. "Well?"

"Just a minute!"

"Is that your answer?"

"No! I—It's . . . Oh, hell." Abderian turned and ran back to the end of the bridge, beside Dolus.

"I take it you are conceding the game," gloated the Riddle-Beast.

"For now," said Abderian. "I'll be back."

"I'll be waiting," said the Riddle-Beast.

FOURTEEN

Those who say I have no use for books have it all wrong. I love books, especially the big, fat ones. You can cut out the inner pages and hide all sorts of things in them.

—KING VESPIN THE SNEAKY

ABDERIAN TURNED TO Dolus, who seemed equally bewildered. "This is incredible. I can't see Maja and the baby. I can't do anything to get the demon baby from Vulka. I've been told I've got to save the throne from plotters, which I have no idea how to accomplish. And now I can't even get into the stupid library to get a stupid book to help me change my brother back to man form! Whatever god is in charge of my life has been taking lessons in helpfulness from Amusia."

Dolus laid a hand on Abderian's shoulder. "We all pass through times of trial, lad. Life's path must cross the Deserts of Despair as well as the Mountains of Majesty."

"Well, right now I'm trying to cross the Rivers of Ridiculousness. That duke offered to help however he could. I don't suppose he's good at riddles."

"He might have the humor for it, but—" Dolus's eyes widened. "My lad, your metaphor has more wisdom than you know. Of

101

course. Crossing rivers, heh-heh. Let us walk down this way,
away from prying eyes."

Abderian took one last glance at the Riddle-Beast. It was
running its tail through its beak and purring. Abderian wrinkled
his nose and hurried after Dolus, who was already some strides
away down a narrow side corridor.

When Abderian caught up, Dolus said softly, "I have an
acquaintance who lives down this way, who I think can help us."

"Is he good at riddles?"

"Sometimes. In a way."

"What does he do?"

Dolus looked both ways and leaned close before whispering,
"Necromancy."

Abderian's mind did flip-flops. That word was so often tainted
with fear and awe. "Why should we consult someone whose main
study is death? Could he throw a spell to kill the Riddle-Beast?"

"No, no," Dolus said quickly. "We won't need him in that
capacity. We oughtn't discuss that subject with the fellow at
all—in fact, don't tell him I told you. But he is a fine scholar who
has knowledge on many subjects and has an excellent memory. He
is often willing to be helpful in matters such as that creature at the
library door."

As they walked along, Abderian tried to imagine what appearance a necromancer would have. Tall and imposing, he decided,
*with dark, penetrating eyes that see the mystery beyond life. He'll
wear dark, hooded robes and speak in a voice deep and haunting.*
Abderian found himself beginning to fear someone he hadn't
even met yet and was about to ask Dolus if they shouldn't recon-
sider, when Dolus turned to a plain, unornamented door and
knocked. Affixed to the door was a small sign written in elegant
calligraphy: *The Evil Genius is IN*. Abderian tugged Dolus's
sleeve. "Uhhh . . ."

"Shush," said Dolus as the door slowly opened.

The person who faced them was a pale, bespectacled wraith of
a man who blinked back at them with bland blue eyes. His lank
blond hair was pulled back in a style of twenty years past, or two
hundred, and he might have been of average height if he had
stooped less. Abderian was about to ask if his lord was in, when
Dolus said, "Good day, Master Rivercrossing. His Highness and
I are having a small problem that we thought you could help us
with."

The pale man bobbed a bow and stepped aside. He mumbled,

in a tenor voice with something of the quality of unoiled door hinges, what sounded like, "Sure, come in."

Abderian followed Dolus into a room cluttered with bookshelves and desk space all arranged like a labyrinth, but with less apparent order. On one table were stacked sheets of parchment, faintly smelling of apple. On the top sheet, Abderian could make out words such as "Enterprise," "ship," and "captain." Abderian presumed it was a treatise on oceanic trade, and he turned back to Dolus.

"It's the Riddle-Beast," Dolus was saying. "We had reason to expect a certain set of riddles, and got something completely different instead."

Master Rivercrossing nodded. "It's been that way ever since the earthquake. Apparently a piece of lintel fell on the beast's head and, well, Salvia's Fifth Law and all that." He looked at them as though he clearly expected that Abderian and Dolus knew what he was talking about.

Abderian blinked and said, "Uh, what?"

"Oh," Master Rivercrossing said, surprised. "You don't . . . Well, Salvia's Fifth Law states that disturbances to magical matrices creates amplified disturbances in the normal space/time frame."

"Uhhh . . ."

"In other words, you don't want to hit magical critters on the head and let them live to talk about it."

"Oh. Right."

"I'm not making this up, you know."

"I believe you."

"Of course it wouldn't have happened if certain people thought to spend more for the upkeep of the library than they do for a royal wedding. Now, let's see . . ." Master Rivercrossing stepped over to scan a bookshelf while Abderian stood deciding if he should take that last comment personally. Dolus seemed to be motioning him to stay calm, however, so Abderian waited.

"Here we are." Master Rivercrossing pulled a thick book from the shelf and walked out of the room into the corridor without another word.

"What . . . Where . . ." Abderian began.

"Come on," Dolus said, smiling. "This should be most amusing."

They followed the pale necromancer down the hallway back to

the library, and Master Rivercrossing strode confidently to the very center of the bridge to face the Riddle-Beast.

The owlish eyes of the Riddle-Beast grew as wide as pie plates. "Oh, no. Not *you*," it whimpered.

"Yes," said Master Rivercrossing, with a wicked grin. "*Me*. I'm His Highness's appointed second. Ask me your riddles."

"Not fair!" cried the Riddle-Beast. "He's got to answer his own riddles."

"Life isn't fair," said Master Rivercrossing. "And may I remind you that in the Castle Charter, Section 21A, concerning the comportment of magical creatures, Paragraph 17, which particularly refers to Riddle-Beasts, states that any person, particularly of the royal family, may call upon a second to take his place in answering riddles. Said second shall also accept the penalty thereof if said riddles are not answered properly."

"Where does—"

"Right here," said Master Rivercrossing, tapping the book he held.

"Oh," said the Riddle-Beast, ducking its head into the ruffled feathers of its neck. "I'd appreciate it if you didn't make that common knowledge."

"I'll think about it. First riddle."

"Uhhh . . ."

"Oh, you remember," said Abderian, enjoying the situation immensely. "It was 'Why did the medium wear ectoplasmic suspenders?'"

Master Rivercrossing raised his brows at the Riddle-Beast. "Gods, not *that* stupid joke. You must have reverted to your Early Sagamore period of programming."

"Not fair!" the beast cried. "They've given you time to think about that one."

"That never bothered you in the old days," said Master Rivercrossing, "when your riddles were always the same. But if you want to give me a different one, that's all right. And I'll answer this for extra credit. A medium wears ectoplasmic suspenders to keep her spirits up. Next riddle."

The Riddle-Beast crabbed from side to side before the library door, burbling to itself.

"What are the white spots between a dragon's toes?" Abderian called out.

Master Rivercrossing swung his head around to look at Abderian with an expression of utter disgust. "You're kidding."

"I'm not making this up," Abderian said.

The necromancer looked back at the Riddle-Beast. "Tell me he's kidding."

The Riddle-Beast fearfully shook its head.

As if the words themselves tasted foul, Master Rivercrossing answered, "Slow maidens."

Abderian winced. *That's Sagamore's humor, all right.*

Master Rivercrossing sighed. "All right, gimme the final riddle. And if it's as bad as the last one, I promise to set up a business as a Riddle Consultant and plague you as often as possible."

The Riddle-Beast trembled but said nothing.

"Let me guess—it's 'How many wizards does it take to change a wall sconce,' right?"

"I know the answer to that one," said Abderian.

"Which answer?" said Master Rivercrossing. "There are at least ten."

"I give up!" shrieked the Riddle-Beast. "I surrender! I can't stand it! *Aaagh!*" With a mighty leap, the Riddle-Beast jumped away from the library door, into the Pit of Itching Moss.

Staring into the pit, Master Rivercrossing murmured, "Gee, and that could have been a lucrative business." He turned and came back down the bridge. Abderian applauded. The pale necromancer looked embarrassed.

Dolus said, "Many thanks. If there is anything we may do or give you in repayment, you need only ask."

Master Rivercrossing thought a moment. "That tincture of Oblivionweed you once described to me—"

"No," Dolus said, firmly.

"Oh. Well, nothing, then." The necromancer waved his hand a little and muttered something that might have been "goodbye" and hobbled down the corridor without looking back.

"What an odd—"

"Hush, Abderian. He suffers under curses of his own. Shall we go in?"

Dolus opened the left set of pages and held the door for Abderian, stepping in behind him. "The librarian here, Master Denileen, may seem an imposing fellow, but I assure you there is no kinder, more patient soul in Mamelon."

Abderian stepped in and saw before him a very long mahogany desk piled high with stacks of books. There were thick tomes bound in gold-stamped leather and thin codices wrapped in vellum. A few, off by themselves, were chased in silver and

studded with cabochon stones. Behind the desk rose shelf upon
shelf of more books, scrolls, and tablets of all description.

"Do people actually read all of these?" wondered the prince.

"Not as many as ought to, perhaps," came a bass voice from
behind the book-littered desk, "but enough to keep me busy."
Like a behemoth from the sea, a tall man of moderate girth stood
and towered over the desk. His placid face was framed in curly
brown mutton chops that came together in a bristly moustache.
His long, thinning brown hair hung in a queue down his back. He
regarded them with the calm gaze of a sleepy walrus. "May I help
you?"

"It is our fervent hope that you may, Master Denileen. His
Highness and I seek a reference work that might explain the more
esoteric forms of magical transformation."

"I see," said the librarian, taking up a pad of scratch parchment
and a quill. He made a brief notation. "Animal, vegetable,
mineral, or all of the above?"

"Animal."

"Man to animal," Abderian added, "and back again."

"Well, that narrows it down a bit," rumbled the librarian.
"Only a quarter of the sorcerous texts in the library might contain
information on the subject."

"How many is that?"

"Oh, about seven hundred."

"Um."

"If you like, I'll call up a listing for you."

"Call up a listing?" said Abderian. "Is that anything like
summoning spirits?"

"In some ways. The method is as tricky and the results are
about as useful. And it does require conjuring the resident demon.
Babbage!" the librarian boomed to the room at large. "To the
front, Babbage. Feeding time!"

From behind the stacks waddled a demon slightly shorter than
Mux, but with a larger belly and rounder head. Its little leathery
wings seemed almost vestigial, but its eyes were very big.
Babbage clambered onto a stool beside Master Denileen and sat,
patiently folding its hands over its belly. The librarian gently
pushed the demon's little button nose. In a high-pitched, nasal
voice it said simply, "Ready."

The librarian brought a sack out from under the table and took
from it a cooked turkey leg. "Here you are, Babbage. Eat hearty,
we've some work ahead of us."

The demon took the turkey leg gratefully in its talons and saying, "Loading," began to munch away.

Dolus said, "Excuse me, Master Denileen, but this must be a new innovation in the workings of a library. What does feeding this demon have to do with finding us a book?"

The librarian, unperturbed, replied, "You see, Babbage's particular talent is his memory. It's quite prodigious. But how well he can use it depends upon how much he has eaten. He can only make full use of his memory on a full stomach. How well he can help us depends upon how many bites worth of memory we make available."

"I see," said Dolus dubiously.

Abderian, finding the discussion uninteresting, strolled along the desk to the far end where he saw a sealed glass-fronted cabinet. Within it, on a marble stand, was a book that fairly shimmered with magic. Eagerly, Abderian tried the cabinet door and found it unlocked. Looking briefly over his shoulder to be sure he was not observed, he lifted the book out of the case and examined it. On a red leather binding, embossed in gold, was the title *Book of the 7 6 5.5 Wizards*. "I wonder what happened to the seventh and sixth," the prince murmured. "And how do you get five-tenths of a wizard?"

"No one knows," Master Denileen boomed from down the table. Abderian jumped, nearly dropping the book. "It used to be seven," the librarian went on. "Then one day the first correction appeared. Some months later, the second showed up. You're welcome to look at it, by the by, but I doubt you will find it useful."

Abderian opened the book randomly and found a recipe for a spell called "Chicken Paprikash," right next to someone's laundry list. Flipping to another page, he saw what appeared to be a bestiary, and beyond that was a comparison of different color magics by the authority Tremble-Javelin. On yet another page was the description of a misshapen tower that had some connection with a very destructive form of red glop. Some pages blurred and changed content while he was in the midst of reading them. Abderian gave up and put the book back in the case. He rubbed his eyes thoroughly and then returned to the others.

Babbage had just set the turkey leg down and, with a delicate burp, said, "Ready."

The librarian fired a rapid list of words at the demon. "Sorcery, transformations, man to animal, animal to man, restoration. Assemble list."

Babbage's eyes seemed to turn inward and he sat very still for a minute or so. Then he looked out again and said "List complete."

"Number of entries in list?"

"Seven hundred and sixty-one."

"I was afraid of that." Master Denileen turned to Dolus. "I can have him name them all and we can be at this all day. Are you sure you couldn't narrow the topic down just a tad?"

"As a matter of fact," said Dolus, rubbing his chin, "I think I can. The particular transformation we have in mind was caused through the use of diagrams or patterns in which magical energy was stored."

"Ah," said Master Denileen. "You might want a book on diagrammatical transformation, then."

"Exactly."

"Babbage, number of entries concerning diagrammatical transformations?"

"Two hundred and three."

"Well, that's better. How much time do you fellows have?"

"This is ridiculous!" Abderian burst out in irritation and boredom. "The change was an accident! We don't even know what really caused it. Something was triggered in the floor of the temple when it belonged to the Lizard Priests."

"Oh," said the librarian. "You should have mentioned that earlier. We received a carton of books from the temple after the Star people took it over."

"I'm surprised they didn't burn them," Abderian said.

"If they are magical texts," said Dolus, "burning might not be wise. Would one of these books contain information on the temple floor?"

"Let's find out. Babbage? New arrivals, Lizard Cult collection. List."

The little demon intoned:

"*Reptilian Taxidermy, a Beginner's Primer*, by Your Most Obedient Serpent, M. Amba.

"*Understanding Your Personality Through Iguana Entrails*, by U.R. Jypt.

"*The Way of the Newt, and Other Heresies*, by M. Slugg.

"*1001 Decorative Uses for Snakeskins*, The Good Lizardkeeping Group.

"*Helpful Hints for Floor Treatments*, by I.B. Saur."

"Stop!" said Dolus. "Describe that one."

"Babbage, give details on Item five."

The demon blinked. " 'Bothered by clashing designs and colors that don't match your creative ideas? This helpful handbook will guide you step by step through the maze of understanding current trends in floor decoration, to help you pick the right floor treatment to fit your overall design scheme.' "

"That's it!" Dolus exulted. "Of course the Lizard Priests would disguise their secrets in the cloak of mediocrity. We must find that book."

FIFTEEN

I suppose the problem with my reign is that I prefer to pay attention to the "good parts." I'd rather conjure haunted castles with my wizard than discuss the number of bushels of turnips produced in a hectare or the throw-weight of an SS-20 catapult.

—KING SAGAMORE

"NO PROBLEM," SAID Master Denileen. "I believe it's still sitting with the others in the 'to be shelved' pile, off in that corner." He pointed to a dimly lit section of the stacks. "They were a bit jumbled up by the earthquake, so it may take some poking around—"

"I'll go find it," said Abderian, feeling very bored and restless. He walked briskly along the desk, drumming his fingers on the wood, then wandered between the tall, dusty bookcases in the direction the librarian had pointed. Not far into the stacks, the light dimmed considerably, and the shelves loomed over the prince, as if they were unfriendly giants contemplating the mortal who walked among them. Like most things in Mamelon, the aisles were not straight; in fact they were quite crooked in spots, and soon Abderian found himself lost in a maze of dusty bookshelves.

At last, he came out at what he assumed to be the far wall of the library, lit only by a tiny window set high in the wall. Curled up at the base of the wall was a reptilian creature, about Abderian's size. It was like a dragon, only its grey-green scales were smoother and shiny and it had no horns. It raised its head and blinked at Abderian. "Yesss?" it hissed.

Abderian gulped. "Pardon me, I pray you. I was—just looking for a book."

"Ah," sighed the reptile. "What sssort of book? There are many here, you know." The creature's talons wriggled, and Abderian could see that it was lying atop a mound of books—had made a nest of them, in fact.

"Well, a book on sorcery . . ."

The reptile nodded encouragingly.

"Actually, it's a book about floor patterns by a priest of the Lizard Goddess Cult, but I don't suppose you—"

"Ah, yessss, I have read that one. I have read all their workssss. I think I may have that one here ssssomewhere." The reptile scrabbled around its nest, searching.

"You . . . read?"

The reptile handed Abderian a small book bound in lizard skin. "Voraciousssly," it replied.

"Um. Well, thank you."

"My pleasssure. Be ssssure to check that out at the dessssk. And sssee that you return it promptly when it'sss due."

"Uh, sure. You bet." Abderian waved the book and put on a brave smile as he stumbled backward into a bookshelf. Quickly he turned and ran pell-mell through the stacks until he came out at the front desk.

"Ah!" boomed Master Denileen. "I see you found it."

"Uh, excuse me," said Abderian, "but, do you keep some sort of dragon in this library?"

"Dragon? Oh, you've met the Book Wurm, then."

"Book Wurm?" Abderian said with a sick expression.

"Yes. It's lived here as long as I can remember. Sometimes it makes a mess of the stacks, but we have very few problems with overdue books."

"I can imagine." Abderian looked down at the book in his hands. Stamped in copper on the lizard-skin binding was the title *Helpful Hints for Floor Treatments*.

"Do you pay it scale wages?" Dolus asked innocently.

"No need," said the librarian with a gentle smile. "It makes plenty of scratch on its own, not to mention a greenback or two."

Abderian sighed. "Dolus, I think we've met your match."

"He'd best not brush his hair then," said Dolus, "else he'd light a fire."

"Some might claim I'm not so bright," said Master Denileen, "but I'm not going to sulphur for it."

"Pardon me," Abderian said desperately, "but I'd like to check out this book and go."

"My apologies, Your Highness," said Master Denileen, bowing. "Death By Witty Repartee is a torment beneath the dignity of your exalted station. Sign here, please."

Abderian scrawled his name in the ledger placed before him and said, "Thank you. Good day, Master Denileen." He motioned for Dolus to come along and he headed for the door.

"Good day, Highness," said the librarian. "See you in two weeks. Or the Wurm will."

Abderian nodded and made a hasty exit, drawing Dolus in his wake.

"I am going to lock myself in my tower," Abderian grumbled to his tutor, "so I need not listen to any more too-clever people."

"Ah, and let His Royal Majesty Sagamore be the only one to comment on your work?"

"On second thought . . ." said the prince. And they hurried away across the bridge, ignoring the Riddle-Beast's whimpers of itching torment in the pit below.

Abderian spent the few remaining hours until sunset in the castle vaporarium, the steam baths being the one place the residents were avoiding in this unusually sultry winter. For a while he was able to let his mind drift with the vapors and be at ease, mulling over the patterns he had seen in the library book.

It was common for users of the steam baths to have certain items placed on the hot stones to impart a particular fragrance to the steam. The ladies tended to prefer flowers or spices. The lords sometimes used garlic, or wine, or aromatic wood. Abderian knew something was odd when the smell of wet leather pervaded the room. He coughed and opened his eyes. The demon Mux was standing before him, looking a little wilted.

"H'lo, Mux. What's wrong? I thought demons liked it hot."

"Dry hot, Master, not wet hot." Mux shuddered and with a grimace of disgust, wiped water droplets from his arms.

"Well, sorry to inconvenience you. What's up?"

"It took me a while to find you, Master. Is there anything I can do for you?"

"No, thank you, Mux. Not unless you know anything about diagrammatical sorcery."

The little demon plopped down beside the prince and said sagely, "Demon magic does not require the scratching or scrawling of funny lines."

"Do demons have magic?"

"How do you think we fly with these flimsy wings?"

"Oh. Well, can your magical knowledge give me any clue as to which of these transformational diagrams in the chapter on "Tailoring Your Appearance to Match Your Decor" might change a man into a bird?"

Mux snorted in disdain and shook his head. "But my common sense, Master, can tell you that staring at funny lines in a book will get you nowhere. Why not go to the temple itself and seek the very spell that did the trick?"

"Do you think Entheali will let me?"

"Remember, she wants to see you, Master. She hopes for your . . . cooperation."

"You're right. And I can try to see Maja somehow, too. Even if I have to sneak up to her room." Abderian reached over and fondly rubbed the demon's head. "Ah, Mux, now I know why I keep you."

"I do my duty," said the demon, with an oddly sad smile.

The many domes of the temple were no longer the dung-mud brown that the Lizard Cult Priests had favored. The Star Goddess acolytes had repainted the exterior pure white. Abderian did not think this an improvement, as now, even in the golden light of sunset, the temple looked like a mass of fungus growing out of the castle courtyard.

The scaly binding of the book of patterns, hidden under his tunic of wine-colored silk, made his skin itch terribly. He knocked on the white painted door and a woman with short blond hair, in a black velvet robe, opened it.

Still a novice, thought the prince. *There's not a single spangle on her.*

"Greetings, Your Highness," said the acolyte with a wry smile. "How may our house be of service to you?"

Deciding he might as well go for broke, Abderian said, "I want to see the Lady Maja."

"I am terribly sorry," said the acolyte with a charming *moue*, "but the Lady Maja is closeted with her infant and will see no one. You may give a message for her to the Star Mother Entheali, if you wish."

"No—I mean, yes. Tell Maja I love her and hope to see her soon. If you've no objection, I would like to visit your Great Hall of Stars to meditate for awhile—assuming you are not conducting services at the moment."

The acolyte smiled. "The Star Rise services do not begin for another half-hour. You may stay until then, if you like."

"That will be fine," said Abderian, stepping across the threshold. "No need to lead me, I know the way."

"Of course," said the acolyte. She bowed and hurried off down the hallway.

She has gone to inform Entheali. They will be watching me. So. Let them watch. Abderian took a right turn and then a left along narrow lime-washed corridors, until a short flight of steps descended into the enormous domed circular room of the Great Hall.

Abderian looked up into the vault of the dome and noticed that the hole made when a chunk of the roof fell in during his fight with the dragon was still there. *Better for observing stars, I suppose*, he thought, *but I wonder what they do when it rains.*

The marble floor, however, was still a mass of lines and patterns. Some were carved channels in the stone. Some were inlaid gold, silver, and copper. Some were painted in garish colors, or stark black and white. Some could not be seen, only sensed. The attempts of the current occupants of the temple to alter or cover over the floor were largely unsuccessful. The lime-wash in one area was cracked and peeling. The plush throw rugs in another area seemed pitifully small in the vast space.

Abderian gazed at the floor, marveling. *It's all still there—the power drained out of a hundred wizards, stored in these patterns, to be used by those who know how.*

Abderian thought it a good thing that the Star Cult made little use of the potential contained in the Great Hall floor. They were nuisance enough as it was. But their attempts at covering over the work of their detested predecessors made Abderian's work tougher. He could not simply look for the pattern he sought; he would have to feel for it with what magical sensing he could, without setting off the spell itself. It would require all his concentration—but at least it would appear that he was, indeed, meditating.

Fortunately, Paralian had told Abderian that his transformation to bird had occurred in the western portion of the room. He walked to that side, stepping gingerly and feeling silly for it. When he reached that end of the Hall, however, he saw that the only pattern the Star Cult had left visible was one that opened gates between sorcerous realms. *No doubt they use that for communication with their goddess, Tritavia.* He remembered the fair woman who sailed a starlit sea in his dreams of long past and he smiled.

Then turned his mind to concentrating on the task at hand and, closing his eyes, shuffled slowly back and forth across the area, careful to walk across, not along, the lines of sorcerous force he felt beneath his feet. Nonetheless, he felt the surge of potential magical power tingle in his bones and it frightened him. He felt himself pulled along certain lines, the spells demanding to be used. *No wonder it was so easy for Paralian to tap into the wrong spell accidentally.* Abderian thought it fortunate that here near the wall there were fewer overlapping patterns, and he began to sense clearly a simple diagram in the area that might be what he was searching for.

Suddenly he felt his right foot stick to the floor, as if welded there. Sorcerous energy arced through his body from the left leg to the right, and he fell over forward from the shock and subsequent lack of energy. *Oh, dung-mother,* thought the prince, *now I've done it. I've set off who-knows-what and unleashed yet another calamity into the world.* "I'm an utterly useless idiot!" Abderian moaned aloud, pounding the floor with his fist.

"Not so," said a deep, ethereal, and frighteningly familiar voice in front of him. "You are a quite useful idiot."

Abderian looked up and saw a muscular red-brown nude man standing before him.

"Well met again, mortal," said Belphagor the Demon King.

SIXTEEN

Do not grieve for the dead. We in the Home for the Mutually Inapparent have enough problems adjusting, without having to listen to you weep and wail about us as well.

> —THE VERY LATE KING SAGAMORE,
> as interpreted by Madam Vellecarcrus,
> the Medium Rare

HEAT RADIATED FROM the Demon King's ruddy skin, and his eyes glowed a blazing white. Abderian slowly crawled backward, finding that his foot was no longer stuck to the floor. He watched Belphagor warily, knowing why he had come.

"Fear me not," said Belphagor, inclining his bald head. "I mean no harm to you."

"No, not to me," breathed Abderian, "but to another. How did you get here? Who summoned you? Entheali?"

"You brought me, yourself." The Demon King pointed at the floor. There, Abderian recognized the pattern for opening gates between realms. It was where his foot had been stuck. "Mux. You had Mux advise me to come here, and you just waited for your chance."

"You see, you are not so useless, and not such an idiot either. But I have little time. For the sake of both our kingdoms, you must tell me where your get of Khanda lies."

"No. You will kill her."

116

"Yes. I must. Surely you understand. Your world is already suffering, as is mine."

"But she's just a baby!" Abderian crawled quickly along the wall, trying now to gather up what sorcerous energy he could, though he was certain it would not be enough to defend himself against the Demon King.

Belphagor closed the distance between them in three long strides and grasped Abderian's shoulders, lifting him off the floor. "Where is it?" said the demon, his glowing eyes burning into Abderian's mind.

"No," the prince whimpered, but already his mind had conjured the picture Khanda had given him of Pokelocken, and added his own memories of the village, the Grey Guild caravan, and Vulka.

"Good," said Belphagor. "All will be well. The matter shall be—"

"No! Wait! You mustn't kill her. She—" Abderian realized he couldn't continue without the priestesses of the temple learning the location of the cursemark.

"I know what concerns you," said Belphagor, "for I see it in your mind. You worry that the child's legacy will create more chaos by its destruction."

Abderian nodded frantically. "We could transfer it . . . take it off her."

"How soon?"

Abderian slumped in the Demon King's grasp. "I don't know."

"In a fortnight, your kingdom and mine shall be uninhabitable. Each hour that passes brings more suffering, and soon the dying will begin. I cannot chance further delay merely because of the word of a mad sorcerer. Fear not. I will make it swift and there will be little pain. It will all be over very soon. Be at peace now." He gently lowered Abderian to the floor and turned away. Dry sobs racked Abderian's chest as he watched Belphagor stride toward the center of the great room.

"The Guild will stop you!" he cried out.

Belphagor stopped and glanced back over his shoulder. "The Guild is powerful. But I am one power it cannot stop." The Demon King continued to walk away.

Abderian rose, stumbling after him unable to free his mind of an image of a tiny red-haired infant dashed against the rocks, or its throat slit, or—"Damn you!" he cried. "Stop! Wait! There must be something—"

"I cannot." A circular area of the floor glowed and Abderian recognized the shape of a teleport circle. Belphagor stepped within the pattern.

"No!" Abderian was filled with frustration, rage, and horror, despite fears that the Demon King might be right. His hands flung themselves forward clumsily and he cried, "May your most precious friend desert you!"

A painful surge of sorcerous energy shot up his legs, through his body and out through his arms, throwing a wispy blue nimbus around the Demon King which then dispersed. Abderian fell to the floor, feeling utterly spent.

For the next few silent moments, a detached part of Abderian's mind said, *"Your most precious friend desert you"? What kind of a wimpy curse is that? Where did that come from? It's not going to stop*—He heard a deep moan in front of him.

Abderian looked up. Belphagor still stood within the glowing circle. But now the Demon King was doubled over, hugging himself tightly. He moaned again and dropped to his knees. The magical light of the pattern suddenly went out.

Abderian crawled closer and saw that the demon's skin was turning purple, and when Belphagor turned a horrified countenance to the prince, the eyes in his face were dull and dark. "What have you done?" whispered the Demon King and a great shudder racked his body.

Abderian slithered closer still. "I . . . I just wanted to stop you. I didn't want to hurt you. What's wrong?"

"Cold," Belphagor whispered, "so cold." The Demon King curled into a ball and rolled onto his side.

Your most precious friend, thought the prince. *A demon's most precious friend is fire.* Belphagor's skin was turning purple-black and sere, and his limbs were becoming thinner. Abderian struggled out of his silk tunic and wrapped it around the demon's shoulders, knowing as he did so that it was a futile gesture. Another shudder shook Belphagor's frame, his bones became prominent and his skin crackled.

Abderian thought desperately. Some of the priestly offices had fireplaces. The prince tried to pick Belphagor up, and found him surprisingly light. Abderian carried the demon across the Great Hall, up the stairs, and raced down the passage, looking for an open door. He found one nearby and burst in, sending the acolytes therein running out, shrieking in horror at his burden. There was a low fire in the grate, and Abderian set Belphagor down in front of it.

"Look," Abderian said, and turned Belphagor to face the flames.

The Demon King opened his eyes and cried out for joy upon seeing the fire, though it made his purpled lips crack and bleed. Belphagor leaned forward and thrust his hands greedily into the flames as if to gather them up. But his cries of gladness swiftly changed to screams of agony as he pulled his hands out of the grate, burned and blackened as the hands of any mortal would be. The Demon King sobbed, and Abderian put his arms around him, desperately wondering what else he could do. The prince murmured a small healing spell, which seemed to ease the Demon King's pain but did not stop the shrinkage of his flesh or the hoarfrost that was spreading on his skin.

"I'm sorry," Abderian whispered, his voice catching in his throat.

Belphagor's eyes opened and he rasped, very carefully, "If I had been you, I might have done the same." The demon's body shivered once more, dry skin rustling on bone, and he became very still. His head fell against Abderian's shoulder, the eyes grey and sightless.

Abderian gently set down the cold, lifeless bundle that had been Belphagor, ignoring the tears welling out of his own eyes. He heard murmurs behind him and spun around. Three acolytes stood just inside the door, with curious, amazed expressions.

"Get Dolus. Bring him here. Now!" Abderian said. Something in his face must have impressed or disturbed the acolytes, for they scurried to obey without a word of protest.

"Ah, Abderian," said his wizardly tutor, shaking his head as he viewed the frozen corpse, "did you have to be quite so *thorough* in stopping him?"

"I told you," Abderian said, "I didn't know what I was doing. I hadn't meant to . . . to kill him."

"You said you were angry."

"Of course I was angry, but—"

"Anger, you see, lad, was what any of those unfortunate wizards felt as their power was drained into the Great Hall floor. Their anger and their desire for vengeance flowed into the patterns along with their magic. So anger is the surest way of releasing that power, particularly against a former ally of the Lizard Priests. Most likely you were temporarily possessed, so to speak, by some wizard's curse."

"How very interesting," said Entheali, behind him. Dolus turned his head and the Star Mother approached Abderian, the star-sparkles on her billowing black robe twinkling in dizzying splendor. Her silver-and-blond hair hung in two thick plaits over her shoulders. "I had always felt the previous tenants of this place were a despicable lot. Now you understand why we have covered over their handiwork."

"And yet," said Dolus softly, "you seem to have some appreciation for the power they had amassed there."

Entheali appeared to ignore him and pointed at the body on the hearth. "What . . . *was* that . . . *thing?*

"He isn't a thing," said Abderian defensively. "He is—was Belphagor, King of the Demons."

"Well!" said Entheali, rocking back on her heels. She frowned deeply, as if searching hard for the implications.

"I suppose," said Dolus, "we should return him to his kin."

"No," said Abderian, "according to my curse, they would reject him." He stared down at the frosty, withered form and said with soft intensity, "We must build a pyre for him."

"I beg your pardon?" said Entheali.

"A pyre," Abderian said louder. "The least I can do, when I made his fires desert him, is to commend his body back to the flames that were his life."

Dolus raised his brows and nodded appreciatively.

"How very poetic," Entheali fleered.

"Do it!" Abderian shouted at her, his fists clenched at his sides. Again he felt some power, fed by the heat of anger, humming in his bones, but he held it in check, willing only that Entheali should see it in his eyes as he glared at her.

Entheali blanched a little and she spread her arms out as if warding the gathering flock of acolytes at her back. "Run along now, girls. We'd best humor His Highness. Gather all the dry wood you can find. Go now. Shoo!" And with that, the Star Mother turned and scooted the black-robed women out the door, herself scurrying out right behind them.

Abderian relaxed his hands and realized he was shaking.

Dolus, his face full of concern, put his hand on Abderian's shoulder. "Go easy, lad," he said.

The prince buried his face in his tutor's shoulder and wept.

• • •

Abderian himself carried Belphagor's dry husk, unmindful of the cold radiating from it, to the platform of wood that had been hastily constructed in the castle courtyard. Ever so gently, he laid the body down. Then he stood back, wondering what more he should do. He saw many curious faces of the noble and servile residents of Mamelon looking on, some with horror, some merely curious. He turned to Dolus beside him and whispered, "No demons wished to come?"

"It would seem they have all vanished," Dolus replied.

This did not reassure the prince at all. A black-robed woman approached him and he asked, "Did the Lady Maja have anything to offer?"

The acolyte pulled a colorful scarf from her sleeve. "She sends you this. She says it once did belong to her sister Khanda."

"Thank you, and thank her for me." Abderian took the scarf gratefully and draped it over Belphagor's body. Stepping back, he said, "I can think of nothing else in this world that he would want with him."

"Then let it be done," said Dolus, "and the grief and guilt with it."

Abderian gestured to a groundskeeper bearing a torch. The man came forward and touched the flame to the pyre. Such was the dryness of the wood, after the unseasonable warmth, that the boughs caught fire instantly, with a great *whoosh* of flame. Abderian's eyes smarted and watered from the light, smoke, and heat, yet he thought he saw Belphagor's corpse relax just a little and the mouth curl into a smile before the flames consumed the Demon King.

Abderian looked away, and saw, at a window in the temple, Maja staring at him. He reached out his arm toward her, opened his mouth to speak, took a step in her direction. But she moved back from the window, closing the shutter.

Maja's face, as well as Belphagor's, haunted the prince as he looked down from his tower window at the smouldering embers of the pyre in the courtyard. *I have done a terrible thing and now Maja is afraid of me. Khanda and all the other demons will hate me. I don't know why I thought I could control magic. I can't. Even Dolus's power gets out of my hands. And what happened in the Great Hall—I shouldn't be trusted around such magic. They should strip me of all sorcery and lock me away somewhere.* For the first time in many months, Abderian considered writing suicide notes again.

He felt Dolus's hand on his shoulder and shrugged it away.

"You did what you had to, lad. No one could blame you."

"They will." Abderian gripped the stone windowsill until his fingers were white and his palms ached.

"Then, at least, do not blame yourself. You were at the mercy of power beyond your control."

"Yes," Abderian whispered. He whirled around to face Dolus. "Yes. Take it back!"

"What?"

"Take back your wizard powers! I'm . . . I'm unworthy! I'll only misuse them."

"Don't give up on yourself so," said Dolus, shaking his head.

"That's right," called out the skull of Sagamore from a shelf across the room. "Stop being such a wannie-woo. You've brought down a dragon and now a Demon King. You'll make a fine young blade of a warrior-wizard, if you don't pummel yourself and lose your edge."

"Shut up!"

"Abderian," Dolus said, shocked.

"My apologies, Your Highness," said Sagamore softly. " 'Twas my duty, as a jester, to try to cajole my liege out of his doldrums. Old habits, it would seem, never die . . . unlike their practitioners."

Abderian lowered his gaze, not knowing what to say. There was a fluttering beside him at the window, and Abderian turned to see his brother the bird peering back at him.

"Hallo," said Paralian. "What's the shouting about?"

"Where have you been?" Abderian retorted.

"Well! Playing spy, if you must know, little brother. Dolus sent me off to Pokelocken to watch a certain Grey Guild caravan. It might interest you to know that the caravan has been 'temporarily delayed' in its passage across the border over The Edge."

"And what might Vulka be doing?"

"So far as I've heard, not a blessed thing."

"Damn!"

"Patience," said Dolus.

"Belphagor said that if something isn't done about the child in a fortnight, both our kingdoms will be uninhabitable. If I hadn't cursed him—"

"The kingdom might be uninhabitable now instead of two weeks from now," Dolus finished. "You have at least bought us time."

"At a dear price," Abderian murmured.

"Paralian," said Dolus, "what are people saying about . . . recent events."

"The freeze-drying of the Demon King, you mean? Fortunately, most people here don't seem to know precisely what happened. They know Abderian killed something strange, ugly, and demonic in the temple, but that's all. Of course, there have been rumors about his dabbling in necromancy, and they think this is just another example. It has them worried, but not yet panicked. Our dear brother the King, when he's not hiding, is in the thick of a bunch of advisors, trying to devise ways of combating the drought."

"And Horaphthia?"

"Still away in the south, repairing some of the earthquake damage. So far as I've heard, she doesn't know yet."

Abderian glumly rested his chin on his hands, his arms lying on the cold stone sill. "And what must Khanda think? She must know by now. Maybe I should summon her and beg forgiveness?"

Dolus coughed behind him. "Er, I doubt it would be wise to open a gate to the Demon Realm just now, lad. Give them time to calm themselves. And take time to rest, yourself."

"I heard you've been working more on my transformation problem," said Paralian. "So when's the big day?"

Abderian said nothing.

"I'm afraid," Dolus said, "Abderian's spell on Belphagor has diminished his magical abilities. It will take a few days to replenish them to the point where it will be safe to make an attempt."

"Ah, well," sighed Paralian. "I guess I'd miss flying anyway."

Abderian lay his forehead on his arms and closed his eyes. *This will not do. I can't see Maja or my son. I can't save the kingdom from traitors or rebels. I can't control magic. I can't change Paralian right now, even if I could. And I can't get my demon child back from Vulka, even though we'll all be dead in two weeks if I don't. No. Something must be done.*

SEVENTEEN

If any of the gods or goddesses lived on earth, people would track mud on their carpets.

—EUTHYMIAN PROVERB

TWO HOURS BEFORE dawn, Abderian rode out of Mamelon's eastern gate, alone. The stablemaster, perhaps fearing a fate like that of the Demon King, had woken up and given the prince a horse, with no questions and many bows and smiles. The Duke of Rosymount had not minded, being a night owl anyway, when he was asked for advice and directions in the wee hours of the morn. For secrecy's sake, Abderian didn't even tell Sagamore where he was going. So it was with a combination of grim determination and delicious freedom that Abderian galloped east through the cool pre-dawn air, toward the Stylus Woods.

Two hours or so later, he entered the woods and followed a well-worn trail according to the duke's directions. Now that the sun was up, the air temperature was warm and pleasant, which meant it would be hot and unpleasant later on. Birds sang in the trees, which were sprouting wilted buds, in expectation of a spring that would prove worse than any summer. The trail, after several turns and bends, opened into a flower-studded clearing. On the other side of the meadow stood a very neat, well-built cottage, almost a tiny manor.

Abderian dismounted and tied his horse loosely to a tree, allowing it to graze. He walked across the clearing to the little cottage and was about to knock when he saw the sign hanging on the door. It read:

> "All booked up for the year.
> Seek ye Valeria the Smithy."
> —Eleanor

Abderian noticed the windows were shuttered and the place appeared uninhabited. He kicked a pebble across the clearing and turned to see Dolus standing right behind him.

"Boo," said the tutor, his expression not altogether kindly.

"Uh, Dolus, good morning. How did you get here?"

"I had to bribe Entheali with the promise of important information. She used the temple floor to send me here."

"You shouldn't have done that."

"If what you've said is true, in a fortnight it will hardly matter, will it? You are my primary responsibility. I see you have decided to seek other advice. Any luck?"

Abderian jerked a thumb back at the cottage. "She's not in. And she probably wouldn't have time to help us even if she was. Do you know where we can find this smithy Valeria?"

"Hmmm. The name is vaguely familiar, but I wouldn't know where to find her."

"Damn. I'm sorry, Dolus. I didn't mean to worry you. I was just hoping . . . Well, I just hate sitting around waiting, powerless, that's all."

"And I can understand your need to get away from things for a while. But, dear lad, you should always tell someone where you are going."

Abderian scuffed his feet in the dirt. "Why am I being blocked at every turn? If Tritavia were a real goddess, I'd pray for her guidance, or at least to tell me which deity's messing up my life."

"Along with everyone else's," Dolus corrected. "In the meantime, let us go look for some firewood so that we can break our fast in this clearing before returning, eh?"

Abderian nodded, still annoyed at himself. Dolus walked into the trees at the south edge of the clearing, so Abderian went to the north edge and poked around the undergrowth. With the drier, warmer weather, there were plenty of branches and sticks and twigs. Abderian could have had an armload in a minute. But he felt more like just wandering, and only desultorily picked up a stick here and there.

After a while, the prince found himself beguiled by the whispering of the wind through the pine boughs and the rattling of the bare branches of maple and oak. Then, to his surprise, he thought he heard the tinkling of little bells above him.

Abderian stopped and looked up. There, hovering among the uppermost branches, wafted back and forth on the breezes, was a small woman. Her diaphanous dragonfly wings glittered in the sunlight and her pale, wispy hair floated around her face. Her ears were slightly pointed, and her long gossamer dress was a grey-blue that matched her eyes. She flitted from branch to branch, working on a tapestry or hanging (Abderian wasn't quite sure what it was) made from spiders' webs and pine cones and stray strips of cloth and leaves, fish scales and butterfly wings, bits of colored glass and metal. Enchanted, Abderian stood and watched the creature as she worked. Finally he breathed, "That's lovely!" And the woman looked down at him, startled.

"I'm sorry," Abderian said. "I didn't mean to frighten you."

"That's all right," said the little woman, in a voice lower than he expected. "I just didn't see you there. Who are you?"

"I'm . . . Abderian. Who are you?"

"I'm a windling. What are you doing in this forest? It can be a dangerous place, you know."

"No, I didn't know. I came here to get help from Eleanor of the Wood, but she's gone. A sign on her door says to seek Valeria the Smithy, but I don't know where to look."

"Oh, I know her!" said the windling. "I can take you to her—she's not far away. This way!" And the windling took off into the trees.

Abderian looked behind him, hoping to see Dolus to tell him of the slight change in plans. But naturally he saw no Dolus and rather than lose sight of the windling, he plunged into the under-growth after her.

Fortunately, the windling led him along a narrow deer path, so while the footing wasn't the best, at least he could avoid the worst brambles and branches. He was only slightly stained and scratched when they came out into another clearing.

This clearing was larger and set on a hillside. In the middle was a cozy two-story cottage with a shed to either side of it. In front, a big, shaggy black dog stood barking and wagging its tail. A lean grey hound barked from a hill behind the cottage. Loudest of all was a tiny hound barking from the cottage door. From the shed on the right, a voice cried out, "Shut up, Max."

"Oh, good, she's here," said the windling, hovering overhead, and she flitted to the shed on the right. Abderian followed, passing several chickens, a cistern with two huge frogs in it, and three shy cats that watched him from a distance.

In the shed, beside an enormous iron anvil, stood a slim woman with a cloud of wavy auburn-brown hair cascading down her shoulders and back. She wore a simple flower-print cotton dress and a leather apron with pockets. To Abderian's mind, she didn't seem the sort to be a smith, until she picked up a hammer and whanged away at a piece of steel on the anvil. Sparks flew and the anvil rang and Abderian immediately decided he would never want this woman to be his enemy.

The prince heard huffing and puffing behind him and he turned around. Dolus was coming through the clearing, setting the dogs barking anew, and the chickens scattering out of his way. "What's gotten into you, lad?" Dolus said between gasps for breath. "Are you truly determined to be free of my company? I see you go tearing off through the woods and it's all I can do to keep you in sight."

"I met this windling who guided me here. This is Valeria the Smithy."

The woman at the anvil stopped her work and looked up. "That I am," she said in a throaty voice. "May I help you? There's a special on horseshoes this week."

"This is Abderian," the windling said. "And this . . ."

"I am Lord Dolus," said the tutor, with a small bow. "Now I remember where I heard of you. Master Rivercrossing thinks highly of you."

"I have had occasion to be of help to him," said Valeria, with a wry smile. "What may I do for you?"

"I'm having some trouble with the Grey Guild," Abderian blurted out. "A note on the door of Eleanor of the Wood referred me to you."

"The Guild, eh?" Valeria said, setting aside her hammer and tongs. "Yes, they can be a touchy bunch."

"Excuse me," said the windling. "But as long as I'm here, could I take a ride around on Killer? I could use the practice."

"Of course. He's in the other shed."

"Thank you," said the windling, and she shot out of the shed and around the corner.

"So," said Valeria, pulling Abderian out of his momentary bewilderment, "it would seem you need my assistance in my other capacity. Come on in." She opened a side door that led from the shed into the cottage and went inside.

"Other capacity?" Abderian said to Dolus.

Dolus smiled. "I understand she has some sorcerous skills that might indeed be quite useful to us. It may turn out we've not wasted time at all. Let's go in."

Just then, Abderian heard the windling cry, "Go, Killer!" He saw, from the doorway, the windling go by astride a gentle-looking black pony with silver trappings. *Killer?* Abderian thought as it trotted merrily into the woods, the windling grinning on its back. Shaking his head, he turned and followed Dolus into the cottage.

Nearly tripping over two of the three cats, not to mention the vociferous Max, Abderian made his way to a large table. There, over several cups of tea, Abderian explained his problem to Valeria. And because of the wisdom he saw in her hazel eyes and the way she was calmly attentive to all he said, Abderian found himself pouring out all his troubles to her, from how he got the cursemark of Sagamore, to the personal problems he was having with Maja, to the unfortunate death of Belphagor.

When he finally ran out of things to say, Valeria nodded sagely. "So, you would like my help in saving the world, eh? That's a slightly tall order." She smiled with a twinkle in her eye. "Well, first off, we need to stir this Vulka out into the open. Get her to make a move so that you can reclaim the child who's the source of this mess. I think we can do something about that." She winked and said, "Come into my study."

In her study, amid the bookshelves, desk, and box of cheeping baby chicks, Valeria pulled up a chair and took from a marble stand an item that appeared to be a steel writing quill. She flourished it, saying, "Mightier than the sword, you know." Taking a sheet of parchment from a stack on her desk, Valeria paused and concentrated for a moment. Then she touched the quill to the parchment. Instantly, the tip of the steel quill glowed and sparked like hot iron struck on an anvil. As Valeria wrote, the lines of the letters burned with flame, though the parchment itself was not scorched, and her hands and arms seemed unharmed. The more she wrote, the more the flames grew until the missive was a small inferno contained within the parchment. With a final flourish, Valeria finished the message and the letters settled down to a dull red glow. "That should get her attention."

"What does it say?"

"Mostly that as prior owner of the contested 'item'—said ownership being provable by sorcery in any court—you have a right to the return of the item within a reasonable amount of time, along with reasonable recompense for time lost dealing with the problem, or Mistress Vulka and her Guild will have to deal with possible indictment on charges of kidnapping and treason. A copy will be sent to the Grand Master of the Grey Guild. Sound good enough to you?"

"Whew," said Abderian.

"If nothing else, having the Grand Master informed of this may light a fire under her. So to speak. While it is true that the Guild is a powerful entity, they hate anything that might tie up their business with legal action, and there's a chance they might investigate Vulka for incompetence."

Abderian had to agree that that should be enough to worry Vulka into action. After Valeria made quite certain that the letter met with Abderian's approval, she wrapped the missive in a piece of chamois and placed it in a blue ceramic box. Striking the box several times, she muttered some syllables that sounded almost like swearing. When she finished and opened the box, it was empty.

"Good. It will be in her hands soon. Care to stay for lunch?"

The sun was high and the weather was very warm, and though Abderian was not hungry, he did allow as how he could use a good nap. So he curled up on the couch, as Dolus and Valeria's companion (a wizened gnome whose name meant something like "to cut short") discussed the bones and leaves one might find impressed upon rocks. Dolus argued they were the artwork of some deity who liked to sculpt, while the gnome suggested that the creatures and plants were once alive.

Abderian peacefully decided this was one conflict he need take no sides in and let the rumble of their voices lull him to sleep.

EIGHTEEN

Fly? What fly?

—MERWIN THE MAGE, later known as "Buzzy"

ABDERIAN WAS CHASING a lizard over a hot, rocky plain. It was more difficult than he expected—sometimes he couldn't even see the lizard and had to guess where it was. And he kept bumping into boulders or tripping over rocks. Abderian wondered why he was doing this and remembered that the Star Goddess, Tritavia, had told him to, but she hadn't said why. He looked up to ask the sky, but it was turning an unnatural shade of grey. Grey shapes that weren't clouds, exactly, shifted to form the face of a great grey wolf staring down at him. Abderian screamed and hunched down among the boulders. His hands and feet grew longer and sprouted fur. His nose didn't want to stop twitching.

The wolf was coming down out of the sky, its paws coming nearer and nearer. Abderian leaped up and bounded across the rocks, moving faster than he ever had before. But to no avail. A wolf's paw came down and pinned him between two stones. The wolf's panting, befanged jaws hovered over him and Abderian waited to be bitten in half.

130

The wolf's head was transformed into Vulka's handsome, weatherworn face and she smiled—a grim smile of victory over a foe. Then she turned and folded herself back into the sky. She was nude and Abderian could see, on her left shoulder blade, a magical mark—a blue-grey line in a pattern of six ellipses connected to a circle. Abderian stared at the mark, knowing it was important somehow, but just then the lizard came back, now twice Abderian's size, and stood over him, blocking his view.

"Hey!" Abderian said.

"Surely you've had enough sleep by now, lad."

"What?" Abderian shook his head and opened his eyes. It was Dolus bending over him, gently shaking his shoulder. "Sorry," Abderian mumbled. "I was dreaming."

"Not pleasantly, from what I could tell. You should be glad I woke you."

"There was something important in it. . . . Oh well."

"Let us get back to Mamelon. If Horaphthia returns and finds us gone again, I fear we'll suffer worse than bad dreams. I've seen to paying Valeria for her services, though deciding what ten percent of saving the world would be was a bit tricky. Come on, lad. Rouse yourself."

Abderian rubbed his face and stood. The cottage was dark and he felt quite disoriented. Valeria entered and said, "I hope you aren't planning on riding through the woods at this hour of the night. Not all the residents here are friendly."

"Oh?" said Abderian, still waking up. "Such as what?"

"Oh, killer raccoons, vampire armadillos, that sort of thing."

"Well, fear not," said Dolus. "We'll take a quicker route back. The priestess Entheali will bring us back to her temple."

"Dolus," said Abderian, "I rode a horse here. I left it tethered over by Eleanor's house."

"Already taken care of, lad. That horse is now stabled here, next to 'Killer.' I gave it as part of Valeria's ten percent. I hope you've no objection."

Abderian had no particular attachment to horses, so he simply nodded, too sleepy to argue. They said their good-byes and thank-yous to Valeria and stepped outside. The warm, dark forest night was full of the chirpings of frogs and insects. Beyond the treetops, the stars overhead were bright. Abderian was surprised and relieved not to see a wolf-face there.

Dolus dropped a star-shaped piece of silver between them and said,

"Shimmer, shimmer little star,
Come and get us, here we are."

Their surroundings went through the now-familiar blurring and
blending until, with only a slight lurch, Abderian and Dolus found
themselves standing in the middle of the Great Hall of the temple.

Entheali, in her hooded, star-spangled robe, stood right in front
of them, arms crossed on her chest. They were surrounded by
other acolytes in robes ranging from pale grey to black.

"So," said Entheali with a cold smile, "since we have interrupted our midnight services in order to do you a service, I trust
you'll be forthcoming as to the information you promised us."

"Information?" Dolus said innocently.

Entheali dropped her arms to her sides, her hands balling into
fists. "No games. Where is the Cursemark of Sagamore?"

"In a safe place," said Dolus, "where neither you nor we can
get to it."

"I will warn you," said Entheali, "that I have empowered the
pattern you stand on to determine if you are telling the truth. Now,
what is this place, and who bears the mark?"

"I don't know—Ow!" Dolus hopped on his feet as though
they'd just been stung.

"How dare you do this!" said Abderian. "When my brother
hears—"

"Your brother the King," Entheali said coldly, "has closeted
himself out of sight. The Queen has not yet returned from her
work in the south. As the highest prelate in the land, it could be
argued that I may act on my own authority, as none higher are
available."

Abderian was certain she could not be correct, but he and Dolus
were rather at the mercy of the power she wielded. And so was
Maja. Belphagor had said he was a higher power than the Guild,
but Abderian doubted that Entheali was. It would be justice to
fling the priestess and Vulka against one another. And it might
prove enough of a diversion to the caravan that he could rescue the
demon child. "The cursemark," he said loudly and clearly, "is
currently protected by a caravan of the Grey Guild, under the
direction of its master, Vulka."

There were whispers around the circle of acolytes, and Entheali
appeared stunned. "The Grey Guild? And does this Vulka have
the cursemark herself?"

"No. The cursemark is borne by an infant who is the daughter of the Demon Queen," he said truthfully.

Entheali, if possible, turned even paler. "I see. That perhaps explains your actions against the Demon King. Well. We must think on this. I will speak to you again soon on what we must do, and how this all occurred."

"When can I see Maja? And my son?"

"Soon. Yes, soon. I must think." Entheali nervously fidgeted her hands a moment, then turned and fairly ran out of the Hall, her concerned acolytes fluttering after her.

When all were gone, Dolus turned to Abderian and said softly, "Was that wise?"

"I don't know. But it seemed to have an effect, didn't it?"

"Yes, she did not appear exactly pleased by the news."

"Perhaps whatever she does will be another spur for Vulka to do something."

"As long as Entheali does not claim to be acting on your behalf."

Abderian did not respond, letting his eyes roam around the domed torch-lit hall. The glow of various patterns that had been used in the midnight services was fading. Others—Abderian noticed one particular dark pattern and grabbed Dolus's sleeve.

"Easy, lad. Still dizzy from the teleport?"

"Look over there! That pattern."

"Which *one*, lad?"

"The circle with six ellipses. I saw that in the dream I just had. It was on Vulka's shoulder. And I've seen it somewhere else." Abderian stepped closer to the pattern and examined it. Without taking his eyes from it, he said, "Dolus, go get the book on floor patterns and bring it here. And bring Paralian, too. I'm ready to try the transformation."

"But Abderian, your energy—"

"I can get it from the floor. I did it when cursing Belphagor. I can do it again for this."

"And you saw how dangerous that was. And it will still impinge on your own capacity—"

"Do it! Please."

Dolus sighed heavily. "As you will, Your Highness."

Abderian did not notice when Dolus left the hall, so absorbed was he in studying the pattern before him.

Half an hour later, Abderian was reading the book of floor patterns and trying not to laugh.

He read aloud, " 'Time for a change? Want to get back to nature? This elegant design is sure to bring out the beast in the man of the house.' Yep, this is a transformation diagram, all right."

Paralian, perched on Dolus's shoulder, said, "And this is the part of the Hall where my change occurred. Looks like we've got a good chance."

"I saw Vulka's transformation from animal to human in my dream. The mark on her back drew itself in this direction." Abderian looked at Paralian. "Ready to try it?"

"Does Sagamore make bad jokes? You bet I'm ready."

"I must, at this point, register two complaints," said Dolus. "One, I still don't think you are ready. Two, you are aware we are being watched, aren't you?"

"One," said Abderian, "by the time I am ready, the kingdom may be in bad enough shape to make it no longer worth trying. Two, let them watch. They've seen me do worse here by now." Abderian knew Dolus feared what the reaction might be when Prince Paralian reappeared in man form. The political repercussions would get interesting, but Paralian just might be able to save Mamelon from Cyprian's negligence. *Assuming I can do something about the cursemark so that the kingdom survives.*

Abderian got down on his hands and knees and sensed for the sources of power in the floor. Surges of magical energy rushed into his hands like puppies to their master at feeding time. Abderian was worried by just how readily the power was available. *I hope it's not some wizard's will eager to do a curse again.* The pattern in the floor began to glow.

"What had you done before," Dolus asked Paralian, "to trigger the spell?"

"I just walked along it, I believe." Paralian fluttered off Dolus's shoulder and landed near the pattern.

"That direction"—Abderian indicated with his head—"should cause the change back to man form."

"All right." Paralian hopped to the top of one glowing loop and began slowly and studiously putting one splayed bird-foot in front of the other, walking the line exactly. "It's a good thing I haven't been drinking," he peeped cheerily, but Abderian saw nervousness in those tiny black eyes.

I don't blame you for being worried. Abderian felt the power he had summoned shift and begin to flow toward the pattern, into its loops and curves just ahead of the little bird. Abderian's own personal energy was ebbing with it and the prince wondered if he would indeed have enough. He now concentrated on the sort of transition they required, just to be sure the spell knew what they wanted accomplished. He heard Dolus chanting a protection spell. *Very wise, considering what we are working with.*

The stride length of a sparrow is very short, and the minutes became very long indeed, as Paralian took little step after little step around the floor pattern. Abderian tried very hard to keep his concentration on the pattern he saw on Vulka's back, its form, how it changed when she changed. Nevertheless, his mind wandered to how she might have become a shape-changer and why the Guild had the wolf as its mascot. What was it like to change back and forth, to be a wolf and then human? How did it affect her life?

Suddenly a shock passed between his hands as though he briefly held a lightning bolt between them. There was a high-pitched shriek and the smell of singed feathers. Abderian collapsed forward, feeling the last of his sorcerous energy draining out through his arms to the floor.

He lay still for long moments, not having the strength to rise. He heard someone's rapid, shallow breathing to his left. Abderian turned his head and opened his eyes. There, panting wetly with a fleshy pink tongue, through a toothy, furry muzzle, sat the biggest brown wolf the prince had ever seen.

"Paralian?"

"Well," growled the wolf, "it's not exactly the change I had in mind, but it's a step in the right direction."

"Abderian," moaned Dolus, "whatever could you have been thinking of?"

"I thought of Vulka and—oh." Embarrassed, Abderian buried his face between his arms. He heard the tick of claws on the stone floor and felt a wet tongue licking his ear.

"Not to worry, little brother," ruffed Paralian. "I can do very well in this shape while you study how to set things right again. I feel stronger already! And smarter. Mayhap I can do some magic while like this. I could be the first sorcerer wolf, hey?"

Abderian smiled sadly and reached up to scratch his brother the wolf behind the ear. "I'm glad you're taking it well. I'm very sorry."

"Don't know about you," Paralian growled, "but I'm hungry. Let's eat."

NINETEEN

Intrigue is a game which is as dangerous for the spectators as it is for the players.

—KING VESPIN THE SNEAKY

"SHE WOULDN'T SEE me."

"Abderian, it's well after midnight. She's asleep. Try again at a more civilized hour and you may get a different response."

Abderian wondered if Maja simply was disgusted by the death of Belphagor and wanted nothing to do with him anymore. He stared down at the bowl of gruel which was all they could badger the sleepy cooks into preparing at this hour. The dining hall was dark and stifling and foreboding. Abderian looked down at Paralian who lay at his feet, contentedly gnawing on a beef bone.

"How can you eat that thing?"

"Damn sight better than what you've got," he gruffed.

"They need to use up the grain before it spoils, Cook says."

"Heh. I wouldn't feed that to a dog."

"You're a fine one to talk."

"Say," said Dolus, "looks as though they're preparing to change the ceiling decorations."

Abderian stared down the length of the room. At the far end was

136

a ladder, beside which was a large basket filled with colorful bits of cloth.

"Let's get a sneak preview, shall we?" said Paralian, and he trotted lazily over to the basket. Grasping one of the wicker handles in his jaws, he walked backward, dragging the basket with him. At Abderian's chair, Paralian stopped and nosed about the multicolored cloth, then pulled out something floppy.

"What have you got there?" Abderian said.

Paralian dropped the pale bundle. "I'm not sure."

Abderian picked up what appeared to be a large rag doll with yellow yarn for hair and an insipidly cute face. The telling clue to its intended identity was the gold paper crown pinned to the doll's head. "I thought we already had a mannequin of Cyprian. A wooden one, better than this."

"Maybe it was broken during the earthquake," Paralian suggested.

"They could have made a better replacement. Cyprian won't like this one."

"I have the uncomfortable notion," said Dolus, "that this is not meant to be pleasing to the King. I notice in this basket there are the territorial banners of various duchies and earldoms: Reedymarsh and Buckland, Jhanemford, Deansland, and Shetter Lea."

Abderian frowned. "I've never even heard of some of those places. Have you?"

"Oh, yes," said Dolus. "I know them all."

"Deansland isn't on any map I've seen."

"It's hidden. It's a secret country."

"Whose idea was that?"

"Oh, just the whim of some dragoon."

"And Shetter Lea?"

"Those tangled lands are ruled by some of the most ancient noble blood in Euthymia."

"Which blood is that?"

"Does it matter?" said Dolus impatiently. "The important thing is that these ducal colors were to be displayed openly in Mamelon. That hasn't happened since the time of rebellions during your father's reign. This is cause for worry, Abderian."

Paralian shook his shaggy head. "Cyprian is not handling things well."

"I guess I will have to talk to him," said Abderian, "though I've no idea what to do, either."

"Perhaps it is this shape you put me into," said Paralian, "but

I know what I would do. I would be tempted to rip a few throats out . . . if I knew which throats to rip."

"You could do that . . . but it would be wrong."

"But not very."

A little blond page stood at the door. He cleared his throat and said, "The Queen Mother Pleonexia sends her greetings to her beloved son Abderian, and requests the pleasure of his company. Immediately."

"At this hour?"

"She's a hermit of the Star Goddess," said Paralian. "What better time?"

"Good old Mum," muttered Abderian.

As Dolus considered this a better hour for sleeping than socializing, he had gone off to his chambers, leaving Abderian and Paralian to walk to the southwestern portion of Castle Mamelon, where the Queen Mother's tower was located.

They came to a long hallway where both walls were painted with wild, running horses. So was the floor (top view of backs and manes) and the ceiling (bottom view of hooves and dust). It gave the viewer unsettling fears of being suffocated or trampled. There came a high-pitched squealing, which Abderian at first imagined to be a horse's whinny. Then two young girls in long, white satin nightdresses, burst shrieking out of a room to their left and came running down the hall toward them.

"Give it back!" shouted the taller, older one.

"Uh-uh," said the younger one, clutching some crumpled paper to her chest and laughing wickedly.

"Amusia, I'm warning you—"

The girls stopped short on seeing Abderian and Paralian blocking their way in the hall. "Make her give it back to me, Abderian," said Princess Alexia.

"You can't make me!" squeaked Princess Amusia. "It isn't hers anyway, and I found it, so it's mine now!"

"Give what? What have you got, Amusia?" Abderian hated to get involved in his sisters' squabbles but he seemed to have little choice.

"Don't you dare tell him!" said Alexia.

"Oh, look, a doggie!" said Amusia.

"It's not a dog, stupid, it's a wolf," said Alexia, "and don't try to change the subject."

"Nice doggie," said Amusia, holding her hand out to Paralian.
Paralian snarled and bared his teeth. *Evidently he's seen what
the girls do to their pets*, thought Abderian.

"He's not a 'nice doggie,' Amusia," said Abderian, pretending
to restrain Paralian from doing something dire. "He's for my protection."

"Well, he's better than that wimpy bird you had," said Alexia.
Paralian growled and snapped at the papers in Amusia's hand.
Amusia jumped back and shook her finger at him. "Bad doggie."

Paralian looked up at his brother with liquid brown eyes full of
loyalty and wounded pride. Abderian found laughter hard to stifle.
"He's only doing what he's supposed to, Amusia."

"What's his name?" I'll bet it's something dumb, like Killer or
Rover or Barfbreath."

"No, it's . . . Paralian."

Amusia regarded Abderian gravely and shook her head. "Sick
sick sick sick sick."

During this discourse, Alexia loomed over her little sister's
shoulder. Suddenly she snatched the papers out of Amusia's fist
and took off running back down the hall.

"Hey!" cried Amusia. "No fair! Give that back!" She went
tearing after Alexia. They both disappeared through a door on the
right.

"Ah, childhood," said Paralian. Remember when you, I, and
Cyprian had tussles like that?"

"How could I forget? It wasn't so long ago, and Cyprian would
deal me worse than tugged hair and nasty words."

"Yes," Paralian said softly, "perhaps best not to remember. Ah,
well, onward to our meeting with Destiny."

"Destiny? With Mother?" Abderian strode ahead down the hall.
He was relieved when they finally passed the south end of the last
north-bound horse, and the mural faded into the wall stucco.

"Of course. You may not realize how much a mystic she has
become since Father died. She doubtless has some fateful premonition for you."

"Oh, no! Not a premonition!"

"I would wager on it."

"Her premonitions are always wrong."

"In the long run or short run?"

Abderian was silent a moment. He had never considered
long-term evaluations of his mother's oracular pronouncements.
In fact, the only one he clearly remembered was her declaration

that "something wonderful was going to happen" the same day he was forced to leave Mamelon because his father had discovered the cursemark on Abderian's arm. The long run didn't look likely either.

Pleonexia met them at the door herself. *The mystic life must agree with her*, thought Abderian, for the full, black, cowled robe she wore hid none of her considerable girth.

"My dearest Abderian," she burbled, greeting him with a smothering hug. Abderian gave her a perfunctory peck on the cheek.

"H'lo, Mum."

"*Rowlror rum*," said Paralian.

"My, what is this? I see you've gotten yourself a dog. Well that's good. A much more suitable pet for a boy than that little bird you used to talk to."

Paralian jumped up on his hind legs, putting his paws on Pleonexia's shoulders, and gave her face a thoroughly sloppy licking. The Queen Mother emitted shrieks of mixed delight and disgust.

"Down, boy!" said Abderian, not too quickly. "Uh, I guess he likes you."

Paralian obediently sat. Abderian had to fight the urge to pet him on the head and say "good doggie."

Pleonexia patted her face with her sleeves. "How very flattering. Now, do please come in, I have something important to tell you."

Abderian entered and stopped, surprised. The roof had fallen in, leaving gaping holes in the ceiling. "Haven't you had someone fix this since the earthquake? Mother, why didn't you tell someone? I could have fixed it for you."

"No, no, Abderian. This is perfect. I could not ask for better."

"Better?"

"Of course better. How else to commune with the Goddess of the Stars than by seeing them directly. This way I may give her my watchful care every night."

And a good thing this weather has been warm and there's been no rain. "Uh, as you wish."

"And how are Maja and the baby?"

Abderian paused. "So far as I know, they are fine, Mother."

"You really ought to marry the girl, you know."

Paralian made a strange sound in his throat.

"Yes, Mother. As soon as she lets me. And I get a few things cleared up."

"Well I certainly hope so. People are talking enough as it is about our family. Have you and Maja thought of a name?"

"Hmmm?"

"For the baby?"

"Oh. No. We haven't . . . talked about it, really." Abderian felt very uncomfortable with the discussion and hoped she would change the subject.

"Are you all right, Abderian? You look a bit run-down. Haven't you been eating right? Getting enough sleep?"

"I'm all right, Mother. It's just—well, I've been worried about Cyprian. And the kingdom."

"I understand, dear. He seems not to be the best of kings lately. The heart is all gone out of him when his wife isn't around. It only encourages all the plotting that naturally goes on. A royal court without plots is like a picnic without ants. Unnatural. Mind you, I like it no more than you do, dear, but to try to squelch it all would require an iron rule such as your father's. We wouldn't want to return to that, now, would we?"

Abderian shook his head. "Was there something special you wanted to tell me, Mother?"

"Ah, yes. I have had a premonition that I must tell you."

Paralian glanced at him, his expression saying, *I told you so.* Abderian suppressed a groan.

"Tritavia appeared to me in a dream!" Pleonexia said. "I saw her drifting on an endless sea beneath a starlit sky."

"Yes, Mother. But what was the premonition?" He steeled himself for an onslaught of turgid poetry.

"She said, 'Tell Abderian to keep out of my temple.'"

After a pause, Abderian said, "That's it?"

Pleonexia blinked and folded her hands in front of her. "Well, I thought that was clear enough."

"Yes, but you—she usually doesn't . . . Oh, never mind. Yes, I suppose she isn't happy with the way I have used her temple. I understand."

"That's good. I told her you were a good boy. She seemed more worried than angry, so you needn't feel too guilty."

Probably worried I'd do something else stupid like turn Paralian into a carrot. Can't say I blame her. But how will I see

Maja? "Thank you, Mother. I will not keep you from your meditations any longer. I think I should go visit Cyprian now."

"Yes, that might buck him up a bit. And really, Abderian, just because I've become a hermit doesn't mean you should feel shy about coming to see me. You and Cyprian and the girls, you will always be my babies, and I miss you so."

Abderian bowed deeply to hide his wince. "Yes, Mum. I'll try, Mum. Goodbye." He quickly turned to evade a fleshy kiss and said, "C'mon Paralian. Come on, boy," and hurried out the door.

It took Abderian until dawn to find Cyprian. The young king had sequestered himself in a lonely little tower that had been dilapidated even before the earthquake. His Majesty sat curled up in a corner of a lancet window, his disheveled blond hair falling over his face, staring out at nothing. To Abderian's eyes, he looked every inch a melancholy seventeen-year-old and not one whit like a king.

"There you are! Do you know how many guards I had to bribe to find you?"

Cyprian grunted, not turning his head.

"Four. And they mostly agreed because I had a vicious-looking wolf—er, hound to back me up. And the one outside the door had to search me before he let me in."

Cyprian shrugged. "Maduro's idea," he muttered.

Considering what Abderian had come to warn his brother about, he could see this as a good or bad thing. "Do you trust him?"

Cyprian shrugged again and said nothing.

"What is wrong with you?" Abderian felt ready to explode with frustration. He wanted at the least to grab his brother by the shoulders and shake him. A slap across the face was an appealing idea, except that it seemed Cyprian might hardly notice it—indeed, might accept it as deserved and request more.

"She hasn't come back," Cyprian said at last.

"She? Oh. Horaphthia." It dawned on Abderian that there could be unexpected drawbacks to powerful love spells. "I wouldn't worry. She should be back soon."

"She should have been back two days ago."

"Oh. Perhaps there was more damage to repair in the south than we thought."

"She would have sent word."

"Well. Look, she's the most powerful sorceress in the land. I'm sure she's not come to any harm."

"No. No harm."

"Well, then, what are you worried about?"

At last Cyprian turned a bleak, red-eyed face to Abderian. "She's left me."

"Oh, come on—"

"Why shouldn't she? To her, I'm just an inexperienced child. She's a better monarch than I am. An infinitely better sorcerer. I sometimes wonder why she agreed to marry me at all."

Abderian did not have the heart to tell his brother it was for the good of the kingdom. He wondered frantically if he could somehow undo the love spell. And then wondered if that was at all wise. "She loves you."

"There is no kindness in lying, Abderian."

"I'm not—look, if you won't believe me, there's no point in my trying to comfort you. Everything will be fine once Horaphthia gets back."

"She won't."

"Stop that!" Abderian's hands started to shape a spell and he pulled his arms tight to his sides. The spell had not felt benign. "I'd better go. Just try to act like a king once in a while, all right? And . . . keep yourself safe. Please?"

Cyprian resumed his purposeless vigil and said nothing.

TWENTY

A wolf at the door is worth two in the fold.

—Lord Dolus

By the time Abderian returned to his own tower, the bell for the morning meal was ringing. He was too tired and disheartened to care. Wearily he pushed open the door to his tower-top room. The hot air inside swept over him like a wave, and he considered staying in the cooler stairwell. But Paralian, panting, squeezed past him into the room and Abderian followed.

"Ah, company at last!" called out Sagamore. "I was nearly going out of my skull with boredom."

"Please, Your Majesty," said Abderian as he flopped onto his bed. "No jests now."

"What, tired? Depressed? Irritable? My boy, that is when jests are most needed. If royal life were a happy life, jesters would have nothing to do."

Abderian thought on this a moment. "You're right. I could use a jest or two right now."

Paralian yawned and lay down on the floor beside Abderian, resting his muzzle on his forepaws.

144

"Ah, so this is the result of your ill-fated transformation. Dolus told me about that when he brought back your library book some hours ago. Do not let it distress you. I've heard so many say it's a dog's life. Anyway, to your jest. Shall I tell you a funny thing I saw just half an hour ago?"

"Sounds good. Carry on."

"While I may be in an advanced state of disembodiment, I hardly consider myself food for vultures, boy. Anyway, I was sitting here minding my own business, not having anyone else's business to mind, when the door opened and in walked a little demon."

Abderian sat bolt upright. "A demon! What did he look like?"

"Oh, a big leathery nose, small, squinty eyes, and droopy wings that I swear could not hold him in flight."

"Mux! That was my demon Mux!"

"Come to think of it, he might have had a voice like that I heard when you first brought me here. But I'm getting ahead of myself. And I might remind you that it is never wise to think a demon is entirely yours."

"So I'm learning. Well, what did he do?"

"He crept in through the door, and looked about him as if fearing someone might be here. I thought of announcing myself, but first I wanted to see what he would do."

"Quite wise."

"Upon ascertaining that no one was about, this . . . Mux hopped up on that stool there and scanned your bookshelf as if looking for something. Then he saw the book that Dolus had returned sitting on your desk there, and his eyes lit up, almost as well as mine do. He made a strangling noise, which I presume was a cry of triumph, for he had the most gleeful grin on his face."

Abderian began to get the disturbing feeling that this was not going to be a funny story at all.

"Well," Sagamore continued, "seeing a mood begging to be broken, I shouted out, 'Ho, there, rascal! Do you need ballast in case of high winds or are they teaching demons to read these days?' "

Paralian barked a laugh. Abderian gripped the edge of the bed and said nothing.

"Well, this Mux fellow nearly drops the book and stares wildly around him looking for me, his mouth open so wide a bat could fly in. I nearly laughed myself off the shelf. Finally he sees me, snatches up the book in his arms and scuttles out the door, as if he's seen a ghost. Isn't that the wildest?" Sagamore let forth an unearthly cackle.

Paralian shook his shaggy head. "Master Denileen won't be pleased."

"Maybe Mux works for the library Midnight Acquisitions Department," said Sagamore.

Abderian struck his bed with both fists. "This isn't funny!"

Sagamore ceased laughing instantly. "I'm terribly sorry. Shall I tell you a better one?"

"You don't understand! The last time I caught Mux reading one of my books it was the book of demon summoning—and not long after, Belphagor appeared. That book he stole tonight explains the power in all the diagrams on the temple floor!"

Paralian stood. "Think I'd better take a sniff around. See if I can learn where he might have gone. Abderian is right, this may be very serious."

"I must be slipping in my beyond-old age," said Sagamore. "It was once a fine talent of mine to know what was funny and what was not."

"That's all right, Sagamore," said Abderian as he opened the door for Paralian and closed it after the wolf stepped out. "You've done me a service by telling me. Now at least I can be more prepared, though I'm not sure for what."

"Glad to be of some service, boy. But I've one small request. Could you kindly assemble the rest of me? Having just the one view here gets tiresome after a while."

"Well, I suppose there's no harm in it." Abderian pulled out the folded cloak containing the rest of Sagamore's bones. He opened it and then fetched down Sagamore's skull and placed that at one end of the cloak. From another corner of the room, he picked up Sagamore's golden sword and saluted the pile of bones. "Arise, my liege."

With a snickety-snick, the bones one by one sorted themselves out of the jumble and reconstructed the whole skeleton.

"Ah, that's better," said Sagamore, executing a graceful pirouette. "Now, have a seat, Your Highness, and I will entertain you in song and dance, and help you to forget your troubles for a time."

Abderian sat back on the bed, and Sagamore posed himself as if holding an imaginary lute. "I shall continue where I last left off." And, clearing an imaginary throat, he began:

There was a young lady of Honeywright Hive,
Of suitors to court her, this lady had five.
There were two sets of twins and one poor, runty lout—
And this one she took so he'd not feel left out.

Sing a ring-diddle-diddle-di do, all ladies are fey.
They'll do what they like, never mind what you say.

There was a young lady of Highcastle Tor,
Of suitors to court her, this lady had four.
They all were quite wealthy, they all were quite old,
She plans to inherit as a widow fourfold.

With a ring-diddle-diddle—

There came a sharp rapping at the door, and a girl's voice:
"Abderian?"

Hoping it wasn't one of his sisters, Abderian motioned for
Sagamore to hide and said, "Who is it?"

"It's Maja."

"Maja!" Abderian arose from the bed and stared at the door,
then looked at Sagamore.

"Ah, an important visitor, I take it?" And before Abderian
could stop him, the skeleton strode over to the door and opened it
wide, stepping neatly behind it and out of view.

With a little frown of bewilderment, Maja stepped in. She
seemed thinner than the last time Abderian had seen her, and pale.
And there was a hint of dark circles under her eyes. Her long
brown hair was unkempt and hung down her shoulders and back.
The burgundy silk dress she wore was loose and billowy. Still, he
thought she looked wonderful. She gazed at Abderian with a wry
smile. "You don't have to show off your magic to me, you know.
What's the matter, haven't you seen a girl before?"

"I . . . I'm sorry. It's good to see you, Maja." Abderian
dared not move, afraid he might somehow frighten her away.

Maja took a few steps toward him. "She finally let me out. I
don't know what you told Mother, but it has so distracted her,
she's not worried about me at all. I found I could just walk out."

"She kept you prisoner?"

"Not exactly. I *was* angry at you. I came to apologize. You
probably think that I think you're monstrous."

"Uh, no. At least, I hope not." Abderian glanced back at the door, relieved to see that Sagamore was content to remain in hiding.

"Well I confess I did, for a while. When you left, I didn't know what to think. And Mother kept filling my ears with wretched possibilities."

"I'm sorry, Maja. I had to. Was the birth . . . hard?"

Maja folded her arms on her chest. "Yes, but Horaphthia made it easier. Now, do I have to stand here all day or are you going to hug me?"

Abderian blushed and mentally kicked himself. Then he went to Maja and hugged her very warmly. "I missed being able to do this."

"I heard that you tried to see me when you came back. You've been fighting some sort of danger. I've become friendly with one of the acolytes at the temple, Lizbet, and she told me the truth about you and the Demon King."

"She did?" Abderian said apprehensively.

"She said he's the one who caused this terrible heat and you killed him because he wanted to kill our child. You were defending me and the baby." Maja looked at Abderian with warm, shining eyes. "You always did like dumb heroics."

Abderian did not know what to say, but he also did not want to disillusion her just yet. He shrugged. "Well. It was nothing."

"Right. Nothing. Modest as well as brave." She gave him an extra squeeze and then stepped back. "But, tell me, why did Belphagor want to kill our baby? Was Khanda jealous or something?"

"No," Abderian said, worried that Maja had already assumed Khanda had a role in it. "I don't want to talk about it, Maja." Abderian glanced quickly at the door and saw a skeletal hand resting on the edge and Sagamore's skull peeping out from behind the door. Maja began to turn to look and Abderian quickly grabbed her hands and led her to the bed. He sat and motioned for her to sit beside him. "So tell me how the baby is. What does he look like?"

Maja thought a moment. "Like a baby."

"Thanks a lot."

"Look, if I say what all mothers say, that he's the most beautiful baby in the world, that won't tell you anything either. He's normal size, the midwives say, and has my color hair. I think he'll have your color eyes. Does that help?"

"When can I see him?"

"In a few days. The midwives didn't think he should be moved much at first. He's with a wet nurse right now. I've been trying to think of a name. Abderian, why do you keep glancing at the door?"

"What?"

"Do you expect someone to come in?"

"Oh, no. It's—well, this is a private conversation and I just want to be sure no one's spying. The way Mamelon is these days . . ." He shrugged suggestively.

"Well!" said Maja, standing, "There's something we can do about that, isn't there?" She walked to the door.

"Maja, no!"

She turned, fists on her hips and an exasperated expression on her face. "Abderian, what's *wrong* with you? I'm only going to shut the door."

Sagamore's unearthly voice called out, "Allow me, my lady." As Maja turned, wide-eyed, the door closed to reveal the Jester King in all his skeletal glory. "Boo."

Maja turned back to Abderian. "I preferred the dead bugs."

"Maja, I . . . he . . . He's a friend—a relative, actually."

"A friend. Who's a skeleton." Maja sighed. "You know, I'm beginning to believe those rumors."

"Rumors?"

"About you and necromancy. One of the acolytes mentioned that you were recently seen in the company of a necromancer right here in Mamelon."

"He was helping me get into the library! It didn't matter that—"

"Ahem," Sagamore said. "Perhaps you have lost your manners in the heat, boy, but I believe introductions are in order."

"Oh." *Might as well get it over with. She'd find out somehow, someday.* "Maja, this is my great-grandfather, King Sagamore. Your Majesty, this is my fiancée, the Lady Maja, daughter of Lord Javel of the House of Thalion."

The skeleton bowed. "Great-Granddaughter of my honored liege, it is an honor to meet you, and I hope you harbor no ill will to one who unwillingly interfered with your family's reign."

Maja bobbed a curtsey. "Um, no, sir."

"Good, because I wouldn't want to offend a cutie like you. And I hated being king. No bones about it, it was the worst time of my dear departed life."

Maja turned back to Abderian. "That really is Sagamore. I can tell by his awful patter. My father used to imitate it in his uglier moods."

Abderian nodded. "I raised his bones with his sword because your dwarfs had wrecked his tomb."

"Oh. I suppose I should apologize for them, but they did have cause to be upset with you, sir."

The skeleton shook his skull. "No need. I accept full blame. If I had a whip, I'd flagellate myself for penance. If I had skin to flagellate."

"Um, Abderian, don't you think bringing him here was a rather stupid idea? Especially now, when the local lords are practically itching for another reason to bring down your family."

"No one else is going to find out, Maja. Only you, I, Paralian, and Dolus know he's here. And once he's helped me with my problems with his cursemark, I'm going to see he's buried safely in the swamp of Castle Doom. Isn't that right, Sagamore?"

"That was our agreement exactly, my boy."

"You see?"

"Cursemark," Maja said flatly. "Problems with the cursemark? That's why Entheali's so upset?" She stepped close to Abderian and looked up into his face. "Where is it?"

Abderian swallowed hard. "I can't tell you."

"Why not?"

"If I told you why not, that would be telling you, that's why not."

"Abderian. If I weren't a lady, I would hit you for that. And I just might, anyway."

"I'm sorry, Maja."

"I could help you, you know. Maybe I could find Onym and he could do something."

"Maja, Onym is cracked as an old doorknob and won't help us."

"Lizbet says you told my mother where the mark is, but Mother doesn't want to talk to me right now."

Thank the gods for small favors. "Look, Maja, I will tell you as soon as I can, all right?"

Maja pressed her lips together, her eyes hard and hateful. "Be that way. Don't trust me, then. Suit yourself. I'll go back to the baby like a good little wife and mommy should do. Maybe someday when you're ready to stop keeping secrets from me and treat me like a friend, I'll consider speaking to you again." She whirled around and went out the door, slamming it shut behind her so hard that it rattled Sagamore's bones.

Abderian sighed, feeling helpless and hopeless. "I only wanted to protect her."

"The trouble with sheltering people from the truth," said Sagamore, "is that the shelter tends to fall down around your own ears."

"So I'm learning," Abderian said softly. He sat down at his desk and buried his head in his arms.

Abderian blinked sleepily and raised his head off his arms. The clock candle on his desk had burned four hours of wax, and outside the window, the sky was deep cobalt blue. He sat up and stretched. *Dozed for longer than I thought.* He yawned and looked around. No sign of Sagamore. No sound of any kind, in fact. The air was very warm and very still. There was a dreamlike quality to everything.

The sudden scratching at the door made Abderian jump in his chair, severely banging one knee on the silverwood desk. "Ow! Just a minute." He rubbed his knee until it felt like he could move, and then he stood, wincing in pain.

There came more scratching at the door, impatient this time.

"Hold on a second, will you!" Abderian rubbed his knee some more, until he was finally able to hobble slowly to the door. "I'm coming."

Abderian leaned on the latch and pulled the door open.

And there stood a wolf—a great grey wolf with pale eyes and very large pointed teeth—growling softly.

Abderian took two steps backward, not noticing the pain in his knee. The wolf followed him in.

When he could breathe, Abderian said, "You're not Paralian."

"No, child, I'm not." The wolf's voice was dark honey on grating stone. Her eyes held certain death.

"V-Vulka?"

The wolf nodded once.

Abderian's breath came in shallow gasps. He had no idea what to do. This was the chance Dolus had hoped for, but he never said what they would do if she just showed up. And after Paralian's transformation, Abderian's sorcerous energy was weaker than it had ever been. It would take many days to recover, Dolus had

said, before they could even consider trying the transformation
again. Abderian's magical knowledge was useless in the current
situation.

"W-what do you want?"

"I dislike boys who act stupid and think it clever. My wizards
trace a certain spell to you. A spell that interferes much with my
livelihood. You will remove that spell. Now."

"I can't, I mean I don't know—"

Vulka bared her teeth and growled louder. The muscles in her
shoulders tensed.

Taking a deep breath, Abderian tried again: "You don't understand. I'll tell you the truth. The baby you have bears the
Cursemark of Sagamore. That mark makes the kingdom follow
the whim of whoever wears it. That's why it's so hot. And it's
going to get hotter unless we take the cursemark off the child. If
we don't, both Euthymia and the Demon Realm will become
deserts and we'll all die."

"You have a touch for the melodramatic, child. But I do not
think I should believe you. We listened to your warning that we
should prepare ourselves against demon attack, only to learn that
you had handily murdered the Demon King yourself. How do I
know that you have not set this heat spell as well?"

"Why would I risk so many lives to influence just you?"

"The child seems to mean much to you."

"She does! She's my daughter!"

"So she might indeed be worth risking lives?"

"Please," said Abderian, sinking to his knees, "you can keep
the child, if you insist, but we must get the cursemark off her or
we will all die! At least let me have her for a little while."

Vulka growled deep in her throat.

"Hold!" came a loud, gruff voice from the doorway.

Abderian opened his eyes and saw a big brown wolf—Paralian,
this time—standing spread-legged and fur bristling on the threshold.

Vulka turned her head to look. Abderian was certain this was
his perfect chance to do something, but he didn't know what. He
jumped toward her, but she swung her powerful head around and
snapped at him, grazing his arms with her teeth. Abderian fell
backwards onto the floor.

"Touch him not!" Paralian growled and moved into the room.

"This is not your business," said Vulka, and she turned fully to
face him.

"It is very much my business. Leave him be."

"Not until I have done what I came to do."

"Then you must leave disappointed."

"I think not."

With sickening dread, Abderian realized what was going to happen. The two wolves approached each other, grey ears and brown ears flattening, two mouthfuls of teeth shining bright. "Please, no," Abderian said softly, knowing he was not heard.

In a moment they were together, in a writhing blur of grey and brown fur. Horrible, soul-rending growling filled the room, as teeth sank into the flesh of neck or shoulder. Abderian tried to find something he could hit Vulka with. He found a fallen piece of ceiling beam, and held it ready to strike. But the wolves moved so fast, around and around, that he couldn't be sure he wouldn't hit Paralian instead.

Then they were apart again. Now, Paralian was between Vulka and Abderian. Paralian backed toward the prince, head lowered and ready should attack come again. As he neared, Abderian saw a wet stain glistening on one shoulder and he felt sick.

Vulka was panting, and lines of deep red marred her muzzle. "What is that one to you?" she said to Paralian.

"He is my brother."

Vulka paused and looked back and forth between them both. "And like a brother you defend him."

Paralian nodded. "To the death."

Vulka narrowed her eyes. Her nostrils flared and her ears came slightly forward. "It is not your death I seek. See if you can talk sense to him. I do not yet accept his story. If he lies, he will be in more trouble than he can imagine. The Guild defends its cargo and its rights with all its power. We will not be toyed with." After one final glare at Abderian, Vulka turned and trotted out the door.

Abderian let his breath out with a whoosh and threw his arms around Paralian's neck. "Did she hurt you bad? Are you all right?"

"Ooooch! Gentle with those arms, will you?"

"Sorry!"

Abderian found some rags and wiped at Paralian's shaggy shoulder and neck, frowning at the bloodstains.

Paralian sighed. "You know, I don't think she really meant to hurt me."

"How can you say that?" Abderian demanded looking at the bloody rags in his hands.

"She could have hurt me far worse. These are only flesh wounds; they bleed like crazy but don't cause lasting harm. If she'd gotten those jaws on my throat or her claws in my gut . . ." He shook his head.

"You think she just wanted to frighten us?"

Paralian looked around at Abderian, one brow ridge cocked. "She succeeded, didn't she?"

TWENTY-ONE

Excerpt from *A History*, etc. by the Princess Amusia:

I miss the demons. There used to be a lot of them in the castle. They showed up when Abderian got kidnapped last year. The Lizard Priests controlled them for a while, but when the Lizard Priests left, there were demons all over the place. They were fun. They would put funny things on the ceiling of the dining hall, and make messes lots of places. But now the Demon King's been killed in the temple. They say Abderian did it, just like he killed the dragon. He ruins everything. I wish the demons would come back.

MANY HOURS LATER, Abderian woke again, on his bed this time. Paralian was curled up beside him, his head on his brother's stomach. Abderian suddenly understood why dogs were so fondly spoken of as companions. He wished he could have had a dog when he was younger.

The setting sun was streaming in through the window and the evening was stiflingly hot. Abderian stretched and let his eyes roam around the room, until they came to rest on Sagamore's skeletal form, leaning nonchalantly against the wall.

"So, you've progressed to lying with dogs," Sagamore commented.

"Wolf," Paralian corrected him.

"Woof woof to you, too."

"Don't you say 'hello' like everyone else?" Abderian snapped. *"Where have you been?"*

"In this incarnation or the previous? Oh, very well. I've been strolling my old haunts, you might say. You people have been

155

letting the place fall down a bit. Not that I mind much. I always thought Mamelon would make a magnificent ruin someday."

"Well you can blame your stupid cursemark for that. Did anyone see you?"

"Quite a few, actually."

Abderian slapped his forehead. "Oh, no."

"Fear not, boy. Some children screamed and ran. A few men laughed, thinking me a wine-borne phantom. A few ladies fainted. Others frowned at me and muttered prayers as they scurried away. Nothing untoward."

"Right," said Paralian. "There goes what's left of Abderian's reputation." He stood up on the bed and stretched.

"And I brought you breakfast." Sagamore took a cloth off a silver bowl on the desk.

Abderian got up and went to look. The bowl contained apples and cheeses and fresh-baked cinnamon muffins. Abderian decided that Sagamore could be forgiven. His stomach reminded him he had missed a few meals the day before and he dug in.

"Could you spare a chunk of cheese for me?" said Paralian, jumping down from the bed and putting his paws up on the table.

"We can do better than that," said Sagamore. From a shelf he brought down a plate on which was a huge, meaty, broth-dripping soup bone. Paralian licked his chops as the plate was set down before him.

"As a king," Paralian said, "you make an excellent steward."

"Thank you," said Sagamore. "Nice to know I needn't have been locked into one career. I'll understand if you wolf your food." Turning to Abderian, the skeletal king said, "So, my miracle-working prince, what wonders do we have on the agenda today, O slayer of demons and translator of birds into wolves?"

Between mouthfuls, Abderian said, "I have to speak to Dolus about Vulka and the demon baby. Where has Dolus been, anyway?"

"Getting much needed sleep, the last I saw."

"Oh. Well, I'll wake him right after dinner. Things are going to get desperate, Sagamore. Vulka doesn't believe me. I guess that letter I had Valeria send only made her madder. I don't suppose there's some way to affect the cursemark at a distance, is there? Sagamore?"

The skeletal king was at the window, looking down at something below. "Well, now, that's very interesting," he said.

"What is? And get away from that window! Someone might see you."

"Ah, now I know how the black sheep of a family feels. Well, Sir Too-Good-For-His-Ancestors, it might interest you to know that there is a small leathery demon down there making the most peculiar faces at me."

"Mux? Let me see!" Abderian jumped up from the table and ran to the window. Sure enough, in the courtyard below, stood Mux, holding a book under his arm. As soon as Mux spied Abderian, however, the demon's eyes went wide with fright and he scurried around the curve of the tower wall.

"I'll be right back," said Abderian, and he rushed out the door and down the tower stairs. The bottom of the stairwell let onto a hallway which led to another hall and so on. Abderian cursed Sagamore's designs that never allowed one to go anywhere in a straight line, but after bowling over two servants and taking one wrong turn, Abderian emerged into the courtyard. He looked around without hope, then saw Mux's leathery face peeking around the tower wall. "Mux! Wait!" Abderian took off running toward the demon. When he next caught sight of him, Mux was tearing across the courtyard, straight to the lumpy white domes of the temple. Abderian gave chase, scattering gravel and startled chickens as he went.

The demon, however, kept his lead, and just as Abderian was catching up, Mux grabbed the handle of the temple front door and dashed inside, slamming the door shut behind him. Abderian reached the door just in time to hear a bolt slam home behind it. Abderian pounded on the white-painted wood and shouted "Mux! Open up! I just want to talk to you!"

Abderian continued knocking for a minute, until he heard movement behind the door, and the bolt scraping back again. But instead of the demon, the door was opened by a tall, thin woman with enormous blue eyes. "You needn't wear a hole in the door, Your Highness. What do you wish?" Her voice was more winsome and childlike than he expected.

"Um, did you see a demon go by in there?"

She blinked her large eyes and smiled with disbelief. "A demon? Why, no. Are you in need of more target practice?"

Abderian scowled back at her. "That's not funny. I just want to talk to him. Let me come in."

The acolyte put one hand on her hip and cocked her head. "Firstly, there is no demon here, so you've no need to come in.

Secondly, Maja expressly does not want to see you, so if that's really why you're here, you can forget it. Thirdly, Tritavia has given word that you must not enter this temple, so I can't let you in. And fourthly, you are so rude that even if I could let you in, I wouldn't." She slammed the door shut in his face.

"But—!" Blowing his breath out in frustration, Abderian stared at the door. He wondered if he knew a spell to magically blow it down. *Even if I did, I don't have the power for it right now.*

"There's a back door to the temple, you know," said a voice at his side.

Abderian whipped his head around, but saw no one.

"Down here."

Abderian looked down and saw a fat white chicken. "Who . . . Onym?"

"Good guess, there, Highness. Exactly right. You seem to be in a bit of a spot."

"So do you."

The chicken shrugged. "I'm used to it. My only problem has been keeping away from the castle cook and an overly amorous rooster. What's yours?"

Abderian felt torn. *Can I trust him? He's the only one who might know what to do.* Squatting down to converse with the wizard-chicken eye to eye, Abderian whispered, "Onym, do you know if there is some way the cursemark can be affected at a distance?"

Onym puffed out his feathers. "If I knew that, I wouldn't be on the outs with Entheali right now. There wouldn't have been that embarrassing scene in the Throne Room."

And you would have been much more dangerous. "Yes, I'm sorry about that."

"Not your fault, Abderian. My magic is slipping in my old age. Say, you don't know if the cursemark has been found, do you?"

"Uhhh . . . I think Entheali knows where it is."

"And she hasn't told me? Oooh, she must be very upset at me indeed. If you're going into the temple, could you tell her how sorry I am and how I'd be grateful to share her company and knowledge again?"

"I'd like to, if I can get in the temple. My demon, Mux, is hiding in there and I need to talk to him."

"Well, that's no problem. I know several back doors to this place. Entheali always preferred that I use them when I came and went."

Abderian could understand why the Star Mother would rather no one saw the movements of this crazy wizard. "Unguarded?"

"Of course. What sort of good back doors would they be if they were guarded? Follow me."

Against his better judgment, and feeling very silly, Abderian followed the chicken around to the back of the temple, where there was only a two-foot wide passageway between it and the castle wall. They came up to a rotting portal hanging askew on its leather hinges. "Try this one," said Onym.

"Do you know where in the temple it leads to?"

"I don't remember, but that's a chicken brain for you. Long on beak/eye coordination but terrible on memory."

"Right. Well, thank you."

"Don't mention it. Good luck catching your demon. Are you going to fry this one, too?"

"No!"

"Oh. Too bad. I wanted to watch. Toodeloo." The chicken waddled back out to the courtyard and Abderian took his chances with the door.

It led onto a dark, very narrow hallway, which Abderian had to turn nearly sideways to negotiate. He could easily imagine the Lizard Priests slipping in and out through routes like this to do their nefarious work. *I wish I'd known about this earlier. I could have sneaked in to see Maja. Maybe I should try to see her now and apologize—tell her the truth. Right after I catch that little thief, Mux.*

The hallway let onto a larger, brighter corridor where Abderian stopped, hearing voices. One was the woman he had met at the front door.

"So I owe him an apology after all, do I? Naturally, everyone else gets to go to bed after Evening Star services so I get to deal with any riffraff who stumble in. Well, you can just use those little leather wings to fly outta here, fella."

"You didn't let him in?"

That's Mux.

"No, of course I didn't let him in. I'm an equal opportunity sentry. I turn them away regardless of rank, birth, sex, creed, or spiritual plane of origin. This means you, too, leather butt. Out!"

Abderian rushed into the corridor, not wanting to let Mux slip past again. "Wait, let me talk to him!"

On seeing Abderian, the woman slapped her forehead. "Oh,

no. Not you too. The Star Mother's gonna mop the floor with me."

"Aha!" said Mux, and dashed away down the corridor.

"Excuse me," Abderian said to the woman as he rushed past her. "Stop, Mux! I'm not going to hurt you. I swear it!"

Mux made a left turn and suddenly Abderian knew where he was headed. The prince followed him past another turn, straight into the great domed room where Paralian had been changed to a wolf and the Demon King had met his doom. Mux walked backward clutching the book to his chest and staring intently at Abderian. The prince stopped at the edge of the vast floor, not daring to walk upon it. "Be very careful, Mux. You don't know what you're walking on. I don't want to hurt you. I never wanted to hurt your king. Just give me the book back, please?"

"Come and get it, yogurt face," said Mux.

"No, Mux. I want you to trust me. It might be dangerous if I walk on that floor. I might accidentally conjure any sort of spell. So might you, if you wander around there. Just walk over here, slowly and carefully, and give me the book. Then we'll talk."

Mux frowned in thought. One step at a time he cautiously walked toward Abderian.

"That's right. Come on, Mux. You'll be all right. Bring the book, there's a good fella."

Mux came within arm's reach and, with a regretful glance at the book, slowly held it out to the prince.

Abderian leaned forward and reached out to take it. Suddenly, Mux lashed out with his other arm and grabbed Abderian's wrist. Flapping his wings and pulling with all his might, Mux dragged Abderian onto the floor. "Got 'im!" the demon cried in triumph.

"What?" Abderian saw he was being dragged over a glowing diagram that had not been visible a moment before. Then the room spun, and his stomach clenched, and his mind faded down into a fuzzy darkness.

TWENTY-TWO

Scaly Mother, bright of eye,
Our blood runs cold in thought of you.
Quicken our souls with your sunlight warmth.
Teach us to shed our sorrows as you shed your skin.
Though you hide your love in dark crevasses,
We leave no stone unturned in search of you.
Save us from the predators of fate,
Send us lots of bugs to fill our belly,
Change the colors of our souls.
Do not forsake us, O Mother of Dragons!
Or we'll be pissed and won't worship you anymore.
Amen.

—Prayer to the Lizard Goddess

THERE WAS NO disorientation this time. No stomach-churning or headache bothered the prince as the teleport spell dissipated. And it was this that Abderian found most disturbing—it spoke too eloquently for the power of the spell.

Ahead of him was rock, dimly lit by torchlight behind him. Stalactites glistened on the ceiling, and the floor looked as though it had, eons ago, been molten. To his right was a wall of hard-packed boulders, earth, and rubble. Amid the stones, a fossil behemoth lay—a ghoulish bas-relief in the dungeonlike cavern.

"I've brought him!" Mux announced.

"You are late," said a terrifyingly familiar voice behind Abderian. The prince twisted around and saw his fears confirmed. There stood a thin man of narrow face and tiny, dark eyes, wearing robes of glistening lizard skins.

"Tingalut," Abderian said.

The High Priest of the Lizard Goddess bowed. "Good to see you again, Your Highness."

161

"I wish I could say the same."

"As do I. If you had accepted my offer long ago . . ." Tingalut shrugged.

"I still don't want to be king. And I don't even have the cursemark anymore. What could you possibly want with me now?"

"Dear me, and I thought your intellect might have matured in the past year, along with some of your other attributes. I understand you are a father now."

"Don't send me any flowers." Abderian turned to Mux. "How did he talk *you* into this?"

Mux raised his little chin defiantly, though there was distress in his eyes. "I gain enough."

"Gain? What gain? Did you know these guys—"

"This honorable demon," said Tingalut, "is helping to renew an alliance that had been unfortunately interrupted."

"A very short-lived alliance," Abderian reminded the priest, "that Khanda thought worth breaking. Mux, what's gotten into you? I thought we were friends."

"Friends!" snarled the demon. "Wizards and demons are not friends! Wizards have books on controlling demons. Wizards summon demons to do their will. Wizards think demons are slaves!"

Abderian had to admit that Mux had a point. "Well, you see, Mux, you may be a fine companion, but demons are often destructive and—"

"Prejudice!" shrieked Mux. "Bigot! Some demons evil, therefore all demons evil. Whadabout mortals? Are all mortals evil?"

Considering Tingalut, Abderian had to concede that some certainly were. "Well . . . But the Lizard Priests think no better of you."

"Ah, but we do," said Tingalut in a soothing, oh-so-reasonable voice. "For his valuable assistance, Mux will be well rewarded. You, by your violent, unthinking action, have deprived the Demon Realm of their king. My sect will see to it that Mux takes his place."

Abderian stared unbelievingly at the ugly, leathery little demon. "You? King? Khanda wouldn't have you on a bet!"

Mux looked offended, then he narrowed his eyes and said calmly, "She will have to."

"What?"

"He is quite right," said Tingalut. "The Demon Queen is

mortal-born, and therefore must have a consort. The more . . . inhuman of demonkind will not accept a mortal-born as their sole monarch. They would force her back into this realm, where she would slowly die."

Ambiguous though Abderian's feelings toward Khanda were, he did not wish her such an unpleasant fate. He felt a sudden flare of anger toward Mux. "Is it prejudice to note that loyalty seems not to be a demonic trait? You're doing well by Belphagor's death."

Mux's eyes blazed with anger and he flew at Abderian, his leathery hands closing around Abderian's neck. "Agh! Lies! Belphagor was the greatest of kings. Dare you say such filth, murderer?"

Abderian could only gargle a response as the little demon tried to choke him, but before long (though not as soon as he could have) Tingalut pried Mux off the prince.

"Now, now," said the priest, "we mustn't compound error with error. The Lizard Goddess steps sideways as she walks, and the death of Belphagor may serve purposes we cannot yet see. Let us not punish Abderian further for his impassioned mistake."

Mux shook himself and seemed to calm down. "Sorry," he muttered.

"'S all right," Abderian rasped, rubbing his throat. Tingalut extended a hand to him, and against his better judgment, Abderian took it and stood. The priest placed a steadying arm across Abderian's shoulders and guided him toward a twisty passageway. "Let us leave Mux to gather himself for now. There is something I'd like you to see."

"I still don't understand why you made Mux bring me here."

Tingalut sighed. "I had heard you had learned much in the past year, but perhaps the reports were wrong. I'll begin again. You have become a father, have you not?"

Abderian stopped dead in the narrow passage, a sinking feeling in his gut. "What of it?"

"No, please don't be alarmed. No violence will be done to you or your son. Keep moving, if you would. It will help you to understand when you see what I have to show you."

Reluctantly, Abderian continued on. Around the next bend, the passage opened onto a cavernous room lit with many torches. Lizard Priests in their glistening, scaly robes stood in a circle around a low altar. The altar appeared to be occupied.

•

"I am told," said Tingalut, "that you have a son, by the Lady Maja. A normal, healthy boy."

Abderian rounded on the priest. "You've no cause for any interest in him. He doesn't have the cursemark either."

Tingalut nodded genially. "I know, I know. Please, join our circle. You see, I am also told that there is another. A girl. A most unusual girl, born of a demon-changed mother. And this girl is yours too, is she not?"

"Do you have spies everywhere?"

Tingalut blinked. "What good are they if they are not?" From his sleeve he drew a small brown lizard of a sort very common in Euthymia. The priest stroked the lizard's chin and clicked at it softly, then let it scramble onto his shoulder. "But, I beg you, stand with our circle and much will become clear to you."

Abderian allowed himself to be guided into the ring of priests and two of the men stepped aside for him. Abderian saw the altar clearly then, and knew he should never have trusted Tingalut.

Horaphthia lay on the altar, her wrists and ankles bound with filaments of copper, silver, and bronze. These ran into the floor of the cave, where they formed inlaid patterns of great complexity. Horaphthia's hair was much more grey than when Abderian had seen her last, and her face was tight in painful concentration. She seemed a hapless insect caught in the web of a horrible, sorcerous spider. Abderian knew just who fit that description.

His spin was swift—his punch quicker than any Abderian had tried before. It should have connected. But Tingalut had suddenly shifted a foot back out of harm's way, and a priest on either side of Abderian held the prince's arms fast.

The high priest seemed unperturbed. "Good. You understand your position now. I know the infant girl has the cursemark, Abderian. Tell me where she is."

"No."

Tingalut shook his head with a sad but knowing smile and gestured at the surrounding priests.

And they all hissed. A loud hiss that filled the cavern with sound like driving rain, water on a stovepan, fire in dry grass. Horaphthia stiffened on the altar, the muscles in her forearms tensing. A viscous white light flowed out of her wrists and down the filaments into the floor, where the patterns pulsed in eerie heartbeat rhythms.

"Stop!" Abderian cried.

The hissing abruptly ceased and Horaphthia sagged on the altar, moaning.

"Very good," said Tingalut. "Now that we understand one another we can get down to business." To the two priests holding Abderian, Tingalut said, "Bring him to my office."

Abderian was escorted to a small grotto where he was encouraged to sit on a sawed-off stalagmite. A low stone shelf served as Tingalut's desk, behind which was a lumpy stalagmite that served as a chair. The only light and heat in the room was from the red-hot coals in an iron brazier. *No wonder the demons and Lizard Priests get along,* Abderian thought glumly. *They like the same environment.*

"This cave," said Tingalut, "was once the den of that mightiest of our goddess's creations, the Great Northern Purple-Spotted Dragon."

"I thought Sagamore's wizard Onym was the only person to create a dragon," Abderian grumbled.

"Let us say he reintroduced the fashion," said Tingalut. "About the only good thing he ever did, too." The High Priest reached beneath the brazier and pulled out a leather sack that had been hanging from it. He slipped his hand into the sack and drew out a large, torpid reptile that he placed on his desk. "This is a spitting dragonlet. They're quite rare, nowadays, which makes them all the more worth cultivating. Camel Breath, here, may seem sluggish, but he's quite warm from being under the fire, and could move very quickly if he chose."

"Did you really bring me here to discuss your pets?"

"I advise you to listen, Abderian. You see, I am going to ask Blinkard and Myrmidon to let go of you and leave. But before they do, I want you to be aware that Camel Breath doesn't like swift movement. It upsets him. And spitting dragonlets, when they are upset, spit a quite deadly poison at whatever is coming at them. You understand."

"I won't try anything funny," Abderian said.

"Excellent." Tingalut waved his hands to shoo the guardian priests on their way. The priests looked nervously at Camel Breath on the desk and did not move. "Idiots, he won't spit if you're going away from him!"

Slowly, both priests stepped back. One of them said, "About the sorceress, Master, she is at the critical stage. Yet it is almost time for the Evening Bask."

"This should not take long," said Tingalut. "If all goes well, you may free the woman before then."

The priests bowed, slowly, and backed out into the passage.

Tingalut folded his hands in front of him. "Where is the baby girl?"

"Don't waste any time, do you?"

"I thought you were tired of chatting about my pets. Would you rather allow Horaphthia to linger on the altar? I don't think she enjoys it much—"

"Stop! A caravan of the Grey Guild has the baby."

Tingalut frowned and rubbed his chin. "An odd choice of nursery. Why did you give her to the Guild?"

"I didn't give her up. The caravan found her where Khanda left her. I tried to get the baby back, but I couldn't. You might as well know," Abderian went on, "that Belphagor, before he died, said that the child will make the two realms, demon and mortal, uninhabitable within a fortnight. I killed him because he would have killed the child in order to prevent this."

Tingalut looked unperturbed. "I am not surprised he told you that. He may have needed an excuse that you would understand. But it is traditional for the King of Demons to destroy his bride's mortal issue, if she has one. They tend to be a jealous lot and consider it unseemly to raise a stepchild of mortal seed. You may ask Mux, if you wish, but I'm quite sure Belphagor was lying."

"I hope, for all our sakes, that what you say is true." *But I doubt it.* "I expect you won't have an easy time getting the child from the Guild," Abderian said with small satisfaction.

"The Grey Guild is known for driving hard bargains. But I think we can meet their price, one way or another. Do not look so glum, Highness. Did I not once say that by cooperation we might help one another?"

"What favor are you doing me this time?"

"The best you could hope for, I think, under the circumstances. We are going to devote all the resources of our cult to your claim on the child. The Grey Guild will find it an offer they simply cannot refuse."

TWENTY-THREE

The client's treasure must be your treasure.
You must guard it like a dragon.
And handle it like a worshipper.
Remember: You break it, you bought it.

—Number Two of the Nine Tenets of the Grey Guild.
Collect them all.

EARLY THE NEXT morning, Abderian stood at the edge of the camp
of the Grey Guild caravan. He had spent the night in the cave of
the Lizard Priests as their "guest." He only saw Horaphthia once,
to ascertain that she was all right. She had been asleep and looked
very old. The only comfort the prince could take during the night
was that the cave was cooler than the outside air. He had hardly
slept at all, and had realized that he had again been offered what
he wanted by people he expressly did not want it from. Even if it
meant the scorching of the world, he did not want Tingalut to have
the power of the cursemark borne by Khanda's infant daughter.

And now, waiting for the meeting with Vulka, Abderian
wondered what he might say to her to thwart Tingalut's plans. The
prince had been dressed in a long tunic of white linen with gold
trim at the neck, sleeves, and hem. A gold circlet had been placed
on his head and he wore gold brocade slippers. He had wondered
just where the Lizard Priests had gotten these garments, but they
had not bothered to tell him and he did not deign to ask. The

clothes were too conspicuous for his taste, and under the morning sun they were too hot. On his wrists were two pairs of bracelets made of twisted bronze-and-copper wire—they looked quite fetching if one didn't know they were enchanted with complex binding spells, as Abderian was all too aware. Just behind him stood the ubiquitous Blinkard and Myrmidon, the latter holding a very heavy silver chest.

Sweat dripped into Abderian's brows as he waited. He worried about Horaphthia. He worried about the heat. He worried about Maja, who would probably find his sudden disappearance another reason to be angry with him. But mostly he worried that he might pitch forward flat on his face from the heat, weariness, and tension, and he did not dare appear a fool again before Vulka.

Fortunately, after a minute, the black-clad bodyguards Stad and Curdrik arrived and escorted Abderian and his guardians to a grey-striped tent set up in the shade of a tall pine. It was just cool enough inside to give some relief, and on a round darkwood table in the center of the tent was a pewter ewer with water drops beading the sides. Abderian nearly smacked his dry lips aloud.

Vulka sat behind the table, dressed in a loose grey silk blouse and trousers. Her handsome face looked a bit more worn and worried, as if she had not been sleeping well. Though her ash-brown hair was still bound in a long braid, stray ends hung around her face and neck. She wore a silver chain around her neck from which hung a pendant in the shape of a wolf's head. Her large light grey eyes seemed very alert, and rather surprised at Abderian's change of outfit.

Beside her on the table was the letter Valeria had written for him. Abderian was surprised that it looked nowhere near as incendiary as it had when he last saw it. The words hardly glowed at all.

Stad and Curdrik placed a carved stool across from her and indicated Abderian should sit there, then they took positions to either side of the Caravan Master. Abderian sat on the seat proffered, and rested his arms on the table, crossing his wrists as though they were bound with rope. He deeply hoped Vulka did not miss the symbolism. *I must show her this is not my idea.* Though he had a healthy fear of Vulka, he now depended on her intelligence to save him, and, perhaps, the kingdom as well.

The Caravan Master's gaze flicked from Abderian's hands to his face, to the priests standing behind him, but her expression revealed nothing. "I am pleased that you have suggested another meeting, Your Highness." This time there was no dubious tone to her husky voice. "My people have done some research into the matter on which we spoke last. And into the allegations contained in your agent's letter. We have come to the conclusion that the best course would be a deal that is to the benefit of all."

Damn. She picks now, of all times, to be reasonable!

"Would you care for some wine?"

Abderian nodded avidly as she poured, and took a long drink from the cup that she handed him. The wine was very sweet and cool. He wondered what magic they used to keep it so.

He felt a tugging at the front of his tunic and saw the little brown lizard Tingalut had given him crawl up his arm and onto his shoulder. Abderian felt no fondness for the creature—it was there to listen. But he dared not brush it away. He saw that Vulka noticed the lizard too, but again she gave no indication of her opinion.

"It is our hope," said Vulka, "to be able to continue our normal course of business shortly, with reasonable recompense for revenue lost while we've sojourned here."

"Yeah," said Curdrik laconically, "our insurance premiums for Business Interruption are horrendous."

"That's enough, Curdrik."

"Yes, ma'am. Shutting up, ma'am."

Turning back to Abderian, Vulka went on. "Naturally, once these stipulations are met, there will be no further harassment of you or your representatives."

"Beyond that which you've already done," Abderian said, despite himself.

Curdrik said, "You think *she's* bad, you should see the Guild's Collection Department."

"Curdrik!"

"Sorry, ma'am."

"May I take care of him *now*, my lady," said Stad. "Please?"

"Soon," Vulka promised between gritted teeth. "Now, Highness, as to your end of the bargain . . ."

"My *representatives* have determined an amount that they believe would be fair recompense." Abderian indicated the two priests behind him.

Vulka's eyes flicked from Abderian to the priests and back. "And does this include the smithy Valeria?"

"No, she has no part in these proceedings. She only wrote the letter."

Vulka frowned. "We have not investigated the background of your current 'representatives.' The Temple of the Lizard Goddess has a varied reputation. I might have to check on their credit rating, which would delay the deal."

"Madam," said Myrmidon, "we are prepared to make an offer which should make a credit investigation unnecessary."

Vulka raised a brow and looked at Abderian.

"My representatives prefer that this agreement not be bound by bureaucratic complications," said Abderian. *They want a secret deal. Say No.*

Vulka regarded him with just a hint of suspicion in her eyes. "That is rather irregular. We will have to give this some consideration."

Myrmidon moved up beside Abderian and placed the silver chest on the table. "If you will but see our offer first," Abderian said. Myrmidon lifted the lid. Revealed within the chest were brooches and rings centuries old, magic crystals taken from the innumerable wizards the Lizard Priests had drained, and gold coins and figurines from an ancient dragon's hoard.

Even Vulka lost her businesslike composure. Her mouth dropped open as she stared. "That is . . . a most generous offer."

Don't do it don't do it don't do it. "Yes, quite unbelievable, isn't it?" Abderian felt a warning tingle from the bracelets on his wrists.

"I believe we should . . . discuss this offer in greater detail," said Vulka.

Blinkard moved up on Abderian's other side, and for a moment the prince feared the priests might do something foolish. Stad and Curdrik apparently thought so too, and stepped closer to Vulka. But Blinkard merely turned to Abderian and said, "Pardon me, Highness. It is nearly time for our Midmorning Bask. If negotiations are going to go on a while, may we be excused?"

Abderian nearly grinned for joy. "Of course you may. Go and bask in peace."

The two priests bowed to him, nodded to Vulka and stepped out of the tent.

Abderian couldn't believe his good fortune. Of course there was still the binding spells in the bracelets to worry about, and the little fellow flicking his tongue on the prince's neck, but Abderian felt he finally had a chance.

"These 'backers' of yours," said Vulka, "seem to want this item very badly. Are their intentions the same as yours?"

How can I safely answer that? "They would cherish her, though not in the same way I would." Abderian tried to let the fear show in his eyes.

"And yet you speak for them?"

"We both speak for the good of Euthymia, though our beliefs on that may differ. That one end would accomplish each is . . . fortuitous." Again the warning tingle in his wrists, stronger this time and Abderian winced a little.

Vulka paused a long moment. "I must consider this offer carefully. In the meantime, should I say hello to your brother for you?"

"Yes, please do!" said Abderian, with a smile full of wild hope. "I'm sure he would love to hear from you."

Vulka was about to reply when the rumbling began. The earth shook and the silver casket danced on the table top. Stad and Curdrik were out of the tent in an instant, and Vulka closely followed.

Abderian stayed seated a moment, confused—then remembered he couldn't possibly be causing this disturbance. "It's the baby!" he yelled and dashed out of the tent after Vulka. And he stopped, seeing that it wasn't the baby at all.

A wide crack had opened up in the earth, just beside the caravan camp. The two Lizard Priests stood next to the crevasse, smiling benevolently. Out of the crack in the earth poured demons. Large, great-fanged, long-clawed belligerent demons were flying into the caravan camp, ripping the roofs off tents and wagons. Few of the men and women of the caravan scattered in panic, however. The wizards among them were busy activating spells and the fighters were wielding whips and swords.

But there were more demons than caravaneers, and the traders had been caught unprepared for such a battle. Abderian thought frantically for some small spell to inconvenience the demons, when he heard a loud click at his wrists. The bracelets had locked together, preventing any sorcerous gestures he might try.

As Abderian stood, helpless, he saw Vulka attacked by a particularly vicious-looking demon. She snapped her whip, but the demon flew in too fast and grabbed her wrist. The demon raised her into the air and slashed down with his claws. She screamed as dark red lines appeared on her abdomen. The demon dropped her and flew on to the center of the camp, where raucous cries of victory indicated that the demons had found what they sought.

For reasons Abderian could not name, he rushed to Vulka's side, where another woman bent over her, speaking softly. As Abderian came up, the woman hissed at him, "Don't touch her! She mustn't be moved!"

Vulka lay on her side, curled up tightly, her face stretched in a grimace of pain.

"I can heal her," Abderian said. His magical energy had only partially restored itself, but even a small healing could help save her.

"Sorcery from without cannot help her," the woman said. "She must be left alone to heal herself."

Of course. Dolus said she was resistant to direct magic. Can I do something indirectly to help? Can I do anything with my stupid wrists locked together? The little lizard on his shoulder began to bite at his neck, and Abderian grabbed the reptile in both hands and flung it away. The Lizard Priests behind him didn't seem to notice. They were absorbed in watching the cloud of demons rising up from one wagon, carrying amongst them a small bundle wrapped in a blanket. *Creative. Dolus always tells me I should be a creative wizard. What can I do?*

Abderian looked around and saw a crate of vegetables spilled open on the ground. He ran to it, finding it more difficult than expected with his wrists locked together, and found a big ripe tomato. He brought the tomato back to Vulka's side and rolled i around in the dirt soaked with her blood. With a fingernail, Abderian cut the tomato as he had seen Vulka cut by the demon. Vulka cried out in pain and Abderian feared he might be hurting her more. He cupped his hands around the tomato and, ignoring the burning from the bracelets on his wrists, began to pour sorcerous energy into the tomato, closing the cuts physically and sealing them magically. Vulka relaxed visibly beside him.

Abderian saw lizard-skin slippers appear to either side of him, and he hurriedly finished his spell. He looked at Vulka, who was staring back, and said, "When you see Paralian, tell him—"

But Myrmidon's hand clamped over the prince's mouth. "Time to go home, Highness."

Blinkard and Myrmidon grabbed each of his arms. The woman at Vulka's side shouted a curse in a foreign tongue. Vulka simply stared, her grey eyes eloquent with understanding.

Abderian hated looking weak in front of her and struggled,

kicking out at his captors. But the binding spell holding the prince's wrists suddenly spread up his arms, down his body and legs and finally into his head, cloaking his mind in darkness, as they dragged him away.

TWENTY-FOUR

Always have some easy-to-make snacks on hand for that unexpected visitor.

—from *An Everyday Guide to Etiquette*
by SALVIA THE SAGE

ACHING AND DISORIENTED, Abderian awoke in a chamber of the Lizard Priests' caverns. The face of the aged woman that hovered over him brought to mind conflicting memories. He recalled waking after a run through the Forest of Forgetfulness long ago and seeing such a face. Yet she reminded him of someone younger. "Horaphthia?" he said, not wishing to believe it.

The sorceress closed her eyes and nodded. Her hair was now very grey and she seemed diminished with weariness. Abderian sat up, noticing that he no longer wore the enchanted bracelets. He put a hand on her shoulder. "Your Majesty—"

"No, Horaphthia will do. I doubt I will be Euthymia's queen much longer." Her voice was less steady than before.

"How can you say that? I'll see that you are healed somehow. You won't die, I swear it."

Horaphthia gave him a look of cold resignation. "A great part of me is already dead. They drained me, Abderian. Sucked up most of my sorcerous power into the damned patterns on their

174

damned floor. Do you know what that means to a sorcerer my age?"

Abderian knew Horaphthia's real age was somewhere in the nineties. She now appeared to be in her late fifties. "So you are using all that you have left . . ."

"Just to keep myself alive. All other magic I have cast will fade rapidly and I cannot renew it."

"The love spell."

Horaphthia nodded again. "Even if, by some miracle, Cyprian still cared for me, it would be unfair for him to remain married to an old, powerless crone. What use to the kingdom am I now?"

"You've never sounded this defeated before. Even when Maja's father made you live in the Forest of Forgetfulness, you didn't let that defeat you."

"This is far more serious, Abderian."

"Don't talk like that. Dolus was drained by the Lizard Priests too, remember, and he hasn't been useless. And I'm going to see that he gets his power back someday."

Horaphthia's face creased in a pitying smile. "Dolus didn't tell you. No, of course he wouldn't, the dear fool. You cannot give him his power back."

"What?"

She shrugged. "The Lizard Priests are nasty as well as thorough. They are jealous of any wizard more powerful than themselves. The very spell by which they drain us makes us unable to take our power back. If I tried, my own energy would kill me." Horaphthia leaned closer. "Do what ever you must, Abderian, to keep them from doing this to you."

Abderian said, "I will," not wanting to believe any of this. "If only we could escape." He looked at the passageway entrance and saw it was blocked by an enormous boulder. "How did that get in here?"

"The same way you did, I expect. *Poof. Shazam.* Instant wedge-in-the-door."

Abderian suddenly wanted to laugh. "But they're stupid! We can get out the same way. You can show me how to draw a teleport circle. Like Dolus, you can teach me and I'll do the spell itself."

Horaphthia gave him a knowing look. "Have you the strength?"

Abderian tried a minor flame-in-the-hand spell. He could only produce a dim flicker. "Not right now. The healing I did for Vulka took a bit, and I was low to begin with. We'll have to wait."

Horaphthia closed her eyes. "By which time, the priests will have returned for us."

"But my magic, along with Dolus's, might be strong enough to fight them off."

"Against the massed power of who-knows-how-many wizards stored in their floor?"

"Oh. Yes, I see."

"Not to mention that they have somehow achieved a link to the power in the temple at Mamelon, as well."

Abderian sighed. "I guess things really are hopeless. And they've got the baby, too."

"Baby?" said Horaphthia, aghast. "They took Maja's baby?"

"No. Not Maja's. Her sister Khanda's." And Abderian at last told Horaphthia the true whereabouts of the Cursemark of Sagamore.

With a deep sigh, Horaphthia sat back against the cave wall and closed her eyes. "Oh, Abderian, if only you had had more trust in me and less shame in yourself."

"I didn't want to hurt anyone."

"Your trying not to hurt anyone has hurt more than the truth would."

Softly, Abderian said, "Belphagor told me the demon baby would destroy the kingdom in a fortnight. Is that true?"

"Demons are creatures of fire—in short, they like it hot. It seems bad enough here in the north, but in the southern duchies, where I went to give assistance, the heat is far worse. Their wells have dried up, the earth is cracked and dry, the sky gives no rain. If they had not already harvested the fall crops, the people would be devastated. As it is, they may not last long, and many will migrate to Mamelon, where resources are already scarce. What do you think?"

Abderian could not reply.

Horaphthia went on. "I did what I could. I conjured up some rain, healed many people, cooled the air for a while. But all my efforts were temporary against the power of the cursemark. My sorcery was soon exhausted, giving the Lizard Priests an easy opportunity to snatch me and drain away what magic I had left."

Abderian placed a hand on her arm. "I am so very sorry," he said, not looking at her. *Why do I destroy the lives of those around me?*

Horaphthia patted his hand. "You meant no evil, Abderian. It the cursemark had been someone else's responsibility, things might not have gone any better."

After a pause, Abderian said, "Why don't they just kill us and get it over with?"

"Ah, you do not understand the ways of the Lizard Cult. Ritual is everything. To let us die without some song and dance would be heresy. Besides, they probably would prefer you alive to be their titular king, clearing the succession for your demonic daughter. As for me, since I am no longer useful or a threat to them, I would not be surprised if they simply let me rot here, forgotten."

"Or let you go."

"Or someday let me go. I suppose they would think that justice—to let me live, powerless, in a world under their control."

"If there's any world left for them to rule."

"Lizards like it hot, too, Abderian. I'm sure these fellows won't mind your daughter's idea of a perfect world."

"I didn't know the priests wanted to push being lizardlike that far."

"Their goal is much the same as that of the Star Cult. The idea is to create an environment suitable for the Lizard Goddess to live in. At least the Star Cult has the good manners to set their goddess on some other plane of existence. The Lizard Cult wants their heaven on earth, so to speak."

"What about future converts? And the demons? I hear they're suffering, too."

Horaphthia shrugged. "I suppose they believe the goddess will spare anyone she thinks important. And the Lizard Priests would like forcing the demons into the same realm as they. The independence and power of the demons comes in part from their having a kingdom on a separate plane of existence. Once here, they are more easily controlled."

"Enslaved, you mean. No wonder Khanda didn't approve of that alliance." Abderian stood and paced around the room, feeling an acute need to do something. "How long was I unconscious?"

"I don't know. I awoke to see you lying nearby. Are you hungry?"

"Um, a little. Why?"

"Then it probably hasn't been days."

"Thanks. Horaphthia, what are we going to do?" Abderian reached up and ran his hands violently through his hair, as if to pull useful thoughts out by the roots.

A shimmering in the center of the chamber startled the prince and he quickly grabbed a rock. In a moment, the blurred air resolved itself into a woman holding a fluffy bundle and a sword. Too late Abderian heard Horaphthia behind him say, "No! Don't—" and he flung the rock with all his might at the visitor.

In a flash of gold, the sword came up and deflected the rock with a loud clang. Behind the sword, Maja's face gaped in surprise.

"Maja!" cried Abderian.

"You idiot! What were you trying to do, brain me?"

The bundle under her arm turned out to be a chicken that fluttered in a flurry of feathers into Abderian's chest.

Pushing the squawking bird away, Abderian rushed to Maja and kissed her. He was relieved that she waited a long time to pull away. "What are you doing here?" he said when at last their lips parted.

"Searching for you, of course. Are you all right?"

"I'm fine," he breathed, gazing at her. Then added, grimly, "For the moment."

"My dear girl," said Horaphthia, coming forward, "you are very brave and extremely foolish."

"Horaphthia . . . is that you? What happened to you?" Maja disengaged herself from Abderian and embraced Horaphthia.

"I'm afraid I've become another notch on the Lizard Priests' floor."

"What?"

"They drained away my power, girl. I am useless, defunct, inert, obsolete, outworn. I am an ex-wizard."

"No!"

"Maja," said Abderian frantically, "we can talk about this later. Can you get us out of here?"

"What? Of course. That's why I brought Onym with me. He pecked out the teleport spell and we used Sagamore's sword to find you. Onym, stop scratching over there and come draw a new circle."

"*Buck bawwwwwk*," said the chicken.

"Onym, that isn't funny."

"*Uk uk uk, bawwwk, uk uk*," said the chicken.

"Not again," said Abderian, slapping his forehead.

Maja sat hard on the cave floor. "I *didn't* pick up the wrong chicken. I *know* I didn't."

"I'm sure you didn't," said Horaphthia. "Onym never tried teleporting while his spirit was transferred elsewhere. Most likely he wasn't aware of the possible effects. Teleportation seems to be a good method for causing the soul to snap back to its original source."

"So now we're stuck—wherever we are."

"We're in a cave occupied by the Lizard Priests," said Abderian. "Their new temple, I guess."

"It is an ancient dragon's lair," said Horaphthia. "An appropriate choice."

"And they're probably going to kill us in an elaborate ritual," said Abderian to Maja, adding sarcastically, "You're just in time to join the party."

For a moment, Maja paled. Then she stood and glared at the prince. "I came because Lizbet told me about Mux and said you might be in trouble. No one else knew what to do to help you. I went to find Dolus and Sagamore, but they just acted confused. A woman in torn grey leather shows up and tells Paralian you've been kidnapped by the Lizard Priests, and that they took your baby—but I knew our child was safe in the temple. I didn't know who to believe! I borrowed Sagamore's sword, hoping I could get Entheali or someone to use it to find you, but she was at Evenstar services and couldn't be disturbed. So I found Onym and I bribed him with some extra chicken feed to peck out a teleport spell to send me to you.

"I came because, in case you'd forgotten, I love you. And I wanted to help you. And I wanted to be with you, even if it means dying some ugly death. Even though you never tell me what's going on anymore. Even if you'd rather I wasn't here. So there's your stupid sword and I'm sorry I bothered and I'll try not to disturb you with my screams when I die!" Maja threw down the Sword of Sagamore at Abderian's feet and she turned and stomped off to the far side of the chamber.

Abderian blinked after her. *Gods, what can I say?* He turned and looked at Horaphthia for support or guidance. Horaphthia shook her head and gestured as if to say, "You're on your own on this one." She turned and walked to the other end of the chamber.

Abderian felt heavy as lead. So many things he wished he could undo. He picked up the sword and walked over to Maja, who was digging her fingers idly into the cave wall. "I'm sorry, Maja. I was only mad because . . . I love you too. I don't want you hurt. Or our baby."

Maja's digging at the wall became more savage. "The woman in grey mentioned a baby. But not ours. What did she mean?"

Abderian sighed. *Guess it's truth time.* "Yes, there is another. That one time Khanda and I . . . you know. She told you at the temple when I slew the dragon."

"I remember," Maja said tonelessly. "When she appeared as the Demon Queen."

"Yes. Well, she had a little girl. But Khanda carried the child while she was changing into the Demon Queen, so the baby was born demonic. And the baby has the cursemark. And that's why everything has been going wrong, and that's why I've been so scattered. Vulka, the woman in grey, found the baby where Khanda had left it. And Belphagor wanted to kill the baby, and I had to stop him. So I've been trying to get the baby back and the cursemark back without anyone getting hurt and I've done a completely botched job of it and I'm sorry."

Maja turned. "You could have told me!"

"I should have." Abderian could not think of what else to say. "If you never forgive me, I'll understand. I'm scum and don't deserve to live." Feeling very sad and very weary, Abderian sank to his knees. "I'm so very sorry," he whispered.

"You idiot," Maja said, at last. "I'm supposed to forgive you for deserting me when I had our baby, for not telling me where the cursemark went, not telling me there was another baby, not telling me what you were doing about it or what danger you were in, and for killing my sister's husband and allowing Euthymia to be wrecked in general."

Abderian bowed his head.

She flung her arms around Abderian's neck. "Just tell me these things a little sooner next time, all right?"

Abderian held her close and gratefully buried his nose in her bosom. Pleasurably muffled, he said, "I promiff."

TWENTY-FIVE

Let what you take in be as a great river flowing to the sea. Let what you expend be as the frugal trickle of a spring in the desert.

Or else the boss will want to have a word with you.

—Number Four of the Nine Tenets of the Grey Guild. Not sold in any store.

ABDERIAN SAT ON the floor of the cavern, tapping the Sword of Sagamore against his palm and thinking. Maja crouched off to his left, trying to convince the chicken to become Onym again. Horaphthia sat very still and quiet to his right.

"I wonder," said Abderian, "if we can hope that Entheali will do something."

"You mean because Mother has the power of the temple?" said Maja.

"Because I told her where the cursemark is. I'm surprised she hadn't gotten to the Guild's caravan before the Lizard Priests."

Horaphthia began to chuckle beside him. Then she threw back her head and laughed outright.

"Horaphthia? What is it?"

"Dear me, how I would have loved to see her face when you told her the mark was in the hands of the Guild!"

"Well, it was amusing but—"

"You see," Horaphthia went on between burbles of laughter,

181

"when she was a young lady, before marrying Javel, she was rather a big spender. I believe her credit rating with the Guild was run well into the ground and never repaid. The Guild might well have cause to seize all the assets of the temple to repay her debts, if they knew where she was. No, I'm not surprised at all."

"I wish I could find that funny, Horaphthia," said Maja, "but that means Mother won't help us."

"I'm sorry, Maja. But the spot I'm in, I must take what little amusement from life I can."

"The spot we're all in," Abderian muttered. Again he let his gaze slowly drift across the room, searching for something to give him a plan, or at least hope. One portion of the wall appeared to be a collapsed passageway. *But it might take the rest of our lives to dig out the fill dirt, and the cave might collapse again atop us.*

Across the chamber, the skull of some huge creature stared sightlessly back at him, trapped forever in its walls of rubble. *Is that what happened to you?* The prince continued tapping his hand with the hilt of the sword, then suddenly realized what he was doing. He stared down at the blade. The jester face on the hilt winked at him in the flickering torchlight.

"Horaphthia, I once overheard an argument over whether strange bone-shaped stones, like those over there, were once alive or were just the product of a sculptor. What do you think?"

"So many such things have been found, I'd say the sculptor would have to be damn prolific. Not to mention having a taste for the morbid. I'd vote for alive."

"Let's find out," Abderian whispered, excited.

"Of course!" said Maja. "I should have remembered. Like those skeletons in Kookluk's lair. And Horaphthia said this was an old dragon's cave."

Abderian raised the golden blade.

"Abderian—" Horaphthia said in a warning tone.

"Arise, ancient beast!" the prince intoned, ignoring her. "Come take possession of your lair once more."

Nothing happened.

Horaphthia shook her head. "I'm afraid you're straining the sword's powers, Abderian. It only commands what lived during Sagamore's reign, or thereabouts. This beastie is a bit out of range."

"Oh."

"Isn't there *some* way to make it work?" asked Maja.

"To animate bones?" said Horaphthia. "Of course. There are standard spells of that nature."

"Well, then."

"Necromantic spells, Maja."

"Oh."

"So what?" said Abderian, exasperated. "Why is necromancy considered so foul?"

Horaphthia stood and blinked at him. "Because it is. For anything living to want to be anything like dead is sick."

"Hmm. But you claim to know such spells."

"I know the general framework of such spells. You can't have been a wizard as long as I . . . was without bumping into these things now and then."

"Will one such spell put my soul in peril?"

Horaphthia looked up at the fossil in the wall. "You'd need a biggie. Let's just say you would have to watch your health for a while afterward."

Maja kicked a stone with her slippered toe. "Maybe we should just blast that boulder out of the way."

"That requires direct energy, which neither Abderian nor I have much of right now."

"Look, I'll risk the necromancy," said Abderian. "Who knows how soon the Lizard Priests will be back, and if we can't escape, I'd like something that big on my side."

Hope and fear warred on Maja's face.

"I won't become evil and awful, Maja, I promise."

"I'm not worried about you, I'm worried about what that thing will do if you succeed."

"We'll only know by trying," said Abderian, eager to at last be doing something. "Show me what to do."

"It's best that I guide you." Horaphthia stood behind Abderian and put her hands on his lower arms. "Raise the sword and close your eyes." As Abderian did so, she spoke low in his ear. "Match your thoughts to the state of being of that which you would animate. You are very old, so old your bones are now stone. The life that once filled and surrounded them is long gone and forgotten. All you know is the cool pressure of the earth around you."

Abderian imagined these things and felt his bones grow cold within him. The outer world drifted away until his awareness was a solid grey darkness. He felt old, indestructible, dead.

"Not that far," cautioned Horaphthia. "Now move the sword in the pattern I direct, and quicken the creature with your life. Fit its feelings to yours. Bring it forth."

Abderian let his arms be guided in a pattern that began as a straight line, but gradually became more jagged, sharp up-and-down movements paced to his heartbeat. He heard faintly the sound of falling rock.

"Abderian, get back!" cried Maja. "It's coming out!"

The prince opened his eyes and saw an enormous skeletal claw issuing from the wall. "Is it all right to stop the spell now?"

"I think you've got him," said Horaphthia. "Let's give him some room."

Together, all three ran to the opposite wall as the giant saurian skull nosed out of the wall, bringing rocks and sand tumbling down and raising clouds of dust. The neck and collarbones followed, then the long breastbone, ribs, and vertebrae. There was too much dust to see it all, but Abderian suspected there was a tail there somewhere as well. A faint shimmer of yellow light surrounded and danced among the bones, resembling a hint of skin here, or sinew there, the pulse of blood or the flicker of thought.

The gleaming reptilian skull turned toward Abderian. In a voice as deep as the rumble of an avalanche and as eerie as winter wind through bare trees, the skeletal dragon spoke:

"Insshaya thassila ahkka stha?"

Abderian swallowed hard, feeling his knees knock together. "Uh, do you speak the tongue of Euthymia?"

"Sthikana theess pastha?"

Abderian jumped as Horaphthia touched his arm. "Of course it won't speak our language," she said. "This creature is millennia old. It was here long before Euthymia was a glimmer in Lungis's eye. It will speak no language we know."

"How do we talk to it?" asked the prince.

"And how do we keep it from killing us?" asked Maja.

"And why didn't you think of this before I called it up?" said Abderian, trying to keep the hysteria out of his voice.

"Hey, I have my off-days, too, you know," said Horaphthia. "Perhaps you could try gestures."

"Right." Abderian got down on his knees and took a begging position. Then he got up and ran to the boulder blocking the passageway and mimicked pushing on it. Then he pointed from the dragon to the boulder and back again several times. He felt like an idiot. It was nothing new.

Throughout his little act, the skeletal dragon watched silently, tilting its skull this way and that. *"Tukka galti kha?"* it said at last.

"It's no use," said Abderian.

"Let me," said Maja. She stood just below the dragon's skull and made noises as if she were eating. She rubbed her belly, then pointed toward the passageway. "Food! Food that way!" She stuck out her hands in front of her mouth and opened and closed them like jaws. She growled, "Munch munch. Food. Yum yum."

The dragon pointed a bony talon at her. *"Ood. Yuh yuh."*

Maja jumped back. "No, not me!"

"Maja," said Horaphthia, "even if the creature could understand you, it has no stomach for eating—literally. Food won't interest it at all."

"Oh. Well, perhaps we could tell it that there are evil priests fouling its den and it should drive them away."

"Right," said Abderian. "You try to act that out."

The dragon lifted its skull as if hearing something distant and moved toward the inner wall. Maja and Horaphthia scattered out of its way. It raised its skeletal paw and placed it, toes spread, gently against the rock. *"Ukkut,"* it said softly.

"Looks like she may not have to," said Horaphthia.

The fossil dragon hissed and turned, crossing the chamber to the wall from which it had emerged.

"No, no, that's the wrong way!" said Maja.

"Leave it be, child. It knows what it wants to do."

Rearing up on its hind bones, the creature began digging at the dirt and rubble. Faster and faster it dug, raising more clouds of dust. Abderian, Maja, and Horaphthia huddled together, holding cloth before their faces in order to breathe.

Soon, sunlight, an evening gold, streamed into the cavern. "I would bet what remains of my magic," said Horaphthia, "that that 'wall' was once the original entrance to this cave." With eerie hoots and grunts, the skeletal dragon pushed away the dirt until it could work its bones through the opening to the outside.

"Our turn," said Abderian, taking Maja's hand, and they scrambled through the opening, Horaphthia close behind. Abderian blinked, momentarily blinded by the sunlight. "Which way did it go?"

"That way, on the path above the cliff," said Maja.

"Cliff?" Abderian opened his eyes and saw a path leading toward the setting sun. To the left of the path was a precipitous drop to a canyon below. To the right of the path was a steep hillside. "Where are we?"

"The northwest corner of the kingdom, I assume," said Horaphthia. "See, to the north lies The Edge."

Abderian turned and looked behind him. The mountains were not so jagged and high as they were in the east, but they were broken by canyons and cliffs, and the hillsides were covered with boulders and weathered outcroppings of rock. Turning his attention back along the path, Abderian saw the bony frame of the fossil dragon slowly round a corner out of sight.

"Follow it, Abderian!" said Horaphthia. "With luck, our friend's sudden appearance should prove a good enough diversion for the priests. You can then seek your child. My guess is they'll keep her in the altar room."

It seemed a good plan to Abderian and it would give him a chance at something else as well. "Right. Maja, stay here."

"Not on your life."

"We don't have time to argue. Well, just stay back, all right?" Abderian turned and hurried carefully along the path. He heard Horaphthia and Maja not far behind. As he rounded the corner, he nearly tripped on the tip of the tail of the dragon. It let out an unearthly roar at the basking priests before it.

The priests leaped up with thoroughly satisfying shrieks of surprise and fear. But instead of running, they prostrated themselves on the flat rocks and sang to the dragon. What Abderian could catch of the syllables sounded like the language spoken by the fossil dragon. *They can speak to it? Oh, no!*

Sure enough, the dragon stood still, and seemed to be listening. Abderian realized he'd best seize his chance before the priests talked the fossil into doing something he'd regret, and he hurried past the great bones to the cave entrance just ahead. As he plunged into the dim interior, he heard shouts of protest from the priests behind him. *Got to hurry. Which way is the altar room?*

With frustrating slowness, his eyes adjusted to the dark and he saw the altar room ahead. He dashed inside and skidded to a halt at the very edge of the magically inscribed floor. Across the chamber, in a hollow in a stone prominence, lay a little red-haired infant.

"Careful, Abderian!" called Horaphthia behind him.

"Yes, I'm going to be very careful," Abderian said, putting one foot out on the pattern-inscribed surface.

"No! Avoid the floor, go around it! Hurry, here come the priests."

"I know what I'm doing." *This is the only way to defeat the priests, Horaphthia. You'll see.* He vividly remembered seeing Horaphthia stretched out on the low stone altar ahead of him. Painfully remembered how the pale light flowed out from her. . . .

And he jumped into the center of the floor, beside the altar, and stumbled to catch his balance. The tripping of his feet quickly became a dance, and he felt his legs out of control, following a path that glowed a pale milky-white. Faster and faster he danced and whirled, as priests gathered and shouted around him. At last his feet slowed as the pattern was completed, and in the second before it hit him, Abderian looked up and saw that Horaphthia knew.

She frowned and whispered, "No."

He nodded. "Yes."

And the full measure of Horaphthia's magical power screamed into his exploding flesh.

TWENTY-SIX

A man can never have too much power. Only too little brains to know what to do with it.

—LORD JAVEL

THE MAGIC FILLED him and burst the confines of his body. It was too much, he could not hold it, yet the magic carried the particles of his being with it. Abderian felt himself expanding outward, unable to feel his arms or legs or any part of him he recognized. He burned without being consumed. He felt like the inside of the sun.

With what senses he retained, Abderian realized he needed a container or a frame. He needed something large enough to support what he had become, or he would expand forever outward to his dissipation and death. He groped blindly with his mind and sensed nearby a suitable frame on which to hang his engorged soul. He flung himself at the object, or rather collection of smaller objects, and he surrounded them, found that they once supported life like himself. He drew on the magical knowledge contained there to become that life. Gratefully he felt himself fall inward, reshaping, resolving into muscle and flesh. He joyfully regained head and body, arms and hands, legs and feet, and tail.

Tail? thought Abderian, wriggling his claws. *Claws?* He opened his enormous eyes and examined his scaly feet and torso. He was outside the caves, where the dragon skeleton had been standing. Before him, several Lizard Priests, prostrate on the ground, cried out, "A miracle! Our goddess returns!"

Behind them, Abderian saw Tingalut turn pale and run to the cave entrance. Horaphthia grabbed the High Priest as he tried to enter, and they wrestled a moment. Then green light flashed in Tingalut's hands and Horaphthia fell aside. Something ancient in Abderian's bones thought *Intruder!* as Tingalut slipped into the cave and Abderian felt his own, massive body moving. In two steps he was squeezing his bulk through the narrow entrance, in time to see Tingalut enter the altar room. With a bizarre feeling that he'd done this before, Abderian followed onto the magically inscribed floor. His dragon eyes, he discovered, were sensitive to sorcery—he could dimly see the patterns and the power Tingalut was drawing out of them. Turning, the High Priest reached for the infant cradled in her grotto.

Abderian did not know dragons could move as fast as he did, whipping his claw forward to grab Tingalut's middle. From the surprise on the High Priest's face, he hadn't either. As the little man struggled in his grasp, Abderian wondered what to do with him. An answer arose from within him, but Abderian did not feel hungry at the moment and found the idea generally repulsive. He looked around the cavern chamber for something to suggest itself.

Out of the corner of his eye, Abderian saw a flash of something colorful. Tingalut had pulled a long black, orange, and red snakeskin from his sleeve and flung one end to the cave floor. He cried out a mystical phrase, and milky white light rushed up the snakeskin and enveloped Tingalut. Abderian smelled flesh burning and realized a moment later it was his foot. With a reptilian yowl, Abderian opened his claw and dropped Tingalut onto the floor, noticing that the priest's robes were steaming. The moment that Tingalut hit the stone, he seemed to explode in a shower of incandescent light.

Abderian felt translucent eyelids move up over his eyes and he squinted against the brightness. He wondered if Tingalut were absorbing more power as Abderian had. But the brightness did not continue expanding. It coalesced, instead, into a column of white light that, like water poured onto parched earth, flowed and was absorbed into the floor. And when the light subsided, there was nothing left behind, except for the priest's scorched robes. One pattern, then another, flickered with light, then all was dark. *Perhaps he had no frame to attach his power to. Or chose to use the floor itself. I wonder where he has gone. Or if he is dead.*

"Abderian, the baby!" cried Horaphthia from the entrance.

Abderian swung his massive head in time to see Mux clamber up and grab the infant in his arms. Abderian uttered a bellow of rage that brought rocks hailing down from the ceiling. Mux cradled the child protectively as the stones hailed down. With only one anxious look into Abderian's eyes, the demon dashed between the dragon's legs. Abderian grabbed for Mux, but was hampered by his concern for the baby. It took all of his concentration to figure out how to turn his massive bulk around in the small cave, by which time Mux had scuttled out the entrance. Abderian squeezed back out and caught sight of the little demon clambering up the hillside above the cave. Abderian the dragon lumbered after him, his enormous claws skittering over the boulders and sending down rockslides behind him. Still, Mux stayed just ahead and Abderian thrashed his tail in annoyance. At the top of the hill crest, Mux confounded him further by spreading his leather wings and launching himself into the air.

"No!" roared Abderian, who instinctively leapt after him. To his surprise, the dragon-prince found himself floating in midair as Mux fluttered like a hummingbird before him. *I don't have wings. I can't fly. What's going on here?* Suddenly Abderian plummeted to the boulders below. Fortunately, he had not achieved much altitude before his fall and therefore only suffered bruises and the shock of too many surprises. Far more injured were his hopes as he watched Mux flapping madly over the next rise, the baby still in his arms.

I wonder how far the border is, Abderian thought morosely. *If they cross it, my spell on Vulka will have been nothing more than delay of the inevitable.* He slithered back over the rise and down the hillside to the cave entrance, where the Lizard Priests waited in silent awe.

"O Scaly Mother," intoned a priest, "our leader is gone. Command us. What is your will?"

Tired, bruised, and disheartened, Abderian growled, "Seek out the demon Mux and bring him and the infant back. You five, you use the floor patterns to seal Euthymia's borders north of here."

"Yes, Cold-Blooded One. We crawl on our bellies for thee."

"Just do it."

The priests scrambled, some over the hillside, some into the cave. Abderian heaved a mighty sigh, feeling very peculiar. He looked around for Maja and Horaphthia in the dimming twilight, and saw them fanning themselves beside a fire. He wondered why. The heat felt quite comfortable now. Abderian ambled over and slid his armored body onto the ground.

"That was well done," said Horaphthia.

"No it wasn't," Abderian said.

"I don't mean your grace and coordination. I meant the use of my power to take on the dragon's form. Your study of transformational magic has served you well."

Abderian snorted. "I'll remember that when I have another go at Paralian." *I wonder how he'd like being a dragon.* "And I should have caught Mux myself, but I couldn't because I didn't know how this body works." He gazed with dragon eyes on Maja, who looked very small and fragile. He very much wanted to hug her and knew he didn't dare. *What if I am going to be a dragon for the rest of my life? I might never hold her again.*

"The priests will deal with Mux better than you could, and can hold a baby more safely. And you have them impressed enough to keep them biddable."

Maja stared back with fascination. "I knew you were destined for bigger things, but I never expected this." Then she frowned and said more seriously, "Are you . . . all right?"

"No. I feel awful."

"Considering the changes you've gone through," said Horaphthia, "I'd be surprised if you didn't."

"Hmm." He glanced away. "I expected you to be angry. For using your power."

"Jealous, perhaps. But I certainly prefer that you have it than Tingalut."

"Tingalut's dead. I think."

"You think? What did you do?"

Abderian described what had happened in the cavern.

Horaphthia rubbed her lined cheeks. "Not dead, I'd wager. Not exactly. But he'll never be able to return to his mortal form. I wonder why he chose that fate."

Abderian remembered one event he had witnessed that was similar. "When Burdalane was killed by the dragon in the temple, he was taken up by Tritavia in the same sort of way."

"So you think Tingalut has gone to his goddess on his own initiative? Sounds possible."

Maja crawled over to him and sat next to his massive head. To his surprise, she gently stroked his scales. "This is going to make our marriage kind of awkward. You'll collapse our wedding bed. And your tail will have to stick out the window; otherwise there won't be room——" Her voice caught and she pressed a fist to her mouth. Then she fell, crying, on his long neck.

"There, there, girl——" said Horaphthia.

But whatever Horaphthia said next sounded garbled in Abderian's ears, and he noticed his sight swimming and dimming. His stomach felt ready to explode and parts of him felt like falling off. *This is it. I'm going to die. All wizardry texts claim that sorcery has its price. I pay with my life.* "Goodbye, Maja," he tried to say, but no longer felt connected to a mouth to say it with. He hoped she and the baby—both babies—would be all right. He wished he could say goodbye to Paralian too. He longed for Paralian to be near, wishing impossibly for his brother to rescue him, to get him out of one last scrape as he had so often before. With his last coherent thoughts, Abderian reached out to Paralian, almost able to see his wolf form in his mind. But the image was not the right shape and another shape was too close. Try as Abderian might to cling to this amorphous vision, he was distracted by the strange and frightening feelings within him. He felt as though he were curling up in a little ball, tighter and tighter, falling ever inward into nothingness.

He awoke to the smell of a garbage heap and the sensation of being slapped across the face with a damp towel. *What afterlife is this?* he wondered. *This is unpleasant, but not horrible. Perhaps I've only fallen to the Hell of the Moderately Incompetent. Or the Hell of the Not Really So Bad But Could Have Been Better.*

Abderian felt something grab the shoulder of his tunic and shake him. *I suppose I ought to see what's going on.* He mumbled something and slowly opened his eyes. Hovering above him, set against a black, starry sky, was the head of a grey wolf. Its eyes and fur glowed red with the light of a nearby fire. "Vulka?" *If she's in my hell too, maybe it's worse than I thought.*

"He's awake!" Vulka barked.

The head of a brown wolf appeared beside hers. "Abderian? Are you all right?"

"Paralian!" Abderian sat up and hugged his brother's shaggy neck. "Are you here, too?"

"Why so surprised, little brother? Horaphthia says you summoned us here."

"Horaph—I did?" Abderian looked around and saw Horaphthia

reclining beside the campfire, just as she had been while he was in dragon form. On the other side of the fire, Maja was stooped over, running her hands over the ground. She looked up and smiled at him once, then continued what she was doing. "Oh. I thought I was dead."

"Didn't you hear me tell Maja that you would only be a dragon temporarily? Perhaps you began the change by then. You could only hold to that large a shape while you had the energy to support it. Once you used that up, *poof*, your body reverted to its previous shape. It would seem, with your last hiccup of energy, you summoned these two."

"Well, I remember wanting to see Paralian. But what is Vulka doing here?"

"Er," growled Paralian, "we were in, um, close proximity to each other. I suppose that's why you got us both."

"We were discussing the best way to search for you and the infant," Vulka put in hastily.

"Vulka is an excellent hunter," said Paralian, "and has skills we could well use. Although, to find you at least, they appear not to be necessary."

"Where is the child?" growled Vulka.

"I don't know," said Abderian. "Mux ran into the mountains with her. I tried to chase him, but couldn't keep up. When I returned, I told the Lizard Priests to search for them and to seal the northern border against their escape."

"Nice work," said Paralian. "And since when have you been able to order Lizard Priests around?"

"Since I turned into a dragon and they mistook me for their goddess. And Tingalut disappeared into the patterns on their floor."

"I don't like the sound of that," said Paralian.

Abderian shrugged. "We think he's gone to Lizard Goddess Heaven, wherever that is."

"It will be on earth, if they don't find the baby soon," said Horaphthia, fanning herself.

"Those idiot priests," said Vulka, bristling her fur, "will not find the demon and the baby. Paralian and I will track her down."

Horaphthia said, "I think you underestimate—Maja, girl, what *are* you doing?"

Maja stood up, a stubborn set to her chin. "The only thing that will really help. We've got to talk to the person who started it all. The one whose fault all this is." She turned, and with a small knife, drew a shallow cut on her arm, wincing a little as the knife scored her flesh.

"Maja!" Abderian jumped to his feet and saw that there was a rough sorcerous circle drawn in the dirt at her feet, into which dripped fresh drops of her blood.

Maja intoned:

> "From the depths of Earth and Fire,
> Demon Realm, hear my desire!
> Khanda, Queen, I summon thee!
> Answer for our quandary!
> By skin of newt and tongue of bat,
> Your little sister wants a chat!"

TWENTY-SEVEN

Demons are Nature's way of telling mortals that it could have been worse.

—TRITAVIA THE SORCERESS

THE DIRT INSIDE the circle turned red and became molten as if heated from below.

Abderian cried "No!" and rushed around the fire, only to be caught in Horaphthia's arms.

"Never stop a summoning in the middle," she warned.

The circle of molten earth sank inward, revealing a black pit. Out of this, seated on her throne of molten gold, rose the Queen of the Demons. But Khanda looked quite different from the night she came to Abderian's tower. Now her gown was black as the blackest coal, and the hem, neck and sleeve edges flickered the red of glowing embers. She had become thin and cadaverous, her fair hair drooping on her shoulders. Her crown of flames seemed smaller and dim.

Khanda raised an accusing finger at Abderian. "You murdered my husband."

Maja stamped her foot. "How dare you accuse him of anything, you baggage! This is all your fault!"

Abderian swallowed hard. "You asked me to save our baby. I did. I didn't want to kill Belphagor, but the child would have died if I hadn't."

"I was a fool," said Khanda, her voice the soft hiss of burning leaves. "Belphagor was right. This child has confounded the Powers of Earth and Fire, and brings disaster to both. While your world scorches with summerlike heat, our realm smothers with air too heavy to breathe, and our fires turn cold and dim."

"Well, maybe we can do something about that if we can get the child back," said Abderian. "Can you summon Mux here? He's one of your subjects, and he has the baby now. Make him give up her up and then we can discuss what to do."

Khanda paused, staring at the prince. "I cannot summon him in this realm. But I can speak with him." She stretched out her thin arms and a vertical oval of light appeared at the edge of Maja's circle. Within it spun swirls of brown, grey, and yellow, finally resolving into an image of Mux squatting among some rocks, a glowing infant on his lap. One of the little demon's wings was drooping and his head was slumped on his chest.

"Mux!" said Khanda. "I command your attention!"

The little demon's eyes shot open. "My Queen!" Reverently, Mux set the swaddled baby in front of him as an offering. "I have your child, my Queen."

"So I have been told, Mux."

"You have also been told the joyous news, my Queen? You are no longer to be a widow. For I am to be your king, in place of our dear, late Majesty, Belphagor. The High Priest Tingalut has foreseen that it must be so. And with the power of this child, we will together rule both realms and found a dynasty that will bring warmth and peace for centuries to come."

Right, thought Abderian, *warm like an oven and peaceful like a funeral pyre.*

"You little fool," said Khanda. "Do you really believe I would accept *you* as my husband and king?"

"It must be so," said Mux, confused.

"It shall never be so. Think you I would marry something that looks like a leather sack filled with potatoes? I would not let my father tell me whom to marry and I certainly won't let some mad priest choose for me, either."

Mux looked stunned. "Your Majesty is mortal-born and does not know our ways."

"Then your ways will change. I will not wed you."

Mux frowned. "But I have the child."

"Kill her."

"*What*?" Abderian roared.

"Destroy the child, Mux. I command it."

Mux scowled back. "You know not what you ask."

"I'm not asking, I'm ordering you. Do as I say."

"How?"

"Whatever way you choose, but make it quick."

Abderian turned to the vision. "Don't do it, Mux!"

Khanda waved her arms again and the vision disappeared. "That is enough. Have I solved your problem, little sister? Once the child is dead, our respective realms can recover and leave each other in peace."

"Has the Demon Realm so changed you," said Horaphthia, "that you are merciless to your own offspring?"

Khanda returned an empty stare. "I have changed with Belphagor's death. I will hurt for the loss of my child, but for the sake of his memory and the survival of our kingdom, it must be done."

"But the baby has the cursemark!" said Abderian. "If she dies, our kingdom will die with her!"

"Even my father never believed that tale. If she dies, the mark goes to someone else, that's all. Fare you well. I have a kingdom to rule, howsoever I may." She sank back down into the pit, not heeding the shouts of Abderian and the others, until the earth appeared over the pit once more.

"Vulka says she has found Mux's scent," said Paralian, "and the vision has given her an idea where he is. We'll hunt him down."

"It will be too late when you find him," Abderian said, sadly.

But the wolves had already run off silently into the darkness.

Abderian sighed and put his arms around Maja.

"I remember my father saying," said Maja, "that if you have to make mistakes, they should be spectacular ones." She gazed up into Abderian's eyes with a little frown. "I guess I win the prize, don't I?"

Abderian caressed her long brown hair. "No. I don't know. Who can say? We had to do something."

For a while, they stood and held each other in silence.

"What do you think will happen?" Maja said at last.

"I don't know. Maybe Khanda and Tingalut were right and nothing will happen. Maybe Onym spread that rumor so that no one would mess with his spell. Maybe the kingdom will just decline slowly. Maybe it will all be over so fast we won't even notice."

"How reassuring," said Maja with a sad chuckle.

Turning his head, Abderian saw Horaphthia sitting very still again, her eyes closed. *Does she hope to prevent the disaster with the last of her power? Will it kill her if she does? Will it matter if she doesn't?* Having just recovered from fearing he was dead, it was hard for Abderian to adjust to waiting for the end of the world to come.

"I've been thinking of a name for our son," Maja whispered. "Dolus told me about that woman who wrote the letter to Vulka for you. I liked her name. It sounded . . . strong. I think Valerian would be a good name for our little boy. Don't you?"

Abderian opened his mouth to reply and found his throat too choked to speak. He held Maja closer and nodded as tears filled his eyes. The wind began to blow around them with greater intensity, causing the trees to moan and their branches to slap and clack together like dry bones. *Here it comes,* he thought.

The slapping became louder right behind Abderian, and Horaphthia said, "Well, what have we here?"

Abderian turned his head and saw Mux wearily laying a bundle down on the ground. "Forgive me, Master," said the little demon.

Abderian released Maja and knelt by the little bundle. "Is she . . . ?"

"See for yourself," grumbled Mux as he flung back a corner of the swaddling blanket. The red-haired baby within blinked in the light. Then she let out a very healthy scream.

Abderian grinned and picked up the baby in his arms. "She's alive!"

"So I hear," said Horaphthia, covering her ears but smiling as she did so.

Maja appeared at Abderian's side and peered over his shoulder. "So that's the little minx that's causing all the trouble," she murmured.

Abderian rocked and shushed the baby and said, "You're forgiven, Mux. Most heartily."

Mux gazed wistfully at the baby. "Couldn't kill her. She kept me warm. I wasn't going to obey the Queen after what she called me. Leather sack of potatoes. Hah!"

Maja clucked her tongue. "You're holding her wrong. You put her head here and hold her bottom like that." She readjusted the infant in Abderian's arms, and he felt a glow of joy. *She likes the baby, too.*

The baying of wolves sounded in the distance. "Don't let them kill me, Master!" said Mux, cringing and trying to hide on the far side of the campfire.

Paralian and Vulka loped into the firelight, their long tongues panting and their eyes intent on the little demon. "Oho!" said Paralian. "All that running and snuffling and the trail leads back to where we started."

"He brought the child back unharmed," said Abderian. "Leave him alone." He realized the baby was getting very warm indeed, and the air around them was hot as a summer's day.

"If you can assure us the demon won't cause any more mischief," said Vulka. "Gods, it's hot. This fur is too warm. Pardon me while I change." There was a shimmer of silver light and Vulka stood, a woman once more, and a gloriously naked one at that.

Maja became intent on readjusting the baby's blanket and stepped in front of Abderian, blocking his view.

"Tell her you won't, Mux," said Abderian.

"By the cold thighs of my ex-Queen Khanda, by the sacred flames of the Lower Abyss of Rhigosys, by the hairy armpits of Sapfu—"

"That's enough," said Paralian. "We get the idea."

"You're right, it is very warm," said Horaphthia. She removed her black *houppeland*, revealing a red silk dress beneath. "Why don't you wear this, Vulka? It's lightweight. We don't want the fellows to be too distracted right now, do we?" She handed the *houppeland* to Vulka and, after a few moments, Maja decided the baby was tucked in well enough and stepped out of Abderian's view.

Vulka, now decorously clothed and seated on a rock, was idly scratching Paralian behind one ear.

Abderian's arms were feeling very warm, and he set the infant in his lap. *It is hot as an oven now.* "Well, we'd better talk about what to do before the kingdom becomes a cookery." He looked Vulka square in the eye. "But you can't have the child back. She's not a 'commodity.' She's a daughter of the Royal House of Sagamore and—"

Vulka tipped back her head and laughed a rich, throaty laugh. "No, Highness, the Guild has learned its lesson. We will not try to sell your babe."

"However," said Paralian, "you might want to consider allowing Vulka to raise the child, anyway."

"Why?"

"You see," Paralian went on, "things are rather shaky in Mamelon right now. What with the disappearance of the Queen," he said, looking significantly at Horaphthia, "and the unseasonably hot weather, and Cyprian's lax handling of affairs, it might take only one more scandal to precipitate open rebellion. Cyprian is not yet a strong enough king to survive that. The babe will get excellent support and education in the Guild. Better than Mamelon can offer, I think."

Abderian frowned, wondering why his brother had switched sides on him. Then he saw how close Paralian sat to Vulka, how she blithely caressed his fur. He didn't know if he ought to be pleased or appalled. "You mean . . . you two . . . want to adopt her?"

Paralian nodded his shaggy head. "You got it." He laid his head on Vulka's lap with a wolfish grin.

"For the record," Horaphthia said dryly, "not that it will make any difference, but I should point out that Vulka is a commoner. Princes, should they choose to remain princes, are not permitted to marry just anyone, you know. Abderian here was fortunate in that Maja is descended from the previous royal house, making her almost a princess. Do you understand what I'm saying?"

Paralian raised his head, and Abderian was amazed how noble his brother looked in wolf shape. "I do. And you are right, it makes no difference. The people of Euthymia believe I am dead, and I've no intention of informing them otherwise. This kingdom has enough troubles without another prince popping up to declare for the throne. Let Cyprian have it."

"And if this poor, confused kingdom should ever need you to lead it?"

"Then they will have to accept Vulka with me."

Horaphthia nodded. "As I thought. Carry on."

"Well, Abderian, will you let us care for your daughter? You may visit whenever you like."

With a sad pang, Abderian realized he was, in a subtle way, losing his brother again. With a loud *ouch*, he realized he had to get the baby off his lap before his legs were seared from the heat. As quickly and gently as possible, Abderian set the infant on the ground. The baby kicked and flailed with her arms and the blanket wrappings fell aside and Abderian was reminded of one very important matter. "We still have to get the cursemark off her somehow."

"I was thinking," said Vulka, "that with Guild training, even as a child she might learn to control it."

"The kingdom won't survive that long," said Horaphthia. "The temperature is tolerable up here in the mountains, but down south, I assure you they are roasting."

"Then why are we just sitting here?" said Maja. "Let's get back to Mamelon and make Onym transfer the mark again."

"That is foolishness," said Vulka. "You cannot remove a magical mark that a child is born with!"

Paralian looked up at her. "This *particular* mark, my dear puppy-wuppikins, has jumped around so many arms I doubt it would notice one more change of address."

"So," said Horaphthia, "how do we get back?"

There was a long, silent pause.

"Could we walk?" said Maja.

"We are four days ride from Mamelon," said Horaphthia, "and we have no food or water."

"But Abderian is a wizard," said Vulka. "He brought Paralian and me here. He can send us all back."

"I doubt," said Horaphthia, "that Abderian has enough magical energy at this moment to light a candle."

Abderian tried it. She was right.

"And what little I have," Horaphthia went on, "is currently in use, preventing me from instantly dying of old age."

"Silliness! Stupidity! Gross underuse of the mind!" said Mux, jumping out of the shadows.

"Does leather-wit have a better idea?" asked Paralian.

"Make the Lizard Priests send you back. They have the power."

They all looked at one another. With an expression somewhere between incredulity and despair Horaphthia said, "He's right. That's what we must do."

TWENTY-EIGHT

Persuasion is like theft. Using tools crude or subtle, one robs a man of his will. If a good thief, you leave no sign that it was you who robbed him. If the best of thieves, you leave no sign that anything was taken.

—KING VESPIN THE SNEAKY

"THEY'RE GONE," MAJA whispered, as they stared into the cave.

So far as Abderian could tell, she was right. Peering around the edge of the passageway into the altar chamber, he couldn't see a single priest. In part he was relieved. He had not relished the thought of holding a torch over the baby's head and saying, "Send us to Mamelon or the kid is toast." *It probably wouldn't have worked anyway. From the way Maja keeps having to set the blanket down, the kid is toast. And likes it.*

Abderian stepped into the altar chamber. Horaphthia put her hand on his arm. "I don't like this," she said, looking about with concern.

"I agree it throws a pebble into the millworks," said the prince. "I guess we'll just have to walk." He saw something gold gleaming on the altar. It was the Sword of Sagamore. "So that's where I left it." He carefully crossed the chamber to the altar. "Just can't seem to lose you, can I?" He picked the blade up, noting there were no dents, scratches, or discolorations. "You've survived this better than I have." He stuck the sword back through his belt.

Paralian brushed past Abderian and padded around the altar, sniffing the floor. Horaphthia walked around the edge of the engraved and polished floor surface, to where a lizard-skin robe lay discarded. Gingerly, she lifted a corner of the garment. "I don't like this *at all*."

"Where did they go?" said Maja.

Abderian shrugged. "Maybe they went chasing after Mux with the others."

"And decided to skip and go naked while they were at it?" asked Paralian, nuzzling another robe.

"I think," said Vulka, walking cautiously into the chamber, "that they have not left this room at all."

Abderian felt a shiver go through him, and Paralian's ears pricked forward. "The huntress speaks," said the wolf. "Now I'm worried."

"Foolishness!" said Mux, jumping into the room. "So they've gone. Use the floor anyway. We do not need them!"

Abderian sighed. "Mux, even if we had the energy to cast such a spell, which between all of us we don't, I don't know which pattern to use."

The little demon ran across the room to an alcove behind the grotto where the baby had been. After a moment, Mux came running back with a familiar-looking book bound in lizardskin. "Here, Master."

It was the library book on floor patterns. *It's almost too bad,* Abderian thought impishly, *that I changed back to human form. I would have liked to see the Book Wurm's expression as he tried to collect this overdue book from a dragon.* He flipped through the pages and toward the back, under the heading "For Getting Rid of Guests Who Over-Tarry," he found a group teleport spell.

"The power of many wizards is in this floor," said Mux. "Use it."

For a moment there was silence as everyone stared at the demon.

"Mux," said Abderian, "if this is another trick . . ."

Mux clapped his hands to his face and pulled on his leathery skin. "No trick! You think I want the Demon Realm smothered?"

"It would seem," said Abderian, "that you've been banished from that realm. What does it matter to you?"

Mux's shoulders drooped. "I know you've reason not to trust me. I listened to Tingalut and he made me think I would be powerful. He lied to me. All the priests lied to me and laughed at me and ordered me around. I only want to help. Will you trust me?"

Paralian snorted. "Not a chance."

"I fear we may have little choice," said Horaphthia. She walked carefully across the floor to stand beside the demon. "Mux, either you and Tingalut have a conspiracy more clever than any I have yet seen, or Fate is more twisted than a snake mating with a corkscrew. In order to save both kingdoms, we have to get back to Mamelon instantly. In order to return instantly, we must use the patterns in this floor. To use the patterns in this floor, we must use the energy in the floor—that of Tingalut and the other priests."

"Well, that sounds fitting to me," said Maja. "Let them pay our fare for the return trip, after what they put us through."

"You don't understand, child. Using other people's energy is a tricky business. You saw what it did to Abderian."

"But we've got to do it, anyway," Abderian said flatly.

"Yes." Horaphthia turned to Mux and asked with a sweet smile, "Mux, since this was all your idea, why don't you summon the energy for us?"

"I thought demons didn't do pattern magic," Abderian said.

"But I'll bet this one has been trained to. Haven't you, Mux?"

Paralian growled and his fur began to stand on end. "If you think I will trust Vulka's life and mine to this conniving little—'

Horaphthia held up her hand. Abderian noticed that Mux seemed surprisingly pale for a demon.

"If Mistress demands it," said Mux, "I will do it. But I would rather not."

"Why?"

Mux looked this way and that at the floor. "It is . . . I don't have the skill."

"You don't have the courage, you mean," said Horaphthia. "But I will trust you. And it is from this trust, not from cruelty, that I demand you summon the power for us."

Mux pouted at the floor. "Yes, Mistress."

"What?" said Paralian. "Horaphthia, how do we know he isn't acting?"

"Because even a demon trained in the thespian arts cannot willfully turn himself that lovely shade of ashen-gray. Whatever you fear, Mux, we will protect you from it. It's in our interest, you know."

"What is it you fear, Mux?" Abderian asked.

"I don't want to get sucked into the floor like those priests," he grumbled.

"Don't worry," said Paralian. "It would probably spit you out again."

"Enough!" said Horaphthia. "We are in some hurry, remember. Let's begin."

Mux gazed up at Abderian soulfully. "Will the Master stand beside me, so if . . . something strange happens he may pull me off the pattern?"

"I'll be nearby, Mux."

The little demon nodded and sighed. He took the book from Abderian's hands, and as everyone gathered in the middle of the floor, Mux found the line he wanted and began to hop and dance, singing an off-key chant:

> By the Goddess of the Snakes,
> Lizards, Newts and Firedrakes,
> Power of wizards, dwarf or gnome
> Help to send these people home.
>
> Mamelon is where they go,
> To the temple there, you know.
> Send them safely, quick and true,
> Just be sure to send me too!

Suddenly Mux's eyes grew very wide and his feet glowed a bright blue. He threw the book to Abderian and put his hands down on the circular pattern surrounding everyone. The pattern lit up with a bright blue light as well. Abderian had to turn his eyes away as the little demon became too luminous to look at. The cavern blurred into an even shade of grey-brown. It felt much the same to Abderian as the time he was brought here from the temple. Somewhere in the distance he heard Mux wail.

The assembled sisters of the Star Goddess Cult seemed quite surprised to have four adults, a wolf, and a baby drop in on their midnight services. Horaphthia immediately singled out Entheali and said, "Seal this floor, now! Don't let magical energy leave it!"

Where's Mux? thought Abderian.

"I beg your pardon," said Entheali. "That is quite impossible. Tritavia needs that energy. Maja, girl, where have you been? What is the meaning of your abandoning my grandson? And who is that shamelessly dressed woman with the dog? And whose child is this?"

Abderian's eyes searched the Great Hall. *What happened to Mux?*

"Seal the floor," Horaphthia growled through gritted teeth, "or your precious Tritavia will sorely regret the sort of energy she receives."

Entheali sputtered, "Are you threatening our goddess?"

Abderian would have loved to listen to the argument longer, but he pushed through the crowd of acolytes that surrounded them. "Mux?"

There was a tugging at his elbow, and for a moment his heart lightened. Then he turned and saw it was Vulka. Her earnest grey eyes were wide.

"Let's leave now, while we can. Hurry!" she whispered.

"I can't find Mux."

"Forget Mux," said Paralian. "Let's get out of here before they look at the baby too closely."

They found Maja eagerly talking to Lizbet. "We've got to find him, wherever he is," she was saying. "It's extremely important, believe me!"

"After what I've just seen," said Lizbet, "I'll believe anything."

Maja turned to Abderian. "We'll search for Onym, and bring him to your tower. Here." Maja handed the blanket-swaddled infant to Vulka and she rushed away, following Lizbet.

"Come on!" said Vulka. With a last glance back around the great domed room, Abderian took off for his tower, Vulka and Paralian not far behind.

Puffing from the heat and the trot up the stairs, Abderian flung his chamber door open and saw Dolus and the skeletal Sagamore standing in the middle of the room. They turned in surprise as Abderian, Paralian, and Vulka rushed in.

"There, I told you," said Dolus. "I haven't lost my touch entirely. Here they are."

Vulka ran to the bed and swiftly put the blanketed infant down. Swearing, she rubbed her arms, where the skin was now bright red. Abderian thought he saw steam rising from the baby blanket.

"I never doubted you, Dolus," said Sagamore. "Ah, is this the infamous infant I've been told about?"

"Yes," gasped Abderian. "We've got to do something about her, fast. The heat's getting worse and worse." Abderian went to the bed and looked at the baby. She was glowing.

There was a thud at the door.

"Horaphthia!" Dolus cried. "Horaphthia? That is you, isn't it?"

The aged woman gripping the door nodded as she gasped for breath. "Not as . . . young . . . as I used to be."

Dolus went to her and took her arm. "What happened to you?"

She locked eyes with him. "The same that happened to you."

Dolus closed his eyes and put his arms around her. "I am so very sorry."

Abderian turned away. *I don't need to cry again now. I don't.* He unwrapped the blanket around the baby and put a corner of his pillow beneath her tiny head. She smiled at him, clearly enjoying all the excitement. *And I wonder whether you're being happy makes things better or worse.* He tickled her cheek and pulled back his hand, slightly burned. "Ow!"

He stuck his finger in his mouth and turned back to the others. Horaphthia was stepping away from Dolus. There was a redness to her eyes and she sniffled. But she pulled herself up and cleared her throat. "Maja and Lizbet have gone to find Onym. I suggest we discuss how we are going to convince that imbecile of a sorcerer to help us."

"Horaphthia, you didn't happen to see Mux in the temple, did you?"

"No, I didn't. Oh. I'm sorry. It must be his fears were right after all."

"No less than what he deserved," Paralian growled.

Abderian turned to his brother, then couldn't decide what to say. Mux hadn't been the most trustworthy of companions, but he had done the right things at the end. And Abderian knew there would be times he would miss him.

"As to this Onym," Vulka began.

"Yes," said Sagamore. "Might I suggest you leave him to me? I was his king for many years, you may recall, and I might yet have some sway over him. After all, I gave him some of his best ideas."

"We know," Horaphthia said sardonically.

"First," Sagamore went on, "I'd like to ask you, Abderian, to allow these weary bones to rest for a little. I've been walking about for days now and I can feel the spell that's holding me up wearing thin. I wouldn't suddenly want to fall apart at the wrong moment. Onym might think I lack backbone. He might even rib me about it. Wouldn't want to appear spineless—"

"Goddess rest ye merry, gentle liege," Abderian said, whipping the Sword of Sagamore out from his belt.

With an indecorous clatter, the bones fell to the floor. Dolus swiftly reached out and caught the skull before it hit the pile. This he placed on the shelf, while Abderian pulled out from under his desk the cloak that he had originally carried the bones in. Abderian quickly and carefully put the bones back in the cloak and tied it up.

He had just finished, and was standing and wiping his brow when Maja appeared in the doorway, followed by the short, rotund, yellow-robed, bulbous-nosed, balding form of Onym.

"At least he's not a chicken anymore," Paralian said.

"A party? For me?" said Onym with delighted eyes.

"Not quite, Father," said Horaphthia. "We need your help."

"Oh, I always love to help—Horaphthia, my dear little girl, what's happened to you?"

"The Lizard Priests drained me, Father."

Onym walked to her and took her hands in his. "Oh, no. Oh, my sweet little thing, how could they do this to you? Oh, no, this will not do."

Abderian felt a wild hope growing within him. "Onym, I have her magical power now—"

Onym swiftly turned on him. "Oh, you nasty boy! How could you—"

"No, I didn't take it from *her*!"

Horaphthia put a hand on Onym's shoulder. "It's all right, Father, he took it from the priests, not me. But we have something more important for you to help with first. You see that baby on the bed there?"

Onym waddled to the bed. "My, my, my. With more children like this, we shan't need fireplaces. She's demon-born, isn't she?"

"Yes, Father. And she bears the Cursemark of Sagamore. The very mark you created."

"She does? How did *she* get it? Why are all these people ending up with things they shouldn't have?"

Abderian decided even Onym ought to know the truth. "It's natural that she had it. She's my daughter, Onym. She inherited the cursemark from me."

"From you? So you did have it all along! Very clever. Your great-grandfather would have been proud of you. So, been sowing your wild oats among the demons, eh? Ooops, sorry Maja."

Maja smiled coldly at the wizard. "What mistakes Abderian made before bringing me to Mamelon have been forgiven."

"Ah. Good, good. Well, this is fascinating. I've never thought of the implications of a demon-born getting the Mark of Sagamore."

"We've already experienced some of the 'implications,' Father, and it's destroying the kingdom. We need the cursemark removed. Now."

"Removed?" Onym said, rubbing his chin. "Well, now, I don't know. I'll have to think about this. There are so many possible complications. I'll have to think."

Onym wandered around the room, chin in hand, as Horaphthia stared after him in exasperation. Abderian sat on the bed, as close to the baby as was comfortable. He felt very tired. The baby was sleeping. "Lucky you," he murmured.

Onym suddenly noticed the skull on Abderian's shelf. "What is this? So you are taking up necromancy, are you?"

Well, if everyone is going to accuse me of it. "Yes, Onym. A little bit."

"Hmmm, I hope you know what you're doing. Exhumation is very rude, you know. This fellow, for example. Did you get his permission first?"

"Yes, Onym. In fact, I saved him from a disrespectful burial. You should be pleased with me. *That* is the skull of my great-grandfather, and your former king, Sagamore."

"Sagamore," Onym breathed, reverently, his eyes wide. He raised his hands to the shelf and gently picked up the skull. Holding it up in one hand, Onym gazed upon the skull and said, "Alas, poor Sagamore. I knew him, Abderian. A fellow of infinite jest, of most excellent fancy. Where be your gibes now? Your gambols? Your songs?"

"The same place they've ever been, you melodramatic nincompoop," said the skull. "Now put me down!"

With a yelp, Onym pulled back his hands in surprise, and once again Dolus had to rescue the falling skull before it smashed on the floor.

"Ever consider taking up medicine ball?" said Sagamore to Dolus as he was placed back on the shelf.

Onym, meanwhile, was on his knees, groveling. "Oh, dearest master," he wailed, "forgive me! I did not mean offense!"

"Onym," said Sagamore, "I have a bone to pick with you."

TWENTY-NINE

I sometimes think that if people put all the time and attention they currently devote to magic, superstition, and the beseeching of their deities into the practical management of their lives, they would be far closer to having what they want.

—SALVIA THE SAGE

"ANYTHING, MY LIEGE!" cried Onym, his forehead touching the floor stones. "Tell me how I may acquit myself in your eyes—er, sockets."

"Eyes will do, thank you. Onym, it's about this cursemark of yours."

"Yours, my lord. I made it for you!"

"You made it for my predecessor, King Thalion, who thought it was a nifty idea to tie a kingdom's health to a jester's heart. Big mistake. He who laughs the loudest hurts the most, and that's a fact."

"You were the finest king Euthymia ever had," said Onym.

"You're too kind," said Sagamore. "But for old times' sake, will you do your old pal, King Saggy, a favor and remove the cursemark from that demon baby before she fries us all to jerky chips?"

Onym rose to his feet and bowed. "If that is what my good liege wishes. To whom would you have me transfer the mark?"

"Transfer?" said Abderian, along with several others. "We want you to dispel it!"

"It's a dangerous nuisance!" said Dolus.

"It's a burden to anyone who wears it," said Paralian.

"It's a pain in the butt," said Horaphthia.

"It cannot be done," Onym said simply. "That mark is so closely tied to the kingdom of Euthymia itself that to dispel it . . ." He shrugged suggestively.

Abderian said, "You mean to say, not only does killing someone who wears the mark destroy the kingdom, but destroying the mark itself does, too?"

"In a nutshell, yes," Onym said.

"An apt way of putting it," grumbled Paralian.

"There are times," Sagamore said, "that you are simply too thorough, Onym."

"Thank you, my liege."

"Then let us decide quickly," said Horaphthia. "Who is the calmest person we know?"

"Paralian had it first," said Abderian. His brother flicked his ears forward, then back, but said nothing.

"It should probably go to Cyprian," said Onym. "He is, after all, the King."

"One moment!" said the skull of Sagamore. "Speaking as the one for whom the mark was made, I claim the right to choose my inheritor. And I think Fate has helped to guide that choice. I offer the cursemark to the most courageous and clever soul among us. Abderian, will you again take the mark upon you?"

Abderian's mouth dropped open. "No," he said softly. He remembered all the pain and trouble it had caused him. "Paralian? Please, it should be yours."

"The cursemark should not leave the kingdom," Paralian said. "If I keep company with Vulka, that would be impossible. And I'm sure you can guess where my choice lies. I chose to give you the mark for good reason, and, for once, I think Sagamore is right."

"I didn't seem to do too well when I had it."

"This past year," said Dolus, "Euthymia was doing fine. And the earthquake and other problems were not your doing at all. I'd say we could do little worse."

Abderian swallowed hard. "Then, if all agree, I'll take it."

Maja frowned. "Are you sure you're willing, Abderian? After all you've been through?"

Abderian put on a brave smile. "Sure, why not? It has made my life so interesting. I wouldn't have met you without it, remember."

Maja paused. "Well. By all means, let's keep life interesting."

"You know it's fine with me," said Paralian.

"I don't think I'm qualified to vote," said Vulka, "but if Paralian agrees, I will trust his judgment."

"As your mentor," said Dolus, "I have something of a proprietary feeling in the matter. And my very biased opinion is that I think you should have the cursemark again."

"Even after all my slips of judgment with Vulka?" Abderian said with a rueful smile.

"Judgment is not part of the question," said Dolus. "Your emotions are strong and healthy and close to the surface. It is better to navigate a boat on a river that is clear and fresh and whose obstacles are visible, than to sail a river dark, turbulent, and muddy."

"Thank you, Dolus."

"Let's do it," said Horaphthia, and she winked at Abderian.

Onym had Abderian stand in the center of his room, draped in a blanket in order to enhance his "similarity" to the baby. Abderian already felt too hot, but he decided not to argue. Onym drew a different design on each of Abderian's hands and a third one on his forehead.

"It wasn't this complicated when Paralian gave me the mark," Abderian complained.

"This is a different case entirely!" said Onym. "Within a generation, the mark can jump like a flea. Across generations, up or down, it's more like dragging a whale out of the sea with a net. Now, hold this." Onym handed Abderian the Sword of Sagamore, which the prince took in his right hand.

Onym now drew designs on the baby's hands and forehead, which was tricky for him to do without getting burned. When he tried to tie silk thread to the baby's wrists, the thread charred and broke.

"She's becoming hotter," Maja said. "The blanket is scorching!"

"Oh, codswallop! I hate it when I have to cut corners. Pomp and ceremony are half the fun of magic. Very well, Abderian, touch the point of the sword to the mark, if you please."

Abderian did so, being very, very careful not to touch the skin of the baby. Even so, he felt some force resisting him, making it hard to aim the blade precisely. Finally, he managed to just barely touch the mark and there was a bright flash. The mark disappeared from the infant's arm and reappeared on Abderian's.

"Ow!" the prince cried, clutching the skin around the mark. "You didn't say it would hurt!"

"It likes you," said Onym. "That's why it moved so fast. Naturally, it didn't have a chance to cool down along the way."

"I see," Abderian said through gritted teeth. Outside there came a distant rumbling of thunder.

"I suggest," said Dolus, "that you calm yourself a bit. Remember your emotions have repercussions once again."

"Oh. Right." Abderian breathed deeply and tried to ease his thoughts.

"It feels cooler already," said Vulka.

To his surprise, Abderian did not feel the weight of the world on his shoulders. As he recalled, he had not felt that either when Paralian had first handed the cursemark down to him a year ago. Abderian looked at his baby daughter. She was returning to normal pink color, but she seemed to shiver a little. Abderian wrapped the blanket around her and tucked it in. He was surprised to feel pleased and proud. He realized that he had missed the feeling of connection to the world which having the cursemark had given him. *I'm actually glad to have it back.*

When he looked back up, Onym was frowning at Horaphthia.

"No, no. My little girl mustn't be such an old lady so soon."

"I'm over ninety, Father."

"For a wizard, that's barely coming of age!"

"Father, my magic was drained from me. I'm . . . not wizard anymore."

"That does not mean you can never be again."

"The Lizard Priests' spells make it impossible for me to take back."

"What their spells do," said Onym, "is to take your spiritual vessel that holds the magic and bend it out of shape so that makes your own power turn against you. Fiendish, these priests are. But there is no need to throw away a golden goblet because it has been dented a bit. No! One pounds the dents out."

"I don't like the sound of that, even metaphorically."

"Nonsense, my girl."

"Now, look here," said Dolus, "with the power the priests have, trying to repair the damage might be as dangerous as the draining itself. You should stop getting her hopes up. I was trained, myself, in the very same way."

"A priest has your power?" said Onym.

"No," said Dolus, "Abderian has it."

Onym stared at Abderian, wide-eyed. Abderian looked at his shoes and blushed. He didn't know what to say.

"Quite the clever thief, aren't we?" said Onym. "You're right, my liege, his cleverness cannot be contested. His morals, however—"

"You're a fine one to talk!" said Maja. "You and my mother tried to steal the cursemark from Abderian and force it on me."

"That was a different matter entirely, young lady," said Onym, puffing himself up.

"Is that true, Onym?" said Sagamore from the shelf. "Did you really try to take the mark from my chosen successor and put it on one of *Thalion's* descendants—no offense, my dear."

"Well," said Onym, suddenly meek, "Entheali and I hadn't realized what a promising young man Abderian was growing into. He had given us some trouble, you understand—"

"He means they couldn't control him, Sagamore," said Maja.

"Let me finish, you impertinent girl!"

"I think I've heard enough," said Sagamore, in a tone colder than a marble tomb in winter. "Onym, you have been a bad boy. I've met quite a few souls in the Land of the Corporeally Bereft who are somewhat miffed at you for some naughty-naughties you've committed in the past. I can give them your address."

Onym looked down and fidgeted his hands. "Entheali and I only meant the best. What would you have me do, my liege?"

"Stop making accusations and get on with setting things right."

"As my liege commands," Onym said, bowing. "Very well, you three sit close together." Onym grabbed Horaphthia's arms and sat her on the bed next to Abderian, then guided Dolus to sit on the other side—though careful not to seat him on the baby. "Now, all three of you hold hands."

"In what fashion?" asked Dolus.

"Whatever is comfortable," said Onym.

Horaphthia leaned over and whispered, "I suggest the Three-Pointed Star."

After some trial-and-error grabbing of hands, Abderian finally seemed to catch the correct hands and Horaphthia nodded, warily, at Onym.

The sorcerer raised his arms and began to speak. Abderian

could not make out the words—although they sounded like those
spoken by the resurrected fossil dragon—but as the room dark
ened, he knew them to be Words of Power. "*Wenthimun issin
thisev venthouz . . .*"

Out of nowhere, darkness boiled around them like thick
smoke. Abderian could no longer see Horaphthia or Dolus. He felt
the same tugging sensations within him as he felt when walking
the Lizard Priests' sorcerous patterns, or when doing an arduous
spell. But this was worse. He felt as if the people on either side of
him were pulling his arms off, yet his arms were not moving. He
felt as though his entrails were being drawn out through his
fingertips. He opened his mouth to gasp—then to scream. . .

Then it was over. His arms felt incredibly light, as if they
wanted to float up to the ceiling. Abderian looked to his right and
saw Dolus sitting tall, more vigorous than Abderian had seen him
in a long while.

"How amazing," Dolus murmured. "It feels better than I re
membered."

Abderian looked to his left and saw a pensive, dark-haired girl
about twelve years of age. "How strange," she said, "why
don't—" Suddenly she stared down at her young form, examining
her hands, her arms, and the gown that was now far too large.
"Father!" The young Horaphthia glared at Onym. "What have
you done?"

"Ah, there's my sweet little girl," said Onym. The wizard
seemed worn out, but quite pleased with himself.

"I don't want to be a sweet little girl!" Horaphthia said, striking
the bedclothes with her prepubescent fists. "Middle-age suited me
just fine, thank you very much!"

Onym merely gazed at her fondly and shook his head. "You
see, my liege, I have not lost my touch, as they say I have. I did
it all at once. Each is healed and has their magical power, and my
Horaphthia has regained her lost youth. Am I not, as they say,
hot?"

"Thou art indeed . . . unique among sorcerers, Onym," said
Sagamore.

"Well I, for one, do not think this is so 'hot,'" said Horaphthia,
jumping to her feet. "Now that I have my power back, pardon me
while I make a few modifications in my appearance."

Her arms whipped around in a rapid series of gestures that
would have seemed impossible from any other twelve-year-old.
She intoned, "Guava, mango, ripe banany, make me neither child

nor granny. Ripe of age, young of heart, make me as I was to start."

Nothing happened. Except that dust crumbled down from the plaster overhead, adding a little grey to her hair, after a fashion.

Sagamore said, "I'm afraid, Horaphthia, you've been mortarfied."

"Very funny," growled the child-sorceress, spitting out dust.

"No, no," said Dolus, frowning. "Your gestures weren't quite right, Horaphthia. It was . . . Oh, it was right in the back of my mind, but I can't recall it clearly. It was—"

"Was it this one?" Horaphthia said, and waved her hands around again. Then she stared at them as if they were strangers to her.

"No, that's the Aiding Flowers to Bloom spell. I know that one well enough. It was, oh, damme—"

Horaphthia stared at Dolus, aghast. "I never learned an Aiding Flowers to Bloom spell."

Dolus stared back, realization dawning on his face.

Both wizards pointed at each other and said, in unison, "You've got my power!" They turned toward the rotund little sorcerer and cried "Onym!"

Onym rubbed his palms on his gaudy yellow robe and blinked. "Did I do something wrong?"

Whatever retort he had coming was forestalled by a knock at the open door. Onym stepped aside and in stepped the young Princess Alexia, her golden gown matching her blond pigtails.

She's grown some, Abderian thought dazedly. *Why she must be about . . . Horaphthia's apparent age.*

"May I come in, Uncle Onym? Mother said it was time."

"Of course, Your Highness."

Alexia's gaze lit on Horaphthia and she broke into a smile bright enough to fry ants. "Oh, Onym, it's true, just like the prophecy! A playmate of my own!" She rushed over and grasped Horaphthia's wrists. "I'm so glad to see you. There's been nobody in the castle my own age to play with!"

"Father—" Horaphthia growled.

"Oh, do you call him father?" Alexia prattled. "I call him uncle. He's so cute, isn't he? Look, here's the parchment on which the prophecy was written." Alexia pulled out of her cabochonstudded belt the same piece of crumpled pink parchment Abderian had seen in Amusia's sticky hands as she teased her sister with it. "I asked Mother to pray to Tritavia for a playmate for me, and she made this prophecy, saying that I would. And Onym promised me that what the Star Goddess sends in prophecy comes true!"

"Father . . ."

Onym gazed heavenward and raised his palms. "It is Tritavia's will."

"I'll get you for this, Father."

"Oooh, do you like nasty games? So do I. I have a little sister who's just horrid. We can get her all you want."

"I suggest," Dolus said frostily, "that we call this a pretty enough jest, and set things back to rights. Don't you agree, Onym? Sagamore?"

"I'm afraid I just couldn't," said Onym. "I'm pooped."

The skull ceased chuckling and said, "And it appears another such transfer would be hard on all of you. Just look at Abderian there."

All eyes in the room turned to Abderian and he felt like crawling under the blanket. "What's wrong?" Then he realized he hadn't moved a muscle below his collarbone since the spell had been finished. He tried to lift one hand, and couldn't. He did not feel paralyzed. Just so very tired. He uttered a soft moan and fell back on the mattress.

"What's the matter? Is he all right?" Fading voices buzzed around him, but a new voice became louder within him.

"Let my rhythms be your lullaby. My spirit shall harbor you safely," said the Land of Euthymia. "Welcome home."

"And another thing," Paralian was saying in the distance, "how are we going to explain that enormous new crack in the castle courtyard?"

Home again, thought Abderian, and he felt himself smile before drifting off to sleep.

THIRTY

The Scaly One steps sideways as she walks.

—DICTUM OF THE CULT OF THE LIZARD GODDESS

THE DAYS BEFORE Abderian's wedding sped by in a pleasant blur. Cyprian finally came out of hiding and certain well-planted rumors gave him the credit for the cooling of the climate and the return to some semblance of normalcy. "He had been in seclusion," it was said, "to perfect the right spells to combat the menace." The strange weather was blamed on the demons, because there were few of them left around and because it was, in part, true.

The disappearance of Queen Horaphthia had been much harder to explain. Particularly since, from the night that Horaphthia had lost her sorcery, Cyprian had forgotten her completely. He had vague memories of a dear love long past, but was utterly surprised when people told him he was married. Abderian wondered how Horaphthia felt about that, but thought it would be rude to ask. The general consensus at court was that she had simply run off to whatever mysterious place she had come from. The unkind ones said good riddance and the kingdom was better off without her.

The kind ones noted Cyprian's personality and said they didn't blame her. The rest shrugged it off as another colorful footnote to Euthymia's already garish history.

And Horaphthia would have eventually browbeaten Onym into returning her to a more mature age . . . except that he seemed to have thrown his soul again. Into a frog, apparently, for all anyone could get out of his recumbent human form was "ribbet ribbet."

Abderian finally got to see his newborn son, and was surprised that the boy looked nothing like his demonic half-sister. Abderian liked him instantly.

Entheali showed some reluctance to continue with the plans for Abderian and Maja's wedding. She felt less interested in a son-in-law who, so far as she knew, no longer bore the Mark of Sagamore. Abderian hinted, however, that he retained connections to the Grey Guild, and they would be quite glad to hear of the whereabouts of past debtors. Entheali then enthusiastically agreed to conduct the wedding services herself, and throw in a hefty dowry in the bargain.

Abderian and Maja's wedding was to take place in the Great Hall of the Temple of the Star Goddess. Abderian had somewhat mixed feelings about this, given his associations with the place. But Entheali had insisted, and that was that.

It was not to be as grand a wedding as that of Cyprian and Horaphthia; Abderian was not the royal heir, after all. But still the elaborate nature of the ceremony required some rehearsal, and Abderian and Maja found themselves in the Great Hall, wandering and waiting for the acolytes to take their places.

"Abderian," said Maja, "one of those patterns is lit up. Is that part of the ceremony?"

Abderian knew that Maja had learned enough about the ceremony to be suspicious. "No, Maja, none of this magic is supposed to be used in the wedding, except as a general blessing. And your mother isn't capable of that sort of surprise. I expect it's left over from the Morning Star services."

"No, I know what that pattern looks like. This light is weird. It's crossing pattern lines. It's heading right for us!"

Abderian turned and looked behind him. A rippling series of triangular-shaped lights came toward them like a sea-dragon across water. Before Abderian could leap out of the way, an invisible something grabbed his leg and Maja's. The floor seemed to fall out from under them and they dropped into a burning, howling darkness.

Abderian blinked and found they were standing in a deserted, rocky wasteland that stretched to all horizons. It was blazing midday, and the sky was as blue as the hottest flame and the air was hot and dry. In front of them stood the thin, snarling form of the High Priest, Tingalut.

Abderian hugged Maja to him and said, "Where are we?"

"A place that is not yet, but will be," said Tingalut. "Tritavia is not the only one with a Paradise. And hers is a false one, for a false goddess. Welcome, you gnat larvae, to the land of the Scaly One, herself."

"Not my idea of Paradise," said Maja. "What do you want with us?"

Tingalut scowled at her. "This place wasn't made for *you*. I want nothing. I only serve The One who asks your presence."

"And I suppose it's only coincidence that you grabbed us just before our wedding," Abderian snapped.

Tingalut shrugged with a smug smile. "It was not I who chose that time for you to walk again among our patterns. Let us say it was my only window of opportunity."

Abderian released Maja and drew the Sword of Sagamore. "You can just throw us back through that window, if you don't mind."

"Ah, but I do mind," said Tingalut. "And what will you do about it?"

Abderian hated to willfully harm anyone. The memory of Belphagor was too fresh in his mind. But he had to show Tingalut he meant business. So he lashed out with the sword, hoping only to gash him a little. He needn't have bothered. The sword went right through Tingalut, with no effect whatsoever.

"You see," Tingalut said, "I no longer really exist, except as a dream of my goddess. To escape your blasphemous meddling, I gave up my corporeal self to the sorcerous patterns. Only the pattern of my soul remains, but I find it quite sufficient. You, on the other hand . . ."

Tingalut gestured and the Sword of Sagamore flew out of Abderian's hands into the Lizard Priest's grasp. Tingalut then lunged with the sword at Maja. The sword bent like rubber, an inch from Maja's silk bodice.

Tingalut stared at the sword in disgust and disappointment, and Abderian grabbed it back from him. "It likes us."

"What a useless object," Tingalut said.

"I have not found it so. Well, if your non-corporeal self cannot harm us, and we can't harm you, it's a stalemate. Why not give up now and send us home?"

Tingalut smiled again. "I am the least powerful piece in the game. Wait until you have seen the rest of the board before declaring it a draw." Tingalut raised his arms in a way that seemed almost a parody of Entheali's invocations to Tritavia.

A dark blur appeared off to the right and sped through the air directly at Tingalut. Before the priest had spoken, he was knocked down by a leather-winged lump.

"Mux!" Abderian cried.

But the little demon did not answer, so absorbed was he in the struggle with Tingalut. Mux had his claws around the High Priest's throat and growled as he tightened his grip.

"I guess one dream can attack the other and have an effect," Maja murmured.

Tingalut left off trying to free his windpipe from Mux's grasp and gestured again. Five priests—the same Abderian had ordered to watch for Mux—appeared in a shimmering haze and pulled Mux off Tingalut.

"No!" the little demon cried, as the priests dragged him away. Mux was scarred and bloodied, looking as though he had fought many such battles already.

The tableau faded again into a cloud of mist, leaving only Tingalut on the ground, rubbing his neck. Abderian thought this might be the perfect moment to try something, though he truly didn't know what. *Some magic, perhaps.* He tried to relax, to let his hands move the way they would, to their own accord—to form the spell his heart conjured, though his own mind did not know it. But his hands did nothing. And Abderian remembered he no longer had Dolus's power, which had been the source of his unconscious spell-casting. All he had was his own power, as yet weak and little trained. That and the cursemark and the sword, and no idea as to how to use them to any effect.

"The problem with dreams," Tingalut rasped, "is that they cannot be banished, and they often come back to haunt you."

Maja went over to Tingalut and kicked him. Her foot went right through him.

"Maja!" Abderian cried, worried for her.

But Tingalut only scowled at her. "Foolish child," he said and painfully stood. Again he raised his arms. "I am done with these, Mother of Dragons. Come and have your will with them. "

For a few moments, nothing occurred. Then a black dot

appeared at the horizon behind Tingalut. And it grew steadily in size. And grew. And grew. Large as a house. Large as a castle. Large as a hill, an enormous reptilian creature towered over them. Her massive head was triangular, with enormous red eyes and long fangs. Her scales seemed black except where the sun's reflection released rainbows of iridescent colors.

Abderian and Maja stared at her in awed and terrified silence. *She is truly the Mother of Dragons,* the prince thought.

"Yes, I am," the creature said, in a voice of thunder. Suddenly, she shrank again to only the size of a castle. "I wanted to be sure I had your attention," she said, in a voice only of roaring wind.

Tingalut smiled beatifically. "No one could ignore you, Great Scaly One. Here I present to you those who have so thwarted your plans, the Prince Abderian and his slut."

"Hey!" Maja said, glaring. "We were going to be married before *you* interfered!"

Tingalut ignored her. "Show them, Mother of Dragons, what happens to those whose acts interfere with the path of your greatest joy!"

"Certainly," said the Lizard Goddess, and she caught Tingalut up in her talons and popped him into her cavernous, befanged mouth. She hardly even chewed before she swallowed.

"Ugh," Maja said and buried her face in Abderian's shoulder. The prince couldn't help but agree and he held her tight.

"Now," said the Great Scaly One conversationally, "we may talk."

"Talk?"

The Goddess shrank again to merely the size of a house. "Is this better for your audible range?" she said in the rumble of a waterfall. "Yes, talk. Chat. Converse. Have verbal intercourse."

"Hey!" said Maja.

"Shush," Abderian said to her. Turning back to the goddess, he said, "What is there to talk about?"

"You, my little princeling. I have had my eye on you ever since Tingalut first pointed you out to me. I have had great fun running races with you since."

"I don't understand."

The goddess's laughter was the rumble of an earthquake. "And you were the one to claim that some deity was setting obstacles in your way, leading you a merry dance."

"Your doing? Why?"

A smile spread across her iridescent, toothy jaws. "It is the way of my kind, from the tiniest lizard to the greatest dragon, to do dances. Some dances are for territory. Some are for mating. Some are paeans to the sun. Some are dances to the rhythms of the universe. Though each dance has a purpose, it is its own reward."

"I'm not a lizard. What is your purpose for 'dancing' with me?"

She lowered her head to the ground and slid it close to Abderian. "I like you."

"Great. Thanks." Abderian was beginning to be very worried by the number of supernatural things that liked him. *Maybe I should start an Appreciation Society, filled with swords and lizards and goddesses with fangs.* "Is that the only reason?"

"No." The goddess sat up on her enormous haunches.

"Well, what else?"

She cocked her head to one side. "I won't tell you."

"Why not?" Abderian was too frightened to lose patience yet.

"Because another trait of my kind is to keep secrets. Secrets of regeneration. Rebirth. Immortality. Do you want to know my secrets?"

"Um, I suppose."

"Good. I like mortals who are hungry."

Abderian shook his head, as if to jumble some sense together from what he was hearing.

"We would like to go home now," said Maja. "If you like us, you will do us the courtesy of sending us back."

The goddess tapped one talon against another and stared at Maja with an expression that was not at all kind. "Perhaps, someday, this will be your home," she said softly. "You," she pointed at Abderian, "have touched the soul of a dragon. You understand, do you not?"

"No," Abderian said. "I do not."

The goddess sighed, creating a great gust of wind. "You are an eggling yet. I am patient. Someday"—she stretched out her foreclaws to take in the whole horizon—"all this may be yours."

"I don't want it."

"We will see."

"Send us home."

"You sing only one tune."

"It's the best one I know."

"Tsk. No appreciation for music."

"But a good sense of rhythm."

"All the better for dancing."

"I won't dance. Don't ask me."

"Stubborn eggling. But clever. You long for your home ground and that is good. Go build your mud nest. Lay your eggs. When you are ready to shed your skin, come seek me."

"Should that day ever arrive, I shall leave no stone unturned," said Abderian.

"See, you do understand. Farewell."

The dusty colors blurred, with a rumble and a lurch. Abderian and Maja stood again in the cool temple, surrounded by anxious priestesses.

"Are you all right? Where were you?" Entheali cried.

Abderian let his breath out and said, "It's neither here nor there. Now let's get on with this wedding, shall we?"

THIRTY-ONE

An Account of the Royal Wedding of His Highness, Prince Abderian and the Lady Maja, by the Court Chronicler, Master Danrathernot.

25th of Crunchy Ice, Year One of the reign of King Cyprian the First.

IT WAS A beautiful evening, here in the courtyard of Castle Mamelon. Lords and ladies, dukes and duchesses, counts and countesses, earls and . . . earlesses, all gathered to stand in the snow at moonlight, awaiting the appearance of the exalted bride and groom. The torches of the crowd flickered against the snow like hundreds of fireflies on white satin seen up real close. While it is quite untraditional to hold weddings at midnight, it is believed by the Temple of Tritavia that it is the most auspicious time for an event to be blessed by the Goddess of the Stars. As the mother of the bride is also the High Priestess of the Temple, and performing the wedding, what she says apparently goes.

So there we were, all up past our bedtimes, waiting for the bride and groom to show. At last, the great double doors of the castle proper opened, and the wedding procession emerged to the great cheering of the crowd. The bride looked absolutely splendid in her white satin jester's outfit, complete with three-pointed cap tipped with gold bells. The open cabbage cart she rode in was made of

226

the finest rough cut silverwood. On the donkey ahead of her rode the groom, Prince Abderian, also dressed in white satin jester's garb, complete with three-pointed cap tipped with silver bells. At his side, in a beautiful silver scabbard, hung the fabled Sword of Sagamore—a treasured family heirloom rumored to do absolutely nothing, but it does look splendidly silly.

As the honored pair reached the center of the courtyard on their way to the temple, the crowd engaged in the traditional "throwing of tomatoes," pelting the bride and groom with the juiciest, ripest fruits and vegetables. Rumor had it that the farmers' market in Pokelocken was sold out of ripe veggies days in advance of this event. And a glorious splattering it was—not a square inch of pristine fabric was spared. By the time the pair reached the doors of the temple, they were a splendid mess. It has been said that this ritual is based upon a long-forgotten ancient fertility rite, but then they all are.

Once inside the temple itself, the Path of Happiness and Joy was strewn with fresh fruit rinds by the youngest sister of the groom, Princess Amusia. And a cute little minx she was, too. You could tell she enjoyed her part by the careful way she placed the rinds so that no two steps could be taken without someone having a slip.

And we were not disappointed. No sooner had the groom entered, still coated with the goopy tokens of the people's esteem, when he took a marvelous pratfall right there in front of the doors. Still smiling, the prince rose and continued down the long, multicolored runner, completing a series of eleven imaginatively executed pratfalls before reaching the altar. Based on past accounts this appears to be a new world record, although there is some debate over whether the twenty-three falls cited for King Vespin's wedding is accurate or not.

The bride made her entrance by climbing the Ladder of Marital Excitement to the top of the whipped-egg-white coated slide. With heartwarming enthusiasm, the Lady Maja flung herself, headfirst, down the chute into a tub of mashed grapes. From this, she was lifted on the shoulders of four acolytes of the temple, who carried her to the His Majesty's side and sat her on a tall stool.

The one possible damper on the entire affair was the High Priestess herself. Entheali was dressed in the most impeccable of black velvet robes, glittering with the chips of diamonds. But it was clear she was not entirely in tune with the proceedings, and her solemnity at first gave an unseemly tone to the proceedings.

"Welcome in the name of Joy, Frivolity, and all High Silliness," she intoned. She then went on to recite the twelve
Anecdotes of Marital Bliss, with an ever-reddening hue to her
face. Fortunately, the Prince and the Lady seemed to be enjoying
themselves immensely and often shared fond and amused glances
between themselves. The High Priestess then proceeded to the
Nine Disclaimers of Marital Duty, which, by the time she got to
the end of the list, finally had her laughing, thus restoring the
feelings of gaiety to the affair.

At last, the words were uttered, "Do you, Prince Abderian, son
of Valgus, son of Vespin, son of Sagamore, take this sweet young
cutie to be your lawfully wedded wife, please?"

Just as he was replying, "You bet your—" a bucket of water
was emptied from the ceiling over the prince's head. The bride
was asked, "Do you take this dumb-but-lovable hunk to be your
etc. etc." She decorously responded, "Sure, where do I take
him?" And the cushion she sat upon uttered a gloriously hearty
raspberry in response. Then the couple lovingly exchanged pies
and kissed amidst the mess. As the assemblage cheered, the newly
wedded couple turned and waved. The bride flung her bouquet of
firecrackers into the crowd, and the prince made funny faces
behind her back.

The parties went on all the rest of the night. Their Royal
Highnesses departed early, but the revels, no doubt, went on till
dawn. Of particular note was the incredible food fight in the
Throne Room, which I think will be unequalled for decades to
come. This is Your Most Obedient Chronicler, saying that's the
way it was, Pickleday, the 25th of Crunchy Ice, Year One.

THIRTY-TWO

Excerpt, etc.:

*So, anyway, Abderian got married and everything cooled down.
It's even snowing. I was mad that Alexia had got that new
playmate, Apu. At least, at first I was mad. But Apu's been
teaching Alexia manners and she hates that, and Apu's nice to
me, so I don't mind anymore. So everybody lived happily ever
after and now I'm gonna go out and play in the snow. Are you
still writing this down? Well, don't, you silly—*

ABDERIAN AND MAJA spent four days in seclusion after the
wedding. They were the loveliest sort of winter days—Mamelon
and the surrounding fields were blanketed under soft, fluffy snow,
and the air was bright and clear and crisp without being too chill.
Those nobles that could, went to their villas in the south,
postponing, for the season, any further problem of revolt.

The priestesses of the temple had their hands full trying to
determine what to do about the Lizard Priests in their floor,
without messing up their spells for Tritavia. Abderian didn't
believe there was too much danger to the Star Goddess. He knew
from personal experience that she had good control over her
haven. Yet the night after the wedding, Abderian dreamed that he
saw a woman with long pale hair, on a boat in a starlit sea,
bending over a little leathery demon and bandaging his wings.

The fifth night after their wedding was bright with full
moonlight and Abderian received a message to meet someone at
the castle foregate. When he walked out, across the Bobbing
Barrel Drawbridge, he saw two dark figures standing in a copse of

229

trees. As he approached, he recognized one as Vulka, dressed in
the grey leathers of a Guild caravaneer. Beside her stood a handsome brown-haired man in jerkin and trousers of brown leather.
His face was strange and yet familiar.

"Paralian!" Abderian rushed to his brother and hugged him.
"This is great!" he said, stepping back to get an eyeful. "When
did you change back?"

Grinning, Paralian said, "Just tonight. And it's only temporary.
Vulka's knowledge of shape shifting sorcery only covers short
term changes. But once I get used to the transitions, I can make it
more voluntary. And Dolus has shown me a few things, though
he's still not comfortable using Horaphthia's magic, and he hasn't
consulted with her any great deal. He's afraid that if he's closeted
with her too much, the court will accuse him of being a child
molester."

Abderian laughed. Then he noticed the wagon and horse team
behind them and his laughter failed. "You're leaving."

Paralian looked down. "Vulka has to return to her caravan.
She's really missed too much time already."

And you're going with her. Abderian felt as though he'd been
told that Paralian had died again. He had no words to say. He
could only nod. He had relied on his brother's companionship for
so long. The air seemed suddenly chillier, and freezing rain began
to fall in fact, icy drops.

"Stop that, now," said Paralian, shaking Abderian's shoulder.
"The kingdom is your responsibility again. Take good care of it."

Her, Abderian thought automatically.

"And I promise we will take good care of your little girl."

"She will be given the best training the Guild can offer," said
Vulka. "And I think they will forgive my long absence when they
see I have brought two such fine recruits." She smiled at Paralian,
and her smile gave her face such beauty, Abderian knew what
Paralian saw in her. Abderian hated her and loved her all at once.

"May I see . . . the baby before you go?" Abderian asked.

"Of course." Paralian walked with him to the wagon and pulled
aside the back tarp. By the light of a dim lamp, Abderian saw the
little red-haired infant swaddled in many blankets, fast asleep.

If only Belphagor could have lived to see she isn't the evil being
he thought she was. *Without the cursemark, she's just an ordinary*
baby, almost.

Abderian gave Paralian and Vulka final hugs goodbye. They
promised to be back for visits when they could, Vulka suggesting

hat if Mamelon started to produce something tradeworthy, they
night make it a regular stop on their caravan route. Abderian said,
'I'll work on it."

Paralian winked and tousled Abderian's hair. "Sagamore knew
vhat he was doing." Then, too soon, he and Vulka were seated in
he front of the wagon, slapping the reins and waving farewell.

Abderian waited until the sleet disguised the tears on his face
efore trudging back through the castle foregate.

Sagamore's funeral was an equally private, but far less melan-
holy affair.

"Are you sure you want to stay, um, awake through this?"
Abderian asked as he wrapped the skeletal king in the finest green
elvet he could find.

"Of course, my boy! How many men have wished they could
e at their own funeral? This is a unique opportunity. I missed my
irst one, you know. They don't allow one a leave of absence from
he Home for Orphans of the Mortal Plane to attend one's wake.
A pity. I hear that mine was a humdinger."

So many were happy to see you dead, thought Abderian with
nixed emotions. Much as he knew Sagamore's role in Euthymia's
roblems, he couldn't help liking the old jester. With a pang,
Abderian realized he'd miss Sagamore too.

"Your Majesty, you know that song you'd often sing for me?
'ou never finished the verses. Perhaps it's too late for me to ask,
ut—"

"Would I finish it for you? Certainly. It's the least I can do. I
ever cared for traditional funeral marches. Bad enough the guest
f honor is dead, without deadening the attendees as well. Let's
ee, what verse did you last hear?"

"Four, Your Majesty."

"Ah, so we start at three. Ahem." So Dolus and Abderian
arried the velvet-swaddled bones of Sagamore through the under-
round passages of Mamelon, followed by Maja and Horaphthia.
As they went, they were regaled with Sagamore's song echoing
ff the slimy stone walls:

> There was a young lady of Hollow-In-Tree.
> Of suitors to court her, this lady had three.
> They all were fat peasants of equal low birth,
> But she chose the fattest to match her own girth.

With a ring-diddle-diddle-di-do, all ladies are fey,
They'll do what they like, never mind what you say.

There was a young lady of Bubbling Slough,
Of suitors to court her, this lady had two.
So proud of their skill were these men of the sod,
That she joined a priesthood and married a god."

The small procession came to a stone door inscribed with
magical diagrams. "Hmm," said Dolus, "I did this one about five
years ago. Horaphthia, could you do the gestures for me? I've
quite forgotten them."

"If they suggest themselves to me." The young Horaphthia
stood still a moment, then her hands waved about in the silliest
fashion Abderian had ever seen. The stone door silently swung
open, and faintly noxious, musty air drifted in.

"You had the most bizarre way of using your sorcery,"
Horaphthia said. "Some of the spells I dream about at night—"

"Being forced into underground hermitage, as I was when
Valgus reigned, will do strange things to anyone's magical study.
And might I add that the spells that your greater power suggests to
me aren't exactly normal, either. For example, why on earth
would you want to conjure string beans?"

"Pardon me," said Sagamore, "but might we have some respect
for the dead? We've a funeral to conduct here. Besides, I can think
of lots of good reasons for conjuring beans. To fill beanbags for
juggling, for example. Now carry on."

"Yes, Majesty," said Abderian and he led the procession
through the stone portal.

Castle Doom was much as Abderian remembered it. It was a
vast chamber lit by a dim greenish glow from magical moulds on
the walls. Its floor was a carpet of oozing, bubbling mud, out of
which protruded ornate columns, chunks of crumbling walls,
empty archways, and twisted staircases all tilted at crazy angles.
Little swamp-fires played can't-catch-me among the ruins, and
unseen bats squeaked in the high, vaulted ceiling. Frogs and
crickets made their music nearby.

"Ah," said Sagamore. "Home."

"You like this place?" Maja asked.

"Don't you?" said Sagamore. "It has such beauty. Such
atmosphere!"

"You can say that again," said Horaphthia, holding her nose.

"What was that about respect for the dead?" said Dolus.

"Look!" Abderian pointed toward the center of the chamber where a gleaming, though green-tarnished in places, bronze boat floated toward them. It was slightly larger than an ordinary rowboat, with a pointed prow and stern. The end of each point was embellished with the trifurcate shape of a jester's cap. "I haven't seen that here before." The boat came up and stopped before the hillock of drier mud the procession stood upon.

"Seen what?" Sagamore asked. His skull popped out of the green velvet swaddling and looked. "Oh. That's interesting. Neither have I."

"A present, my liege!" said a nearby bullfrog. Abderian jumped and took a step backward. "Dolus, that isn't—"

"Onym!" Horaphthia and Maja said in unison.

"I thought *I* was supposed to be the croaker at this party," said Sagamore.

"I threw my soul here the better to be prepared for your arrival," said Onym the Frog. "And though doing magic while in amphibian form was an interesting challenge, I am pleased to present to you the results. A boat for making that Great Crossing, to keep you afloat on the Sea of Eternity, to—"

"Thank you, Onym. I heard enough of that sort of thing on the Other Side. Now, if you fellows will just give me the heave-ho onto yon barque, we may finish this business."

So Abderian and Dolus put the bones of Sagamore into the bronze boat.

"You have one more verse, Majesty," Abderian reminded him.

"Ah, yes.

> "There was a young lady from Bullcastle Run,
> Of suitors to court her, this lady had one.
> He was handsome and courtly, quite rich and well-bred,
> So this girl ran off with the blacksmith instead.
>
> With a ring-diddle-diddle di do, all ladies are fey.
> They'll do what they like, never mind what you say."

Abderian and Dolus stood back and Dolus pulled a small scroll from his sleeve. Ceremoniously he unrolled this and read:

> "Noses are red, poets are blue,
> If you'd seen where I'm going then you would be, too.

Ashes to ashes and dust to dust,
Stand clear of the way, lads, it's Deathland or Bust."

Horaphthia and Maja stifled giggles as they placed flowers on
top of Sagamore's velvet shroud and then stood back. Abderian
raised the blade of the Sword of Sagamore and said, "Are you
ready, Your Majesty?"

"Ready as I'll ever be. Shove off, me hearties. Good night,
ladies. Farewell, Dolus. Be good, Onym. Take care, Abderian, of
yourself and this silly kingdom. I have great hopes for you, you
know."

"I will do my best," Abderian said with a wry grin. "Rest in
peace, Your Majesty." Abderian saluted with the golden sword.
There was no apparent change except that the room suddenly
seemed more silent. Dolus began to push the boat back into the
swamp, when Abderian said, "Wait!" Abderian laid the Sword of
Sagamore among the flowers on the shroud. "Here is my farewell
gift."

"Are you sure you don't want to keep that?" said Dolus.

"You did make good use of it," Maja added.

"Well, it is *his* sword," Abderian said. "Besides, it's mostly
good for raising old bones, and that would just lure me down the
wicked path of necromancy." He winked at Horaphthia. "I'm
better off giving it back."

"A noble gift!" said Onym the Frog. "A wise decision. Sagamore indeed chose well."

Abderian snorted and, despite himself, blushed at the praise.
He turned and helped Dolus push Sagamore's funeral barque out
into the muddy water. From somewhere overhead, a disembodied
voice sang:

"There was a young lady from east of the sun,
Of suitors to court her, this lady had none.
But spare her your pity, this maid was not sad,
For she preferred ponies to make her feel glad."

Abderian threw a rock into the water beside the boat. "Go to
sleep!"

Maja and Horaphthia fell on each other's shoulders laughing.
After a moment, Dolus and Abderian laughed with them.

"If you don't mind," Horaphthia said finally, "I would like to get back to fresh air. I'm sure this atmosphere is unhealthy for a growing girl like me. And, Father, we must have a talk."

"Not just yet, my dear," said Onym, staring after the boat with worshipful amphibian eyes. "I wish to stay and . . . commune with my lord awhile longer."

"Suit yourself," said Abderian, and he took one last look at the boat. It was sinking slowly into the mud out in the center of the chamber. Just before the ooze covered it over entirely, there was a flash of green-gold, and the Sword of Sagamore levitated from the funeral barque. As if waved by an invisible hand, the sword saluted him. Then it unceremoniously plopped back into the mud and disappeared from sight.